DEATH BY DARWIN

PREQUEL TO THE CHRONICLES OF JONATHAN STEEL

BRUCE HENNIGAN

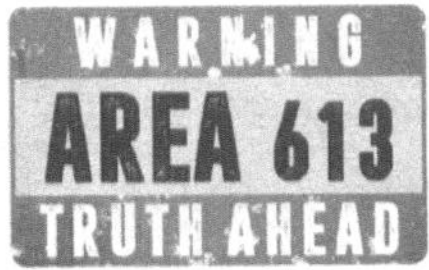

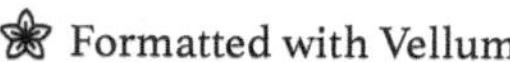 Formatted with Vellum

TRUTH VERSUS MYTH

For the time will come when men will not put up with sound doctrine. Instead, to suit their own desires, they will gather around them a great number of teachers to say what their itching ears want to hear. They will turn their ears away from the truth and turn aside to myths."

2 Timothy 4:3-4

1

D arwyn Paleontology Institute
Dallas, Texas
12:34 A.M.

DR. WALLACE DARWYN threw himself into the stairwell, slammed the door behind him, and gasped for breath. Blood ran across his face from the gash on his forehead and stained his gray beard. He wiped away the warm fluid ,with the back of his hand and noticed more blood streaming down his arm. His lab coat was in tatters and the only thing still intact was his name tag. He had lost his glasses somewhere down the hallway that led from his office. He tried to calm his breathing and listen for the approaching sounds of the thing that chased him. Maybe it would pass the door to the stairwell and continue on down the hall.

Clack, clack, clack.

The brittle sound echoed in the hallway on the other side of the door. He crouched down beneath the door's glass window and tried to calm his ragged breathing. A shadow passed over the window and he held his breath. He looked up into the eye of the devil himself!

Something heavy thudded against the door and he stifled a scream as he watched the door handle twist. The thing could open doors?

He shoved away from the door and slid on his own blood. He tumbled down the stairs and pain lanced across his back as he heard one of his ribs crack. He coughed and sprayed salty blood on the wall. Climbing to his feet on the lower landing, he hurried down the stairs as the door above flew open. He glanced in horror at the shadows of claws playing across the wall beside him.

Darwyn burst out onto the second floor walkway overlooking the display area. Just hours from now, the sunlight of a new day would have illuminated his greatest triumph. But, all of that had changed. A ringing sound came from his shirt pocket. His phone! In the horror of the moment he had forgotten his cell phone! He fumbled for the phone and it shot out of his bloody grip across the floor and under the bottom edge of the railing along the walkway. He fell to his knees and crawled after the phone but his hands slid out from beneath him. His head butted against the railing overlooking the exhibit below. Through the towering prehistoric foliage that reached to this level, he glanced at the empty display stage in horror. Bright spotlights meant to showcase his greatest discovery illuminated a faint, blinking light. His cell phone had fallen to the floor below and was still ringing. Dr. Darwyn pulled himself up on the railing. His back ached with the lacerations and his heart pounded with fear. He had to get to his phone.

Clack, clack, clack!

Darwyn pushed away from the railing and stumbled across the bloody tiles trying to remember the location of the next stairwell. He stopped at the midpoint of the walkway as the clacking grew louder. Suddenly, a spine tingling warbling reaching across the millennia to stoke his fear. Below him, The cell phone rang again and he stopped to catch his breath.

Clack, clack, clack!

He turned to stare into the face of his murderer. The blow caught him just beneath his breastbone and something sharp and long pierced his heart as he was lifted up and over the rail and tossed through the air. He fell through the gentle embrace of palm fronds and lacy ferns and thudded on top of his cell phone. Pain surrounded him and he managed to focus on the thing hurtling down upon him from the walkway above. For a brief moment, he wondered if he would meet God. He got his answer.

2

———————

"Happy Holidays!"

Ruth Martinez felt the cup of eggnog slip from her fingers and tried to catch it before it shattered on the fireplace. The creamy fluid splashed everywhere splattering her black jeans and covering her boots. It sizzled as it ran into the fire and surrounded her with the odor of burned milk and rum.

"I didn't mean to scare you."

She turned and pushed her short, brown hair out of her face and glared at Bryan Nicholas. He towered over her in his perfectly starched denim shirt and his perfectly creased jeans. His chocolate colored eyes glittered with the hint of mischief. His dark hair was, yes, perfectly combed.

"Bryan, you scared the life out of me!"

"Well, who can blame you for being a little twitchy after the year you've had?" He sipped at a cup of eggnog.

A cold wave ran over her and she looked away. "I'm not twitchy."

"Sure you are, Ruth. You can't be blamed for being a bit nervous." He stepped into her line of sight and leaned down to look into her eyes. "Admit it. You had the best defense move of the year. Why, if you hadn't have gotten Drake off, your name wouldn't be in competition with mine for the next partner."

The cold wave quickly warmed. "What do you mean by that?"

Bryan shrugged. "Your record hasn't been, well, stellar, Ruth. Now, I, on the other hand have singlehandedly bested the record for the number of settlements in one year held by Grace Pennington, of all people."

"Quantity isn't everything, Bryan." Ruth said lamely. Was he right? Was her name in the completion simply because of the Drake case? She hoped not. In spite of the victory, she did not consider it her finest moment.

"Ah, I see doubt written all over your face." Bryan said. He placed a hand on her shoulder. "Drake's acquittal, thanks to you, while dramatic and newsworthy, wasn't our firm's shining moment. I'm sure you can't forget what he got away with."

Ruth stepped away from his hand and felt her heart race. "How dare you bring that up? Do you know what I went through? Can you imagine how I feel knowing the man I defended did those things?"

"You have to learn to sleep at night, Ruth. Just rest in the knowledge that you won your case. That should be enough." Bryan frowned and sipped some more egg nog. "But, it still eats away at you, doesn't it? That is why you are not ready to move beyond a lowly associate to a partner. Want to know why?"

"Not from you!" She tried to turn away toward the fireplace but he was there again, his face pressed close to hers.

"You still feel guilt, Ruth. You don't know how to put away your conscience."

"At least I still have one."

"And, that is why I have been chosen as the next partner." He straightened and beamed.

"What?" Ruth glared at him.

"Ruth, where would we normally be right now? Christmas eve? Exactly where our fathers demanded we would be, at home with the rest of our family members gathered around the tree all smiling and hugging and mugging and holding our dinner down while he spouts sentimental clap trap all the while knowing how disappointed he is that we aren't living up to his grandiose expectations." Bryan's face reddened and he snared a passing servant by the shirtsleeve. "Brandy! Now!" He slammed the empty cup onto the waiter's tray.

Ruth drew a deep breath trying to wrap her mind around Bryan's claim. Had the firm already decided? Was she out just like that? And, how mad would her father be if she was late for Christmas dinner? And, mixed in with all of those chaotic thoughts were the memories of Reginald Drake. She shuddered and hugged herself.

Bryan regained his composure and wiped his face. He smiled at the servant as the man handed him a snifter of brandy. "Ruth, dear, there's only one reason I would abandon my family gathering for this party. Grace has made her decision."

"But, she said she wouldn't make up her mind until the first of the year." Nausea gripped her and she stared at the glowing embers of the fire. Bryan being here could only mean one thing. Grace Pennington, founding partner of Pennington, Foster, and Birmingham, one of the most respected law firms in Dallas, had chosen the next partner. Her face grew warm and she clenched her fists. "You're lying, Bryan."

"Why don't you ask her yourself?"

"I will!"

"There's the fiery side of Ruth Martinez! You go, girl!" He shouted and the odor of brandy washed over her.

"Where is she?"

"Well, she just talked to me in her library. She basically told me--" he paused and sipped his brandy as a pitying look came over his face. "Well, let's just say the best man won."

Ruth felt the tears sting her eyes. She balled up her fists and drew them to her chest. How could Ms. Pennington have done this? She pushed passed him and headed through the milling crowd of office personnel that filled Grace Pennington's home. She stopped just short of the library doors and drew a calming breath. She felt warmth behind her and looked over her shoulder into the eyes of Bryan Nicholas.

"I wouldn't do this if I were you. It's just not like you. You're not ruthless. Pardon the pun." He whispered in her ear.

Ruth shoved him away and pushed aside the pair of sliding doors. She stormed into the gigantic library and marched up to Grace Pennington's huge mahogany desk. Grace was dressed in a bright red Christmas cowboy shirt. Her short, graying hair framed her face. She was studying something in a folder and she looked up over her forest green reading glasses at Ruth.

"Ms. Grace, I want a word with you. Right now!"

Grace blinked and took off her glasses. It was only then that Ruth noticed the man sitting across the desk from Grace. The man's hair was short and reddish blonde and his eyes were averted to the floor. He wore a faded pair of jeans and a red Hawaiian shirt over a beige, long sleeve tee shirt.

"Ruth? What is the meaning of this?"

"You promised you wouldn't make the decision until after the first of the year. And, now I understand you've chosen Bryan Nicholas over me. I want to know why!" Ruth blurted out. Her lips were trembling and she felt the tears trickle down her cheeks.

Grace stood up, her tall willowy frame smartly dressed in velvet dark green jeans to offset the red shirt. The jeans matched the color of her glasses. She walked around the desk to the library doors. Bryan Nicholas stood just outside the sliding doors with a sly grin on his face. He disappeared from sight as the doors thudded together. She returned to her desk and closed the folder.

"Ruth, when are you going to learn not to buy into Bryan's lies?"

Lies? Ruth felt her cheeks sting and her heart pounded. The jerk had set her up! He had done this to her deliberately. She searched the library for a dark hole to crawl into.

"Oh, I'm such a fool!" She turned and tried to walk calmly toward the doors, every muscle in her body screaming for her to run from the room; to run out of the huge palatial mansion surrounded by acres of horses and cows; to drive her small, cheap car back to Austin, Texas to her mother and father and three brothers.

"Stop!" Grace barked.

"Should I leave?" The man spoke quietly.

Ruth turned and Grace settled behind the desk. "There's no need for that, Mr. Steel. You should hear this. Ruth, sit. Now." Grace gestured to the other empty chair.

Ruth collapsed into the chair and tried to sit upright and stiff. "I'm sorry. I shouldn't have fallen for Bryan's manipulations."

"No, you shouldn't have. I thought you trusted me, Ruth." Grace chewed on the ends of her reading glasses as her bright, green eyes flared with emotion. "I chose you from law school for this firm, didn't I?"

"Yes."

"I said you could become one of the best attorneys in the state, didn't I?"

"Yes."

"And, what did Bryan Nicholas say? Did he say any of these things about you? Has he, in any way tried to encourage you?"

Ruth blinked away the tears and felt her anger build again. "No."

"Ruth, I chose you because you have balance. Bryan is all cold intellect and cunning. He has compassion only when it serves his purposes. With Bryan, everything is a game of impressions. I know that is what is supposed to happen in the courtroom, but I have built this law firm on thinking outside that box. There is a place for balance and compassion and humanity. You exemplify that."

"Thank you, Ms. Grace."

"I have not spoken to Bryan Nicholas tonight. But, the two of you will soon know the truth so I will tell you there is one partner undecided. I'm for you, Ruth. And Foster is for Byran. You and Bryan each have one vote. Birmingham's will be the deciding factor. And, since you and Bryan seem to have this bull-chasing contest going on, Birmingham has an idea how we can settle it. Bryan, get in here!" Her voice strengthened.

The doors slid aside and Bryan stood just outside. "I hope you don't mind. I was eavesdropping." He sauntered into the room and placed the empty brandy snifter on Grace's desk.

"Who said you could drink my husband's brandy?"

Bryan blinked and shrugged. "One of your servants?"

Grace glared at him. "I will not have you using my name in your games, Bryan. You try this again, and I'll have you cleaning out the record boxes in the basement for the next two years. Understand?"

"Yes, ma'am." Bryan said quietly.

"That's much better." Grace said. "Now, Bob Birmingham made an absurd suggestion to me just this morning. At first, I was against it. But, we all known how pig headed Mr. Birmingham can be. So, there doesn't seem to be any other alternative. In order to get his vote, one of you will have to beat the other."

"Well, there's not a game I can't beat Ruth at." Bryan said smugly.

"This is not a game." Grace said. "A man's life may be at stake."

"I hope he's not another Drake." Bryan said. His smile faded under Grace's stare.

"I've heard enough about that case. Understand?"

Ruth paled and tried to melt into the chair. Grace tapped her fingernail against the desktop. "Have either one of you heard the news this week about Dr. Wallace Darwyn?"

Darwyn? Ruth sat forward. "Isn't he that wealthy scientist who was murdered?"

"Yeah, the head of that dinosaur institute." Bryan said. "I heard his associate wanted Darwyn's job. Killed him with a dinosaur claw."

Grace nodded. "Yes, Dr. Wallace Darwyn founded the Darwyn Paleontology Institute. He was to have opened the doors the next day with a huge show featuring his newest discovery, a dinosaur named Annieraptor of all things. Named after his late daughter, it seems."

Ruth's mind was working furiously. Why was Grace bringing this up at a time like this? Grace slid the folder toward Ruth.

"Here's the deal. In order to get Birmingham's vote, the two of you will take on this case. Mr. Nicholas, you will be on loan to the D.A.'s office per their request. Seems they've got you in their sites. Now, I know you have loftier plans, but this could be a feather in your cap and look good on your resume. The case is a slam dunk and you will lead the prosecuting team for the duration of the trial."

"About time they saw me for my true potential." Bryan reached for the folder. Grace placed her hand on his.

"Not so fast. That folder is for the defense." She looked at Ruth.

"You want me to defend the murderer?" Ruth blinked quickly. "Against Bryan?" Her heart raced. She couldn't go through this again!

"Yes." Grace leaned forward. "Ruth, I am convinced this man is innocent."

"But, you said the case was a slam dunk." Ruth's heart raced. "I heard about it on the news. The murderer was found hunched over Dr. Darwyn's body with the claw in his hand! He ripped open the man's chest!" She stood up and gasped for breath. Drake's leering face swam in her sight and she shuddered. "I can't do this! I can't go through this again!"

Grace stood up. "Ruth! Listen to me!"

Ruth pressed her hands against her eyes and chased the memories away. The bloody hands. The bloody face. The blood stained teeth. Drake's shark cold eyes.

"I told you she wasn't ready." Bryan said.

"Bryan, shut up!" Grace said loudly. "Now, Ruth, sit down. Take a deep breath. This is what you need to do. This is what you must do! You have to move on. And, I'm telling you this man is innocent."

Ruth drew a deep breath and fought to control her racing heart. Was Grace right? Could she do this? Did she really want to be partner badly enough to go through this again? Bryan placed a hand on her shoulder and she jerked away from him.

"Looks like I'm the one getting the best Christmas present, Ruth." He winked and the sight of his lopsided smirk chased the doubts away.

"I'll do it for one reason." She stepped toward him. "To shut up your arrogant face!"

"That's enough!" Grace shouted. Ruth plopped into the chair and Bryan nodded.

"You're right. We need to save the maneuvering for the courtroom."

"Here is the D.A.'s assistant in charge." Grace handed him a business card. "Give her a call today and report to their office Monday. From this moment on, you are no longer on the payroll, Mr. Nicholas. Sorry, that means no Christmas bonus."

Bryan's smile returned and he tucked the card in his shirt pocket. "I think I just got my bonus. Happy Holidays everyone." He slid the doors closed behind him as he strutted out of the library.

Ruth slumped forward in her chair. "I'm sorry Ms. Grace. He knows how to push my every button."

"Dear, you must find a way to beat Bryan Nicholas. You can start by pushing his buttons." Grace slid the folder closer to Ruth. "This is for you."

Ruth opened the folder. The first photograph ran red with blood. She gasped and pushed away the other memories. This was different. This was new. This could not hurt her. The body of Dr. Darwyn was draped across a diorama surrounded by rocks and ferns in the shadow of a tall dinosaur statue. His shirt had been torn into shreds and his eyes were dull and lifeless. Huge rips in his chest wall exposed rib and lung tissue. She felt nausea rise and drew a deep breath to calm herself.

"Is she up to it?"

Ruth jerked. She had forgotten about the other person in the room. She turned to look closely at the man sitting next to her. She was startled by his bright, turquoise eyes and the intensity of his voice. He seemed to be a bundle of tightly coiled muscles just waiting for release.

Grace looked away from the departing Bryan and tossed her glasses on the desk. "I'm no fool, Mr. Steel."

"I didn't come here to help with a murder trial. I came to see the artifact you bought for your husband's Christmas present."

"Yes. We've had this discussion already." Grace sat in her chair. "You'll find me rather formidable, Mr. Steel. As I told you, I'll gladly show it to you if you help with this investigation. When you called and asked to see me, I contacted my friend, Dr. Lawrence."

Steel flinched. "You're checking up on me? That was smart."

"He said you are very capable and you have a private investigator's license. You want the artifact, then that's my price."

Steel straightened in his chair and leaned back. He placed his hands in his lap and sighed. He turned to look at Ruth and she felt the heat of his stare penetrate her face.

"Can you do this?"

Ruth closed the folder and tried to speak. She opened her mouth and closed it several times. Get control, she thought. "Ms. Grace has faith in me." She said weakly. Did she really? Or, for that matter, should she have faith in her? The world had just turned upside down.

"Faith is the key word, Ruth." Grace said. "The accused, Dr. Frank Miller is a Christian. Dr. Darwyn is an atheist. Bryan will quickly paint the picture of a crazed, religious zealot seeking to stop the opening of the Institute."

"What?" Ruth shook her head in confusion. "But, you said Dr. Miller was the main associate. Why would he work at an institute whose devotion to paleontology he might oppose on religious grounds?"

"Exactly!" Grace nodded and leaned forward. "This is not about religion. It is about a scientist fudging the facts for his own personal gain. According to Frank, Dr. Darwyn's claims regarding this Annieraptor are false. He wanted Dr. Darwyn to come clean. That's all. No religious conflict at all. But, you and I know Bryan, Ruth. You know the wedge he will drive between perception and the truth."

"And, he knows me." Ruth nodded. "He'll use my convictions against me."

"You have conviction?" Steel blinked. "I like that. A person of integrity. You refuse to compromise your values."

"And that is why I want her as my new partner." Grace said. "This case has become more than just trying to get a good friend acquitted from a murder I am sure he never committed. It has become my last chance to keep integrity as an integral part of this practice. Ruth, please accept this case. I will give you all the help you need.

According to my old friend, Dr. Cephas Lawrence, Mr. Steel is a reputable investigator with quite a bit of knowledge of faith related concepts. And, I have faith in you."

Ruth placed a hand on the folder and sighed as her heart raced. She glanced over her shoulder at the doors. Run home to Austin or stay and fight? Did she have a choice? "I'll do it."

3

Ruth checked her watch as they waited for Dr. Frank Miller to be retrieved from his cell. It was almost eight o'clock and she had hoped to be on the road to Austin in time for Christmas day.

"You'll make it, dear." Grace Pennington patted her arm. "I made arrangements for my private jet to take you home as soon as we are finished tonight. You'll be snug in your bed by midnight."

Private jet? "Ms. Pennington, you continue to amaze me. A private jet? And, you left all of those guests at your house at your own party."

"And, they will never know I'm gone." She waved her hand and sniffed. "Most of them won't remember they were at the party tomorrow morning! Their Christmas present will be a huge hangover. Now, please call me Grace. I felt it was terribly important that you meet Dr. Miller tonight before the rush of the coming holiday week swept through."

"I wondered about that." Ruth settled into a chair on her side of the table in the meeting room. "This is very important to you, isn't it?"

"Frank is like a son to me. His mother was one of my childhood friends."

The door opened and Jonathan Steel walked in. His turquoise eyes burned with irritation. "You lost me in the traffic."

The look on his face chilled Ruth. "I forgot you were following."

"Don't do it again." He said. He drew a deep breath and leaned against the wall. His face was red and she could see the rapid beating of his heart in the arteries of his neck. Why was the man so angry?

The inner door opened and Dr. Frank Miller was ushered in. He wore a yellow jumpsuit and his hands were shackled. He had shoulder length hair and a goatee of dark brown. His intense eyes were drawn instantly to Grace.

"Officer, we won't be needing the shackles." She said coldly.

The officer accompanying Miller undid the shackles and stepped out of the room. Miller came to Grace and she enveloped him in her arms. They stood there for a long time and Miller's shoulders shook with emotion. When he pulled away, he wiped at his eyes.

"Thank you so much. I didn't kill anybody, Aunt Grace."

"I know, Frank. Have a seat and let's get to it." She reached into her coat and pulled out a card. "Oh, by the way, Merry Christmas."

Miller took the card and sat at the table. He studied it and tears dripped from his eyes. He opened the envelope and read the card inside. He wiped at his eyes and laid the card on the table. "Thank you. You might as well take it back. They won't let me keep it."

"Do you want me to, uh, tell, uh, anyone anything?" Grace said awkwardly.

"No." Frank said. "We both know what I've lost in getting the Institute up and running." He sat in the chair opposite them.

"This is Ruth Martinez, one of our up and coming junior associates." Grace said.

"You're not representing me?" Miller leaned forward and ran a hand through his long hair. "You don't understand, Aunt Grace. They want the death penalty."

"I can't represent you, Frank. You know that. Conflict of interest. There are some other senior partners but they specialize in litigation and contract law. Ruth has experience in criminal defense and she is very dedicated." Grace cleared her throat. "She was our lead attorney in the Reginald Drake murders." She reached out and placed a hand on Frank's. "If she can get that man acquitted, your case will be a piece of cake."

Ruth swallowed. Was that why she had been chosen? Before she could speak, Miller reached across the table and took Grace's hand. "I don't know what you're talking about, but if you trust her, that's good enough for me."

Ruth digested these remarks and tried to compose a response. Miller interrupted her thoughts.

"Who's he?"

"Jonathan Steel." Steel said without moving.

"Mr. Steel is an investigator with special skills in the area of evil." Grace said. Ruth looked at her and then back over her shoulder at Steel. Had she said evil?

"Just know that Mr. Steel comes highly recommended and I believe he is exactly what you need on this case." Grace said.

Steel pushed away from the wall and came up to the table, towering over Ruth. He reached between Ruth and Grace and offered Dr. Miller his hand. "Jonathan Steel, Dr. Miller. I will do whatever I can to help. That's a promise. And, I always keep my promise."

Ruth felt the man's intensity roll off him like hot air and she leaned away from his muscular arm. Dr. Miller shook Steel's hand.

"I need a miracle worker, Aunt Grace. They found me over Wallace's body with the claw in my hand. I was just trying to save the man."

"Just a minute, Dr. Miller. Do I have your permission to record this conversation?" Ruth asked.

"Sure."

She reached into her satchel and took out a digital recorder. "Dr. Miller, tell us everything that happened that night."

"It was a week ago tonight. We were having a party for the staff to celebrate the upcoming opening of the Institute to the public. Wallace wouldn't call it a Christmas party. He wouldn't even call it a

Holiday Celebration. You see the word holiday comes from 'holy day'. Wallace was a staunch atheist. He made Richard Dawkins look like a Sunday School teacher."

Miller sat back in his chair and studied his hands. "Well, at the party, Dr. Darwyn unveiled his newest dinosaur discovery, Annieraptor. We had all seen the prototype figure that was to be displayed in the center of the atrium. But, he had added feathers. Feathers! Wallace had added feathers!" Miller stood up and tossed his hair back. He paced across the room. "He added feathers!"

Ruth glanced at Grace and the older woman shrugged. "Dr. Miller, you'll have to explain the significance of that to us."

Miller stopped and looked at them like they were simpletons. "Wallace has always been fascinated with Bambiraptor, a dinosaur fossil discovered in 1993 in Montana. It had feathers. Turned the world of paleontology on its head. Here was the missing link between dinosaurs and birds." Miller crossed his arms. "Well, experts later concluded that Bambiraptor was a member of a group of bird like creatures that most likely had feathers due to phylogenetic bracketing. You see, subsequent discoveries confirmed that small dromaeosaurid dinosaurs like Bambiraptor were fully covered in feathers." He stepped toward them, gesturing with his hands. Ruth could imagine him standing in front of an auditorium filled with students. He would make a good expert witness. He pointed a finger at them. "But, according to the fossil fragments I examined, I do not believe Annieraptor was a dromaesaurid dinosaur. No feathers! But, that didn't seem to have bothered Wallace. Did you know he even named the dinosaur Annieraptor to remind people of Bambiraptor? Can you believe?"

Before Ruth could ask for further explanation, Steel spoke up. "So, the two of you disagreed on this feather issue?"

Miller leaned on the table. His face was red. "I don't expect you to understand. I don't mind disagreeing on the issue, but Annieraptor's fossils had no evidence of feathers! Not even quill buds! But, Wallace was determined to ride the publicity train by passing off his discovery as a feathered dinosaur. More donations! More attendance to his displays! He was becoming a regular P. T. Barnum!" Miller pounded the table top. "He sacrificed his scientific credibility on the altar of fame and money! He betrayed science!"

Ruth sighed and tried to wrap her head around this information. "So adding feathers was Wallace's idea and was not supported by the evidence?"

Miller's eyes lit up. "Exactly! Don't you see? He was so desperate to prove his point, he cheated. When I saw Annieraptor unveiled in all of her hypocrisy I was enraged. We had an argument right there in front of everyone and I went up to my office to write a letter of protest."

"Just for my information, Dr. Miller, what is your area of expertise?"

Miller straightened and calmed down. "Well, at the Institute, I serve two functions. I have experience in programming. I helped some of the staff complete the programs for their respective areas of interest. But, my real expertise is in paleobotany. I study prehistoric plants. Wallace hired me to study coproliths and gastroliths."

Ruth raised an eye in confusion and Miller pressed on. "I'm sorry. Coproliths are fossilized feces. Gastroliths are fossilized contents of the stomach. By studying these, we can determine what kinds of food the dinosaurs ingested. That's why I'm at the Institute. To study the plants and make sure the final exhibit had flora and fauna as close to the time of Annieraptor as possible."

"How long were you in your office?"

Miller shook his head. "I don't know. Until about midnight? That's when I heard the screams. I came out of my office and went down the hall to Wallace's office. There was blood. Lots of it. I followed it down the hall to the stairway and out to the walkway overlooking the exhibit. I was horrified. Dr. Darwyn was down on the diorama at the feet of the Annieraptor statue. He was covered in blood and the claw was sticking out of his chest. I ran down the stairs and checked his pulse. He was dead. When I pulled the claw out of his chest, everyone showed up at once. The staff still in the building. The night security guy. And, the police. Someone had called 911. That's when it all went south. Someone started taking pictures of me holding the claw. Before I knew it, the police had tased me and that's all I remember until I woke up in a holding cell."

"You had means, motive, and opportunity." Steel said quietly behind them.

"Wallace and I may have disagreed on things, but I would never kill him. What would be the point?"

"To stop the exhibit." Steel stepped forward to the table. "You're a religious man, aren't you?"

Miller nodded. "I am a Christian, yes."

"Old earth or young earth?"

Miller perked up. "Somewhere between old earth and TE."

"If you're TE, you wouldn't have problem with feathers."

Grace shook her head. "Sorry, but TE?"

"Theistic evolution." Miller sighed. "A discipline that accepts the principles of evolutionary processes such as mutational advance but with the guiding hand of a transcendent intelligence. More or less. Some believe more guidance others believe less. And, Mr. Steel, I had a problem with fudging the data. I am a scientist. This has nothing to do with my religious beliefs."

Ruth was looking back and forth between the two men and her eyes came to rest on Grace. Grace smiled. "Now you know why I hired him."

"Aunt Grace, we can't make this about creation versus evolution. I will lose. They'll paint me as a fanatic."

"They will do that anyway." Steel stated quietly. "Everyone knows how dangerous religious fanatics can be. At least, that is the public perception." He placed a hand on Ruth's shoulder and she flinched. "Just get ready, Ms. Martinez. It will be the Scopes monkey trial all over again."

Miller slumped into his chair. "This can't be happening to me. We'll have the ACLU and the National Geographic Society and the National Institute of Science all over this. They'll open up their purses and they'll bury me. They'll bury me!"

Grace reached out and touched his hand. "No, they won't Frank. We will win this. Do you know why?"

Miller looked up at his Aunt Grace. "Why?"

"Because we have truth on our side."

Grace sat back and crossed her arms. Feathered dinosaurs? Creation versus evolution? What a Christmas present this had been!

4

J ONATHAN STEEL

MY NAME IS JONATHAN STEEL. At least, I think it is. Grace Pennington gave me this digital recorder to keep track of everything I see, say, and do. She said to keep it separate from my cell phone; business versus personal. I'm not sure how much I'll use this. Everything I put on here will go to Ruth Martinez.

Okay, let's see – Grace has this thing set on voice activated recording and I'm not sure how to change it. Oh, well. Sorry if something I say offends anyone. I'm not a diplomat. I pretty much say what I think.

Ruth Martinez. Hmm. I'm not sure about her. She seems, what is the word, passive? No, that's a bit harsh. Seems she's gun shy. Something spooked her in the past. I'll have to help her get over that if she is going to win this case. I need to examine the artifact and head back down to Orange Beach. I need to be at the beach house. After all, it's been one year today.

After I decided to start helping people, I had taken the RV left to me in the will and upgraded it as my center of operations. It gave me mobility and a place to live while I looked for it. After the party, Grace allowed me to park my RV next to her stables. All the necessary hook ups. I unhooked my SUV from the back of the RV and made sure it would start. Night was falling and it was Christmas Eve. That meant something to people. At least, people with family. I wouldn't know.

By ten o'clock I had the RV hooked up to water, electricity, and sewage. I went inside and stared at the clock above the computer monitor sitting on the kitchen table. It had been exactly a year to the hour. My heart raced and my face warmed. I had been searching for it for over a year now; the thing of evil that had stepped into my life and destroyed everything I cared about. The pounding on my door finally pierced my stillness. I opened the door. Mrs. Grace Pennington stood on my doorstep bundled in an ankle length coat.

"I was beginning to think you'd fallen asleep."

"Come in." I motioned to the only seat in the RV, a desk chair sitting in front of my converted kitchen table. Grace climbed into the RV and looked around. She smelled of cinnamon and spice.

"I won't stay long. Just wanted you to know I dropped Ruth off at the airport and she should be in Austin before midnight. I don't guess you have plans for Christmas dinner?"

"I don't do Christmas."

"I'm sorry. I thought you were a religious man."

"It has nothing to do with religion." I said. "Just bad memories."

"Well, if you change your mind, we are eating around 1 PM in the main house. We'd love to have you." Grace said.

"Thank you for the offer."

"Cephas said you would act like this. You can't spend every day alone, Mr. Steel. You don't have to speak to any of us. Just come and eat and at least not be alone. If you want to, you can sit in the kitchen away from my family."

My eye twitched in irritation. "Cephas has a lot of room to talk. Locked up in that high rise building of his." I imagined the tiny, old man staring out the window of his New York City building at falling snow alone with all his arcane artifacts and weird collectibles.

"Oh, he won't be alone." Grace said. "He told me he was feeding over 200 homeless in the neighborhood. But, if you insist on spending tomorrow in total, abject misery so be it. I know what you lost a year ago. Cephas told me. But, you have to ask yourself what would she prefer for you to do on the anniversary of that tragedy? Don't give this evil being who destroys lives the pleasure of keeping you in misery. I'll expect you at 1. Okay?"

Cephas and his big mouth. The man was supposed to be my mentor, not my therapist. I tried not to smile. She was insistent. "Fine. I'll be there."

Grace nodded and stepped back out into the cold darkness. I closed and locked the door behind her. I walked through the kitchen and the short hallway to my one and only bedroom. I paused before the photograph hanging on the wall. It was of a father and his adult daughter. My eyes misted and I reached out and touched her face.

"I'll do it for you. But, that's the only reason." I said hoarsely.

5

R uth studied her reflection in the patio doors of her parents' home. Her hair was in disarray. Her face was lined from the scarce four hours' worth of sleep in her childhood bed. She wore her favorite flannel nightgown and bunny slippers. If only she could return to that simple time in her life when her greatest care on Christmas morning was whether or not Santa brought her the perfect gift. But today was a different kind of Christmas morning. She slid the patio doors open and stepped out onto the lake house balcony. Bright sunlight reflected off the blue gray waters of Lake Travis and the air smelled crisp and clean. Steam misted from her coffee cup in the cool air and she hugged her flannel robe around her. The past twenty-four hours were a surreal memory of spilled egg nog, murder and a strange man with turquoise eyes. She settled into a chair and sipped her coffee. It had cinnamon in it. Her favorite.

The door opened behind her and Mark, her brother, sat down beside her. He was a foot taller than her and currently enrolled in medical school in Houston. He wore a burnt orange Texas Longhorn sweatshirt and white sweat pants. He was ruggedly handsome with dark skin, jet black hair, and piercing brown eyes.

"I'm impressed, Sis."

"Yeah, I forget how lovely it is out here on the lake."

"No, with you. Let see. You fly home on Christmas Eve in a private corporate jet. You are met at the airport by limousine and driven all the way to the south side of Austin to Lake Travis in the dead of night, a feat that rivals anything Dad would have pulled off." He held a glass of milk in his hand and motioned to her cup. "I toast your success."

"It was just Grace Pennington. She promised to get me home by Christmas."

"Ah, yes, the powerful Grace Pennington. Did you know one of your partners sued my surgery attending last year? It cost the man his position at the medical school. Now, he's in private practice doing body piercings." He gulped his milk. "That settlement probably paid for your jet." He not only looked like their father. He had his temperament.

"Mark, I haven't seen you in months. Do we have to fight?"

"Of course not. Since I am the only one of us who isn't going into law, I should just keep my mouth shut."

"That's not a bad idea." Ricardo Martinez stepped onto the balcony and towered over them. Ruth looked over her shoulder at her father. His hair was a light gray and his face was regal with high cheek bones and a straight nose. Somewhere in their ancestry, his DNA had been passed down from an Aztec king. He was a tall, handsome man who had started out in the state attorney general's office and now was a high-level state court judge.

"Mark can't resist being the rebel." Ruth sipped more coffee. In spite of her attempt at peacemaking, acid boiled in her stomach. "After all, he's the baby."

"Okay, you win." Mark stood up. "At least Mother wanted all of us to be doctors. I'm sure she will understand."

"You always were her favorite." Ruth sighed.

Mark grunted and continued to drink his milk as their father patted Ruth on the shoulder. "Good morning, pumpkin. Feliz Navidad. Sorry for Mark. He can't resist making a good situation bad."

Mark glanced at them and shook his head. "Three out of four of your children as attorneys should make you happy, Dad. I'm sorry for being the disappointing one."

"Well, that's yet to be seen. If you can possibly make it in the top ten percent of your class and if you can find the perfect residency in neurosurgery, say at Duke, then I won't be disappointed." Their father said.

"Duke! Really?" Mark sat forward and squinted an eye. "I ought to look at UCLA just to tick you off."

Martinez shrugged. "You'd have to be in the top five for that."

Mark stood up stiffly. "And you don't think I have it in me?"

"I never said that."

"Well you just wait and see." He stormed around the rocker and slammed the patio doors together.

Ruth shivered. "You did that on purpose, didn't you?"

"I'll take any form of motivation he will respond to." Martinez sat in the rocker beside her. "If I recall, that particular move didn't work on you."

"I didn't need motivation, Dad. I was always in the top three percent."

"Unlike Bryan Nicholas. He was in your class, wasn't he?"

Ruth flinched. "Who told you? I only found out last night."

"His father has always had it in for me ever since I beat him out for my first state circuit judge position. He called before midnight to gloat." Martinez patted her arm. "But, I told him that Bryan was about to grab a tiger by the tail!"

Ruth felt the morning chill seep through her robe and she sipped more coffee. "I'm glad you have confidence in me, Dad."

"You beat impossible odds already this year."

Ruth nodded and the twisted face of Drake reared itself in her memory. She chased it away. "I got lucky. That girl didn't. I won all right, but at what a cost?"

"He hasn't tried anything again, has he?"

"No." Ruth looked at her Dad. "The FBI have him under constant surveillance after the parking garage incident." She looked quickly away. She had never told anyone what really happened that day. She couldn't. She wouldn't. "Anyway, this case is more of a slam dunk than Drake was." She sat forward and put the empty coffee cup on the balcony railing. "Grace is convinced our client is innocent. I've met him, and I believe he is innocent. But, my opponent is Bryan. Only one of us will become the next partner."

"Is that why you took the case?" Her father asked.

"Yes. And, no. I'd love to beat Bryan at his own game. Just once."

"Tell me about the case."

Ruth gave him the short version of what little she knew. Her father stood up to lean against the balcony railing. He looked out over the dark blue water of the lake. "Bryan's very ambitious, like his father. He will go for the emotional, Ruth. He'll play this out as a bigoted, judgmental Christian versus enlightened, atheist scientist. You'll need to get the Bible belters on your side. Choose the jury wisely. Forget the science and defend the man."

"My client will appear superstitious, backwards; petty and vindictive. It will make him look guiltier."

"Is he innocent?" Her father asked.

"Does it matter? You taught me not to ask that question."

"And yet, you do ask that question. You care about who you defend."

Ruth sighed. "Can you blame me? We both know what happened after Drake's acquittal. It's hard for me to sleep at night."

"There are many things in life to lose sleep over. You have to ask yourself, Ruth. Are you always one hundred percent certain your client is innocent? I don't think you can ever be that certain. It is why we use the term, 'guilty beyond a reasonable doubt'. You can't afford to doubt yourself. This man's life is in your hands, guilty or innocent."

Ruth looked up at her father, his stern features illuminated by the rising sun. "I know, Dad. I know." Ruth stood up and joined him at the balcony railing. She sighed as she studied the mesmerizing waves of the lake. "I've been a Christian since I was ten, Dad. I've just never thought much about the science of it. It has never really mattered."

"Until now. My suggestion is to let the prosecution play their creation/evolution debate card. Let them make your client look like an idiot. If you weigh the jury in your favor with just enough devout religious people, they'll come over to your side."

Ruth picked up her cup and sipped the last cold swallow of coffee. "It always boils down to a game of impressions, doesn't it? What happened to the truth? When did we lose it?"

Her father put his arm around her. "It's the 21st century. Very few people believe in absolute truth anymore. The only thing certain in this case is if you lose, your client dies. And, that is the truth."

Ruth gripped the cup so hard, it shot out of her hand like a lemon seed. It fell down the rocky slope below the lake house. The porcelain cracked and tinkled as it tumbled to the water's edge.

6

J ONATHAN STEEL

Mrs. Pennington told me to go by the police station the day after Christmas and pick up the evidence portfolio for the defense. They have to share the evidence with the defense, she told me. I was aware of this provision and I was determined not only to get the portfolio but to actually see the evidence. I knew we were entitled to that. I know I was instructed to bring it back to her. But, I wanted more. I wanted to SEE the evidence for myself.

I arrived at the main Dallas Police station downtown and was directed to the homicide division to a Detective Jones. I arrived at her desk and she pushed aside a Christmas gift on her desk.

"Juan is putting the moves on me." She nodded at the gift. "He fancies himself a lady's man. But, he's nothing but a glorified nerd on loan from the F.B.I. Now, what do you want?"

"I'm Jonathan Steel and I work with Ruth Martinez. Defense for Frank Miller. I'm here to see the evidence."

The short, African American woman with shocking yellow hair wore a Dallas Police uniform and weighed no more than 120 pounds soaking wet. "I'm Detective Citronella Jones and I'm with the homicide division and I don't care."

I was expecting as much. Maybe defuse the situation with a little humor? I had to plan these things. Spontaneity was not one of my strengths. "Interesting name."

"My mother loved the smell of citronella. All my life, I've kept my hair this color. Way I figure it, honey, is to roll with it. Own it. My friends call me Nella. But, you can call me Detective Jones." She sat back and steepled her fingers before her face. "Now, I know I have to cooperate with the defense. I know I have to help out Ms. Martinez. But, I don't have to like it. She did a number on us with the Drake case and we haven't forgotten. Eight months of work down the drain on the day of closing arguments. Now, this Dr. Frank Miller may have done one better than Drake. He committed one of the most heinous crimes I've ever seen."

"Heinous?" I said.

"What? You don't think I can use big words? The poor sister who worked her way up through a white man's world? Is that what you think?" Jones' eyes had grown wide with anger. Okay. Where was my diplomacy? What had Cephas told me once? You can get more with honey than with vinegar.

"I didn't mean anything with that remark. It just seems you've made up your mind about the guilt of our client." I said.

"Of course I have." Jones cleared her throat and sat back in her chair. "Sorry for the speech."

"I sort of liked it." I said. She raised an eyebrow and tilted her head as she studied me some more.

"Honey, it's my job to be biased. It's my job to arrest them when the evidence is convincing." She tapped her fingernail against her desk. "And, the evidence here is overwhelming. And, heinous." She leaned forward and raised an eyebrow. "Almost as convincing as it was against Drake."

"Who?" I was tired of hearing about this Drake character.

"You don't know about Drake, do you?"

"No."

"Ask your boss and maybe she can tell you why we are not highly motivated to be cooperative with Ruth Martinez."

"You have no choice. We are allowed access to the evidence." I said.

"We'll see, honey." She sat back and examined her fingernails. We waited. I blinked. She studied her fingernails some more and then glanced at me. I took out a small notebook I had picked up at a convenience store and tried to push my growing anger away. "Detective Jones, when can I see the evidence?" I said quietly.

"You can visit the evidence lock up and look at what we have, but, honey, that's all. You can touch but you can't keep." Jones said.

"I wouldn't dream of touching anything so, uh, heinous."

She finally smiled and leaned forward onto her desk. "Well, how can I say no to a man with those eyes? Where did you get those gorgeous peepers?"

"Peepers?" I said irritably. She sniffed and sat back in her chair.

"Fine. You're a P.I., right?"

"Yeah. I'm sort of a private investigator."

"Sort of?"

"I have a license. Occasionally, I use it to help people."

"For a price, I'm sure."

I glared at her. "For nothing. I don't need money."

She frowned. "Honey child, we all need money. What world are you coming from?"

I shrugged. "I wish I knew."

"Now, that's an intriguing answer."

I glanced down at my notebook. Even my handwriting still looked foreign to me. "I have amnesia."

"Oh." She continued to study me and sighed. "Sometimes, when I see all of these 'heinous' crimes, I wish I could have a little amnesia, honey. Where'd you get that name? Not from a porno movie, I hope."

"I got it from the FBI. They created me a new identity."

She fell silent and tapped the desk with her fingernails. "Well, Mr.

Jonathan Steel, let's get you to the evidence room." Jones led me through the hallways of the police station to a remote room. A window covered with thick wire separated me from a large room filled with shelves. Jones spoke with the man behind the wire and then motioned me forward. His name tag read, "Juan Destillo, F.B.I. Crime Technician."

"Juan is on loan from the feds. He'll give you thirty minutes, Mr. Steel. See you later." She walked away and Juan studied me like I was some insect trapped in amber. He was a slight man with unruly, dark hair and eyes that glowed with the menial power he had been given.

"Identification." He extended his hand through the slot at the bottom of the cage window.

I pulled out my wallet and handed me driver's license. For a moment, I studied the photograph of the strange man staring back at me from my own license. Jonathan Steel. Turquoise eyes. Lean face. Short, reddish blonde hair. Who was I? I was staring at a photograph of myself but also at a stranger. Juan handed the driver's license back to me after scanning it into his computer. "License?"

"I just gave it to you."

"P.I. License." He said tersely. My face warmed with anger and I tried my best to suppress it. Not always successful there. Now was not a good time to throw a temper tantrum in a police office. I handed him my P.I. License. He scanned it in and handed it back. "What is someone from the F.B.I. doing in a Dallas Police Department evidence lock up?"

He glared at me. "Empty your pockets."

I grit my teeth. I placed my keys and cell phone in a bowl along with the notepad and pen. "What did you do?"

"Got a gun?" He ignored my question.

"No." I said quietly.

Juan glanced at me and frowned. "A P.I. without a gun? You're either very, very good or very, very stupid."

I looked away. I was back in the gun club shooting range. My hands were clasped around the pistol. The target had six neatly placed holes in the forehead. I was an expert marksman. I remembered dropping the gun as if it were a poisonous snake. Who had I shot in the past? Couldn't remember. "I don't own a gun."

"What did you say?"

I glared at him and said a bit too loudly. "I don't own a gun!"

Juan stiffened and a shield of suspicion arose between us. "That necklace. Gotta go." He pointed at my neck.

I swallowed and slowly took the necklace from around my neck. The tiny gold cross glittered in the fluorescent light and spun slowly on the chain. Stop them! Don't let them win! I closed my eyes and tried to chase the image of her dying eyes from my memory. The necklace had been a gift from me. Now, it was a reminder of sorrow and regret. I placed the necklace carefully in the bowl.

"Girlfriend?" He sneered.

If the cage hadn't been between us I would have broken his nose. "She's dead."

"Sorry." He put the bowl aside and nodded at me as if acknowledging my grief. I hated it. "Sexual harassment. That's why I'm here. Made a pass at the wrong agent." He motioned to the door to the evidence room and pushed a button unlocking it.

I pushed through the door into the room. Juan stood behind a counter and handed me the pen and notepad. "You can get the rest when you leave. Row 12, section 7, bottom shelf. Boxes labeled Darwyn. With a 'y'."

I took the pen and notepad and began searching for the boxes. There were two boxes labeled Darwyn. I brought both boxes back to Juan's counter. He pointed to a table next to the counter. "You can examine the contents at that table. Do not open any evidence envelopes. Do not take any pictures. You have thirty minutes."

I wanted to point out he still had my cell phone so, of course I couldn't take pictures, but my anger was only now becoming manageable. I sat down at the table and opened the first box. The top item in the pile of evidence was the claw sealed in a plastic evidence bag. It was painted a dappled brown and was stained with old blood. Darwyn's blood.

I picked it up. The thing weighed five pounds easily and the curved shape was over six inches in total length. I tried to imagine how I would handle such a claw as a weapon. I could grip the base like the handle of a scimitar but trying that made me realize how unwieldy it would be. Too much forward weight. I played around with various grips and found if I grabbed the base of the claw in my palm and allowed the hook to protrude between my index finger and middle finger and over the back of my hand, I could use it in a backhand swing. I tried it, swinging my arm from side to side. Still, the claw was very heavy. It would take considerable force to drive the claw into a man's chest. Could Miller have done this? Maybe. If a man was angry enough, he was capable of anything. I should know.

I sifted through the remainder of the evidence. Blood swabs, photographs, Dr. Darwyn's blood stained lab coat. His ID was still clipped to the pocket. I studied the man's photograph on the ID. Regal features under gray hair. His chin seemed to be raised in a haughty attitude. He thought highly of himself. Maybe I was over reacting.

In the bottom of the second box, I found the camera. The evidence label said it belonged to Dr. Styles. Photos of the fight at the party perhaps? Definitely incriminating evidence. And beneath the camera was Darwyn's cell phone. The screen was cracked and coated with clotted blood. Had he tried to call 911? Had someone called him to warn him of his imminent death? I had to get those phone records.

"Time's up." Juan said. "You can leave the box there. I'll have to inventory the contents to make sure you didn't take anything."

I placed the items back in the box. "You were watching me the whole time."

"Yes, I was." He said. "There's a portfolio on Jones' desk with photos of the evidence and copies of everything we've gathered so far. That's all you get from us, partner."

Partner? Oh, yeah. I was in Texas. "Can I have my stuff?"

Juan pushed the bowl toward me. I scooped up my stuff and headed out of the evidence room. Detective Nella Jones was seated at her desk. I plopped down in the chair in front of her desk. She looked up from her laptop.

"I thought we were done."

"Folder for me?"

"Oh, yeah." She opened a desk drawer and rummaged inside. "It's here somewhere. Found it!" She slid a small folder across the desk. "Sign the release on the top that you picked this up for the defense."

"This is all we get?"

"Honey, I let you handle the evidence. You need to see it again, bypass me and go straight to Juan."

I took the folder and drew a calming breath. "Dr. Darwyn had a cellphone. Can we get the phone records?"

"You'll have to talk to the carrier for that." She said coolly.

"Don't you have them?"

"I might."

"Will the carrier give us the records?"

"If you subpoena them. Ask your attorney, honey. You're new at this, aren't you?" She leaned forward and rested her hands on the desk.

"Sort of. Thanks."

"Did Juan make you angry?" She asked.

I felt my cheeks grow warm. "How can you tell?"

"Your fists are clenched. And, I can hear your teeth grinding from across the room. You know, he has that effect on people. Sometimes I wonder about him." She went back to her laptop. "See you later."

I waited for the "partner". It never came. I tried to relax my fists and marched out of the building. Get a grip! Don't lose it at a police station. The last thing I needed was to land in jail. Again!

7

————————

R uth gasped as she stepped into the law firm conference room. Jonathan Steel sat at the table, his eerie eyes fixed on her. "Did I scare you?"

"I didn't know anyone was here. Our offices are closed for the holidays." She said.

Steel wore a long sleeve tee shirt and a pair of mirrored sunglasses perched on his head. "Grace told me to meet you here."

Ruth hugged a stack of folders to her chest and wished she had worn something other than her tattered sweat shirt and jeans. She shook her head. Why did she feel that way? The folders slid out of her grip and papers and photographs spilled out onto the table. Steel stood up and began sliding papers toward her side of the table.

"How was your holiday?"

"Nice. I went home to my parents' lake house in Austin." She slid into a chair and tried to sort through the folders. For some reason her face felt hot. "What about you?"

"I stayed in my RV at Grace's ranch." Steel sat down again and the mirrored sunglasses on the top of his head reflected the harsh light above the table.

"By yourself?" Ruth stacked papers and photos.

"Yes."

"Any family?" Her face cooled down.

"No."

"Friends?" She said hoarsely.

"No."

"Oh, well no one should have to spend Christmas alone."

"I wasn't alone. Grace invited me for Christmas dinner." He said.

Ruth paused. Ms. Pennington and Jonathan Steel at the family dinner table? She shuddered.

"Rat ran over your grave?" Steel said.

"No." Ruth tore her gaze away from those eyes. She shuffled through the photos and lined them up in front of her. "It's just these pictures. Disturbing, you know."

"We had TexMex." Steel said.

Ruth couldn't look at him. "Uh, so you met Grace's husband?"

"No. He was on call and he was at the hospital."

"Well, he's one of the best neurosurgeons in Texas." She glanced at him and tried not to shiver again. She had met Grace's husband and she balked at the idea of him and Steel in the same room. Both men were uber intense!

Ruth studied the photos on the table. The first images made her nauseous. They showed Dr. Darwyn's body draped over fake rocks. His shirt was torn and ripped and huge gashes covered his chest. Blood was everywhere soaked into his torn dress shirt and the remains of his lab coat.

"I saw these at the police station."

"You went to the police station?" Ruth asked.

"Mrs. Pennington asked me to pick up the evidence folder for you."

Ruth drew a deep breath. Grace had done what she should have thought of to do the moment she took on the case. She was slipping already. She focused on the photos.

"Whoever did this really ripped him up." She said.

Steel tapped a photo of a very sharp, curvilinear claw covered in clotted blood. "How can one man do all of this with one claw? It looks like bone but according to the analysis, its metal."

"If it was made of metal, it must have been pretty heavy."

"It was. I held it. If he held it in his hand like this." Steel pointed to the base of the claw. "By putting the base in his hand and letting the claw slide out between his index finger and the middle finger all he would have to do is rake it backhand across something. Let the weight of the metal and the sharp edge do the damage."

Ruth shuddered as she tried to imagine the claw ripping through her skin. "But, there was a blood trail all the way from his office, which I think is on the third floor. Both men appear about the same size. Surely Dr. Darwyn could fight off Dr. Miller."

"Yes, the blood trail bothers me, too." Steel sorted through other crime scene photos. "The trail began in the hallway just down from Darwyn's office. That must have been where he was first attacked. He ran down the hall, into the stairwell, and out onto the walkway overlooking the exhibit." Steel lined up photos to recreate the grisly blood trail.

"Then he fell." Ruth said.

"Or, was pushed and landed on the rocks in the exhibit. The autopsy said his back was broken by the fall."

"So he would have been paralyzed." Ruth said.

"Then, the killer took his time coming down from the walkway to literally rip the man's heart out with this claw." Steel picked up the photo of the claw again. "I wonder how much strength it would take to pierce skin and bone with this."

"Maybe not strength. Maybe adrenaline fueled fury."

Steel glanced at her. "Fury, I understand."

Ruth blinked in surprise at his sudden intensity but the moment was broken when Grace Pennington stepped into the conference room and smiled at them. "So, where are we?" She wore a long denim skirt and a bright, red turtle neck sweater. Her green glasses perched on top of her head.

"Not in a very good position. We were just talking about the supposed murder weapon." Ruth said.

Grace sipped at a blue and gray coffee cup with the Dallas Cowboys' star on the side as she settled at the table. "I doubt very seriously that anyone of Frank's stature could do that amount of damage with this metal claw."

"We were just talking about that. Someone else must have done this." Steel stood up quickly and began to pace around the room. "Someone larger and stronger."

"Who?" Ruth said.

"I don't know." Steel said. "We need to interview the members of Dr. Darwyn's staff. We need to find out who was there the night of that party. And, we need to see the layout of those offices. I want to see the blood trail."

"The prosecution cannot keep you from interviewing anyone." Grace said. "The Institute is on lock down until this trial is over. All of its assets are tied up in the legal outcome of Dr. Darwyn's finances."

Ruth put her face in her hands. "So much to do and only two weeks until we go to trial. Mr. Steel, would you make arrangements for us to tour the Institute tomorrow and interview all of the main personnel?"

Steel had paused by the window, his gaze focused on something far away.

"Mr. Steel?" Ruth said.

"Someone very strong. Almost supernaturally strong." He whispered.

Had the man said supernatural? Ruth glanced at Grace and she only smiled.

"I told you he was special."

Steel nodded and returned to his seat at the table. "Of course. I won't take no for an answer."

"Don't hurt anyone, Mr. Steel." Grace said.

"What is that supposed to mean?" Ruth glanced at Grace.

"I don't always play nicely with people." Steel slid his sunglasses down from his head and covered his eyes. "I have a bit of a temper."

"Okay!" Ruth gathered the photos back into their folders and tried to hide her shiver. "I'll interview Dr. Miller a bit more. I'd like to know why he was still at the Institute at midnight."

"I can answer that one." Grace said. "He was living out of his office."

"What?" Ruth glanced at her. "Why?"

"It is complicated."

"Can you uncomplicate it for us?"

"Frank is in the midst of a rather contentious separation from his wife. He moved in with me while he tried to settle his financial situation. His wife tried to get her hands on his property so he sold it all out from under her. Then, he declared bankruptcy, moved out of my house to save me the trouble and moved into his office. Everything he now owns is in his office. He's been sleeping there for the past two weeks." Grace said.

Ruth nodded and her face warmed with growing anger. "This is why you claimed a conflict of interest?"

"Yes, Ruth. I was going to tell you everything."

"Now, I have a potentially hostile character witness for the prosecution." Ruth shook her head. "Any more surprises?"

"No, dear." Grace said quietly. "Now you know why I chose you to defend Frank. You're level headed. You're quiet and unassuming."

"In stark contrast to his wife?"

"Ruth, this changes nothing." Grace stared at her with those intense green eyes. "I want you to defend Dr. Miller because I truly believe you are the best person for the job. I regret that I have had some dealings with Frank in the past two months but I can't change that. He came to me and asked for help and we will help him. I can help from behind the table but you must be the face of the defense. You must be calm, informed, and rational. It will make the prosecution's claims seem outlandish."

"Unless Dr. Miller blows up on the stand." She slammed the folders down on the table.

"Seems I'm not the only one who can lose their temper." Steel almost smiled.

"You think?" She said.

8

The Darwyn Paleontology Institute was close to the state fairgrounds in a long, three story building. The building at one time had featured some of the most impressive art deco architecture in the city. The front façade still featured carvings of cavemen and dinosaurs from its earlier history as a museum. The rear of the building had been renovated and a tall, cylindrical glass domed addition protruded from the ancient brick structure like a huge boil on the hind end of an ant.

Ruth and Jonathan Steel entered the foyer of the building and were greeted by a tall, African American security guard in a blue uniform.

"Ms. Martinez? Mr. Steel? I'm Henry Johnston, the head of security."

"We spoke to you earlier." Ruth said. "Thank you for arranging our visit with the staff."

Johnston frowned and his tiny mustache arched downward like a caterpillar. "They weren't very happy about it. One of them called the D.A.'s office and was told they had to allow you to speak with them. But, I wouldn't hold any hope they will tell you much. A lot of secrets around this place. Now, I am to escort you throughout the building and make sure you do not touch any of the crime scene."

Ruth looked around at the foyer. The two opposing walls were covered with a mosaic of bright stones depicting cavemen attacking a woolly mammoth on one wall and a T. Rex attacking a Stegosaurus on the other wall. "These mosaics are very impressive. How old is this building?"

"It was built between the two world wars for school children. It closed back in the 1970's and was abandoned until Dr. Darwyn purchased it three years ago."

Steel motioned to three security kiosks with metal detectors lined up across the entrance. "You have a high level of security."

"One can't be too careful nowadays." Johnston said and tried to smile.

"Who would steal dinosaur bones?" Ruth asked.

"Oh, it's not the bones Dr. Darwyn was worried about. It was his technology."

Steel pointed to a far corner where a red light blinked on a security camera. "You have security cameras?"

"State of the art. We can keep up to two weeks' worth of video logs."

"Were they working the night of the party?"

"We thought they were." Johnston motioned them through the metal detectors. "Just leave your purse and your phones in the bowls."

Ruth placed her purse in a bowl and walked through the detector. A green light blinked. Steel dropped his keys and his phone in another bowl and walked through. An alarm squawked and Johnston pointed to his sunglasses.

"I'm afraid you'll have to take them off."

Steel pulled the sunglasses from his face and his eyes gleamed with anger. He walked back through the detector and tossed his sunglasses into the bowl. This time when he walked through the light blinked green.

"Good." Johnston smiled again and motioned for them to retrieve their stuff. "Now, if you'll follow me I'll show you our security kiosk and the monitoring system." He walked over to a desk in the corner and turned a computer monitor toward them. "The system was working fine before the party. It was the first time we'd used it. We booted up the system to try it out. We didn't realize it at the time but the live feed was working but the images were not being recorded correctly. When we replayed the recording for the police, there was nothing but static."

Johnston took the mouse and moved a scroll bar at the bottom of a video image. The main camera over the security kiosk showed people streaming into the foyer and showing their invitations to one of the security guards at each kiosk. The image then exploded into static black and white snow. "The only people coming through the main entrance were staff, family, and specially invited friends. And, some media. But, the system only recorded about five minutes' worth of images. A glitch in the system. We got the main hard drive back from the police and our techs can't find any images on it."

"Where did these images come from?" Steel tapped on the monitor.

"They're stored in the RAM of the security computer."

"Mr. Johnston, I can subpoena that hard drive, but I'm sure you'd want to be cooperative with us. Can we take it and have someone look at it or will you make us jump through the hoops?"

"Well, Ms. Martinez, I have to be honest. There is some video footage on the main hard drive from a couple of days before during our testing. But, the rest of the footage shows static. I don't think you can find anyone more qualified than our people." He shrugged.

"I know someone." Steel said. "A security expert. If information has been erased or corrupted, he can recover it."

"Very well." Johnston nodded. He retrieved a playing card sized metal slab from a desk drawer. "It's a solid state drive so no mechanical failure. If you'll just sign this log that I turned it over to you." He handed Steel the drive and made a notation in an old school ledger. Ruth signed her name next to the date and time.

"Thank you, Mr. Johnston. We're just trying to get to the truth."

"Good luck with that." Johnston said cryptically as he took two plastic cards from a tray next to the monitor. "Visitor tags. Just place your index finger on this reader." He motioned to a fingerprint reader next to the monitor.

"Fingerprint?" Ruth touched the glass face of the small monitor and a green light played over her finger.

"Each visitor pass is keyed to your identity." Johnston swiped the visitor card through a slot on the side of the monitor. On the screen, Ruth's picture popped into view. It had been taken by a small camera on the top of the monitor. Johnston handed her the ID. He paused. Above her picture the name, Dr. Wallace Darwyn appeared. "Sorry for the name mix up. This must be one of Dr. Darwyn's extra I.D.s."

"Extra?"

"He was constantly misplacing them. I keep a few extras with his ID on the RFID chip in the card. For now, you can use it. Just clip it to your lapel."

Steel ran his finger over the reader. "Seems a bit severe."

"Dr. Darwyn insisted. There are lots of proprietary secrets in his labs." Johnston handed Steel his ID card. "With the RFID chip, we can track anyone, anywhere."

"Dr. Darwyn was wearing an ID the night of the murder." Steel clipped the ID to his tee shirt. "I saw it in the evidence box still attached to his lab coat. Did you track his ID the night of the murder?"

"When the recording software went down, so did the tracking software. But, that part of the system is back up and working. See?" He pointed to a second monitor. It showed a revolving set of line drawings of each floor of the Institute. Blinking orange pixels were attached to names of the staff. Johnston touched a key on the keyboard and the image paused on the first floor. He pointed to the three dots in the foyer. One had Jonathan Steel's name beside it. Another had Security Chief Johnston. And, a third had Dr. Wallace Darwyn beside it. "We can follow you anywhere in the building."

"Did you know Dr. Miller?" Ruth asked.

Johnston's face went slack and he averted his eyes. "Yes, I did."

"What do you think of him?"

"Nice man with a bit of a temper. Very high strung when it comes to his area of expertise." Johnston said quietly.

"Do you think he killed Dr. Darwyn?" Steel asked bluntly.

Johnston glanced at Steel and shrugged. "I really can't have an opinion on that. Shall we go upstairs to the offices? The staff are pretty busy and we have to be finished by noon."

Johnston led them across the foyer to an employee elevator. They rode up two floors to the third floor. They stepped out into a reception area. A small woman sat at the reception desk. White hair was pulled back into a severe bun. She wore a high-necked sweater and a dark blue blazer. Her eyes were magnified by huge, white rimmed glasses.

"Mrs. Greely, this is Ruth Martinez and Jonathan Steel. They are defending Dr. Miller." Johnston said.

Greely stood up quickly and planted her hands on her hips. "Why did you let them in here? Traitor!"

"Josephine, that's no way to talk to our visitors." Johnston said.

She glared at Ruth. "You're defending that horrible, horrible man?"

"Yes, ma'am." Ruth said.

"Shame on you! He killed Dr. Darwyn and he deserves to be fried in the electric chair. Fried to a crisp!" She sat in her chair and turned her back on them.

"Well, we know where she stands on Dr. Miller's guilt." Steel whispered in Ruth's ear.

"Mrs. Greely, we'd like to ask you some questions about the night of the murder." Ruth said to the back of her head.

"I wasn't here. I was at home. In the quiet." She sniffled. "I wasn't invited. Only the technical staff. Now go away!"

Johnston shrugged and ushered them down the hallway beyond the desk and paused before an office door. "That is Dr. Darwyn's office at the end of the hall overlooking the Cretaceous Garden in the back of the Institute." Johnston pointed to a yellow tape draped doorway. "These," he pointed to the nearest office doors. "are the other four main professional staff."

The office door behind him opened and a tall, blonde haired woman stepped out. She was studying a clipboard. She wore a light green lab coat over a flowered blouse and lilac pants. She looked up at Johnston with some surprise.

"Mr. Johnston, I thought I asked you to get my office moved down the hall before Friday? You haven't even started." Her gaze drifted to Ruth and then locked on Steel. Her eyes widened. "Who are you?"

"I am Jonathan Steel. This is Ruth Martinez."

"Well, you I could use to move the file cabinet. But you," she glanced at Ruth, "are way overdressed for moving office furniture."

Ruth started to protest and Steel interrupted her. "Where do you want your stuff moved to?"

"To Dr. Darwyn's office, of course. I'm the new director of the Institute." She checked off a few items on the list on her clipboard. "I know the police tape is still up, but I had the janitors move all of his furniture out and down to storage. What little the police left."

Johnston cleared his throat. "Dr. Trudy Morrant, I'd like you to meet Ruth Martinez, Dr. Miller's attorney and her assistant, Jonathan Steel."

Dr. Morrant's eyes widened and then narrowed. Tension seemed to drain out of her body and she looked away. She bit her bottom lip and let the clipboard hang by her side. "This looks bad, doesn't it?"

"Not at all." Steel said. "I'd understand why you'd want to move into your boss' office only two weeks after he was murdered. It makes perfectly good sense to me."

Morrant glared at Steel and her body tensed again. She tucked a loose strand of hair behind an ear and smiled at Ruth. "I'm very busy, Ms. Martinez. I have an Institute that is now leaderless and locked down by the police. We're bleeding money every minute some paying customer isn't walking through our doors."

"I thought Dr. Darwyn's Foundation took care of operating costs." Steel said. Ruth glanced at him. Where did he learn that?

"The Foundation is tied up in probate in the aftermath of his death. We won't see another penny until that is over with. True, we have some emergency funds, but they'll last us only a few more days."

"So, you are the new accountant?" Steel asked. Ruth opened her mouth to protest but Dr. Morrant cut her off.

"Accountant? Do I look like a pencil pusher to you?" She pointed her finger at Steel. "I have a Ph. D. in paleontology. My area of expertise is in skeletal reconstruction."

Ruth put a hand on Steel's arm. The muscles were tense and tight. "I think what Mr. Steel meant to ask is if you are the chief financial officer now."

Morrant dropped her hand and drew a deep breath. "Sorry. I've been under a lot of stress. As the acting director, I have to know about finances."

Steel walked past her and looked in through her open door into her office. "Do you want me to move a file cabinet?"

The tension faded from Morrant's face and she cast a confused look at Steel. "No. You're not even bonded."

"Seems there's plenty of room for us to sit down so Ms. Martinez can ask you some questions." Steel motioned into the office. "Or, do you agree with Mrs. Greely that Dr. Miller should die?"

Ruth flinched at the remark and opened her mouth in anger. Steel glanced at her and there was a tiny shake of his head. Morrant started to speak and then bit her bottom lip again. "Sure. Let's go inside and I'll give you a few minutes."

So, Steel had a knack for catching people off guard. But, still, Ruth had lost control of this process. She needed to have a few words with the man. Once they had asked a few questions, of course. They settled into two chairs facing a huge wooden desk. The shelves behind the desk were covered with books and models of dinosaur skeletons. One wall of the office was covered by a huge flat screen monitor. Morrant glanced at her watch and then settled into her office chair. She tossed the clipboard on the desk and pushed her blonde hair behind her ears.

"Just so you'll know, I graduated from U. T. Austin top of my class. I am the world's leading expert on dinosaur skeletal reconstruction. I got to where I am because I'm smart, educated, and motivated. I didn't buy my way into this position. I am more than qualified to run this Institute." She waved a hand over what appeared to be a desk mat and the monitor on the wall sprang to life. A swirl of bones cascaded across a black background. Morrant touched the mat and the bones began to move and reassembled themselves into the completed skeleton of an upright, walking dinosaur. The image of the dinosaur then began to spin and suddenly sprang outward in a three-dimensional hologram. Ruth gasped.

"My specialized program. This is what I do. Taking care of the finances and trying to run the Institute are jobs I'd rather have left to Dr. Darwyn. But, he is dead. And, gone." Her voice broke and she blinked away tears. She drew a deep breath. "Now, what are your questions?"

Ruth tore her gaze away from the dinosaur skeleton dancing in the air just inches above Morrant's head. "So this is what you do for the Institute?"

Morrant leaned forward and touched a nameplate. She turned it around. "I am the Director of Skeletal Reconstruction. I take the fossils found at a dig site, scan them into my program and reconstruct the final skeletal model of the animal with three-dimensional print-ing. We then use that model for the further reconstruction efforts. As to my working relationship with Dr. Darwyn I would say I'm third in charge. Dr. Miller was the assistant director."

"And now that both of them are out of the picture, you're the alpha?" Steel asked. Ruth glared at him but his eyes were riveted on Morrant. What did he mean by alpha?

"What are you implying?"

"Nothing. I'm just asking a question. I thought I would use language a paleontologist would be familiar with. Most dinosaur groupings are female and there is always an alpha female."

"The answer is, 'yes'. I am in charge." Morrant said testily.

"In one of the textbooks you authored, you somehow draw the conclusion the skeleton of a dinosaur can reveal if it is the alpha."

She leaned back. "You're well read, Mr., what was your name?"

"Steel. Dr. Adrian Drake seems to think you put too much comparison on your skeletal remains to mammalian models. No one is clear about the pecking order in dinosaur herds."

Ruth leaned forward and cleared her throat. Who was this man? And, how did she lose control of this conversation. "Mr. Steel is not going to ask you anymore questions, Dr. Morrant. We'll make this short and to the point. Are you surprised that Dr. Miller is accused of killing Dr. Darwyn?"

"That's an odd question." Morrant said tearing her gaze away from Steel. "Look, they never got along very well. That's the way Wallace preferred it. He liked to surround himself with experts who disagreed with him. He said it kept him sharp. Dr. Miller is a religious fanatic. What can I say? I knew it the moment I met him. I would never have hired him. He wanted to decorate the foyer for Christmas! Really? We're a scientific establishment, not a fairy tale theme park. And, we all know that religious fanatics can snap and become psychotic. Just watch any movie. Or, the nightly news."

"And we all know movies represent the truth." Steel said. Ruth glared at him and his eyes met hers. She shook her head slightly and felt her face warm.

"Now, Dr. Morrant, were you at the party the night Dr. Darwyn was murdered?"

"Yes." Morrant seemed to deflate. She fidgeted with the desk mat and the monitor went blank. The three-dimensional dinosaur skeleton disappeared. "Wallace had asked me to accompany him. As a date. I was a little uncomfortable with it, but we had grown fond of each other. You know how it is in a professional relationship. You try to keep it formal, but sometimes, the lines get blurred. I was standing there beside Wallace when he unveiled Annieraptor. That was when Frank went ballistic. He rushed across the Cretaceous Garden and immediately verbally attacked Wallace. They got into a very heated argument about feathers. Feathers! Of all things, Frank got all caught up on the feathers! The man has no sense of imagination."

"How long did they fight?"

"About five minutes. Wallace tried to calm him down, but he

wouldn't hear it. That's when Frank shoved Dr. Darwyn and he tripped over a rock in the display room. Frank stormed off upstairs to his office. Wallace insisted he wasn't hurt and finished the party."

"When did you last see Dr. Darwyn?"

Morrant blinked and a tear slid down her right cheek. "I walked him up to his office. It was about ten P.M. He was really tired and distracted. Frank was waiting in the hallway to speak to him so he, uh, he kissed me on the cheek and told me he'd call me the next day. That was the last time I saw him alive."

Ruth watched Morrant wipe the tear from her cheek. Her eyes were riveted on the desktop. "I think that's all I need, Dr. Morrant. Thank you for your time."

She stood up and Steel remained in his seat. "I'd like to ask one last question." He whispered. Ruth gritted her teeth and before she could speak, he stood up and leaned across the desk toward Dr. Morrant.

"Who owns the rights to your program?"

Ruth opened her mouth to protest and then glanced at Morrant. She stiffened and leaned forward.

"What do you mean?" Morrant asked.

"You said you created this three-dimensional program. Do other universities and museums use it?"

"Yes." Morrant blurted out.

"How much do you get paid in royalties?" Steel leaned closer.

"Nothing. The Darwyn Paleontology Institute owns the program." Morrant slowly stood up.

"The crowning achievement of your career and Dr. Darwyn took it from you and let others use it. I assume he charges them?"

"Yes."

"You don't like that?"

"No. But, I signed my rights away when I took this position."

"And, Wallace," Steel said the name with sarcasm, "wouldn't give you back the rights, would he?"

"I think I've said enough. I have to get my office moved. Mr. Johnston?" Morrant moved from behind her desk and opened the door to the hallway. Johnston glanced in. "Mr. Johnston, I'm done with our guests."

Ruth found herself breathing heavily as she glanced from Steel's intense stare and Morrant's pale features. She didn't know whether to be furious or pleased. They left the office and Johnston closed the door behind them.

"Would you like to move on to the next staff?" Johnston asked.

"Yes." Ruth glared at Steel. "But, first, I need to wash my face."

9

———————

Steel was leaning against the wall when Ruth came out of the
women's restroom. She glanced around the corner into the
hallway and Johnston waited just out of earshot. She looked
up at Steel's bright, turquoise eyes.

"What was that all about?"

"Ms. Pennington was right. You need help." He stated.

"I'm in charge of this investigation, Mr. Steel."

"And, you aren't seeing it."

"Seeing what?"

"She is guilty?" He looked down at her.

"Of what?"

"Murder, maybe. Selfish advancement for sure. She developed
that software to find herself the perfect position that would gain her
the most in money and position. She just didn't read the fine print in
the contract. She lost control of her program."

"And you think she killed Dr. Darwyn for that?"

"Maybe. She was seducing him to get into his good graces. I wonder
what she gets paid by the Institute. Of course, now it'll be much more
since she will be in charge of the money. Power, sex, money. Powerful

motivators for murder. She'll make sure the control over her program returns to her. She has gained a lot with Dr. Darwyn's death. You know what I call that?" He tilted his head when he looked at her.

"What?"

"Motive."

Ruth closed her eyes and rubbed her temples. The man was giving her a headache. "Steel, she's not much bigger than I am. There is no way she could have ripped Dr. Darwyn to shreds with that claw."

"No, but maybe he wasn't the only man in her life." Steel pushed away from the wall and disappeared around the corner.

JOHNSTON LED them down the hall and paused in front of a glass door across the hall and slightly down from Dr. Darwyn's office. He poked his head inside and then motioned them in. Across a chrome and glass desk stood a pudgy African American man in rimless spectacles. His short, gray hair covered his head and extended down along his jaw line in a gray beard and trim mustache. He wore a light red shirt and a blue bowtie.

"I'm Dr. Mitchell Grant." He said as he came around the desk. "It's a terrible time for us all and I do hope I can help Dr. Miller."

Ruth introduced herself and Steel as Johnston stepped back out into the hall. Grant motioned to a couch to the side of his desk. The walls were covered with paintings of the human body stripped of flesh in various poses. A model of a human baby sucking its thumb sat on the shelf behind the desk. Its skin was absent and all the muscles and vessels were bright colors. Ruth gasped and tried to swallow back nausea.

Grant noticed as he moved behind his desk and shrugged. "I'm sorry you find my display distasteful. It's a resin injection model of the human body. Polymer preservation. Surely you've heard of it."

"I have." Steel said. "An anatomist has filled an entire museum with these sculptures. They're real people who agree to have their bodies injected with a resin substance."

"Thousands have signed up to be models once they've died." Grant smiled as he sat down. "I'm on the list."

Ruth swallowed again and took out her notebook. "Well, that's nice, Dr. Grant. We'll make this short. We would like to talk to you about your relationship with Dr. Darwyn and Dr. Miller."

"Well, that should be easy. Dr. Darwyn hired me about nine months ago to work with Dr. Morrant on her skeletal modeling program. My work is in kinesiology, the science of muscles. I fill in all the muscles, tendons, and ligaments. I study bone structure to determine how and where musculature is located. I give the skeletons the means to move, you might say."

He stood up and turned a flat panel computer model around so they could see it. The image of the same dinosaur that was on Dr. Morrant's screen filled the center of this one. Grant touched the screen and the skeletal model began to rotate slowly.

"You saw this model already?"

"In Dr. Morrant's office." Ruth said.

"Well, I take her three-dimensional model and I disconnect all the bones and study how they articulate with each other. I look at the grooves and insertion points on the bones and determine the size and dimensions of muscles. Each muscle is a function of its work load and movement; it's biomechanics." Grant touched an icon on the screen. Two bones in the leg of the dinosaur separated from the image and zoomed forward.

"This is the femur and the tibia articulation. I outline the insertion points and using my own program, determine how and where the muscles insert on the bones." He touched another icon. A yellow highlight pulsed on the bones and then a reddish muscle grew out of thin air and connected the two bones. The bones then moved through various ranges of motion and the muscle contracted and elongated with the movement. "As I said, Dr. Darwyn met me at a national conference about a year ago and was impressed with my program. He offered me a job and money to complete the program development."

"Is this program just for dinosaur bones?" Ruth asked.

"Oh, no. This is just a stepping stone for me. Dr. Darwyn knew that, but he had what I didn't. Money. I hope to continue to develop this program to go with other adaptive technology that is surfacing, that of artificial muscles. Imagine if we could reconstruct bones for an amputee and then place artificial muscles on those bones and give a person back their leg! The problem with prosthetics is that no matter how hard we try, the prosthetic does not move or perform naturally. My work will, in time, correct that problem. Muscle and bone will be replaced perfectly matched to the patient."

Grant leaned forward. "Researchers in Japan started with an artificial human skeleton that was then covered in bundles of a proprietary multi-filament artificial muscles. These multifilament bundles contract and expand like real human muscles when an electrical current is applied. You see, by controlling different groups of these muscles at different times, the skeleton's arms, legs, and head can all be made to move similar to how a real human can. But, the research is still light years behind where we need to be. I want to be on the ground floor of this developing technology. Dr. Darwyn has given me a chance to complete my work."

"And, your personal relationship with the man?" Steel asked.

Dr. Grant frowned. "Let's just say he's not very chummy. Driven. Focused. He's just not the most hospitable human being."

"Did you ever have a disagreement with him?" Ruth asked.

Grant looked away and pursed his lips in thought. He studied the top of his desk for a moment. "We don't always get along here at the Institute, Ms. Martinez. We're all a bit egotistical when it comes to our areas of expertise. Yes, we've had disagreements mostly on academic and scientific matters, but that is all." He finally looked up at her and a weak smile creased his lips.

"What about Dr. Miller?"

Grant leaned back and sighed. His smile became genuine. "Ah, Frank and I are good friends. We both share a love for football, soccer, and German chocolate cake! I want to help him. I can't believe he killed Dr. Darwyn. He's passionate but he isn't a violent person."

"Dr. Grant." Steel said. "You seem to be an expert on muscle and bone interaction. Have you seen the wounds on Dr. Darwyn?"

Grant frowned. "I was here the night he died. I came up to my office to finish up some work halfway through the party and fell asleep at my desk. When I heard the sirens I ran downstairs." He paused and swallowed. "I saw Dr. Darwyn's body as they packed him up and took him away. His wounds seemed quite extensive. Personally, I don't see how any human being could have done that. The sheer ferocity of some of the wounds, particularly on his back, suggests a killer with enormous strength and agility."

"Would you be willing to testify to that?" Ruth asked.

"Yes. Anything to help Frank. Listen, Ms. Martinez, he didn't kill Dr. Darwyn. I would stake my reputation on it."

"You may have to."

JOHNSTON LED them past the next office and into a huge, well lit room. Counters were scattered about the room and were covered with computer screens and electronic wiring. Fiber optic cable and metal littered the room. It looked like a robot had exploded. Johnston took them back to the rear area of the lab. A man was crouched down between two bins of computer components. He was tossing things over his shoulders and cursing loudly.

"Dr. Styles? Dr. Styles!" Johnston shouted.

The man stopped throwing things and whirled to face them. He was young, perhaps in his late twenties with spiked hair and a nose ring. He wore a blue tee shirt under his stained lab coat. "Live Loud and Party!" was written in white letters across his chest above his jeans and sandals. A hand bore a perversion of the Vulcan salute.

"What? I'm busy trying to find the Feldercarb 360 that Mazie supposedly put back on the rack before I fired her!" His face reddened and then he took in the sight of Ruth and Steel. "Oh, you're the defense guys."

Ruth introduced them and Johnston shook his head as he left the lab. "I'm Burton Styles. Mechanical engineer." He shook her hand and left a smear of white grease on it. He glanced at her hand and reached for a red rag and unceremoniously shoved it into her hand.

"I'm kind of busy so if we can get on with it?" He pushed himself up onto a lab counter and shoved aside a nest of wiring and metal rods so he could sit.

"Sure." Ruth pulled out her notebook. "What do you do here?"

"Mechanical engineer? I just told you." He glanced past her and seemed to be searching for something.

"And why would a dinosaur institute need a mechanical engineer?"

Styles rubbed his face and left a patch of the white grease on his cheek. "Uh, because we build recreations of the dinosaurs. Who do you think takes Grant's muscles and Morrant's bones and puts them together? Huh? Someone has to do the hard work of actually pulling off what they create on their nifty little computer screens, right? It's not just modeling clay and pipe cleaners, you know."

Ruth looked over at Steel. The man's face was crimson and she saw a muscle twitch in his cheek. "Dr. Styles, what was your relationship with Dr. Darwyn?"

Styles hopped down from the counter and pushed her aside. He crouched over a black bin of wire and pulled out a thick, green tinted metal rod with two areas of flexible joints. "Here it is!"

Steel reached over and jerked the rod out of his hand. With his free hand, he grabbed Styles by the front of his tee shirt and lifted him up back onto the counter. He plopped him down very hard and Styles' teeth rattled. For the first time, the man's eyes focused on Steel.

"The lady asked you a question. I suggest you pay attention."

Styles blinked away his fear and it was replaced with indignation. "Hey, who do you think you are? I'm calling security."

"He's right outside the door. You can scream after you answer the question." Steel growled.

Ruth gently pushed Steel aside and tried to regain control of the situation. "Dr. Styles, we'll be out of your hair in a few minutes and you and your Feldercarb 360 can have lunch, if you want." Steel backed away and bumped up against a cabinet. Glass tinkled and Styles hopped down from the counter and rushed past him to catch a glass flask filled with an oily substance. Something white rolled along the bottom of the flask. "Would you stop rampaging through my lab like a bull elephant?" Styles gingerly placed the flask back on its pedestal. "I have quite a few volatile chemicals in here, not to mention delicately tuned instruments. You're one dropped test tube away from a fire!"

"You're avoiding the question." Steel said. The chemicals in the room weren't the only thing that was volatile.

Styles looked from Steel and back at Ruth. His anger faded. "Fine. The old man and I didn't always see eye to eye. He didn't appreciate my ability. I had ideas for improving things and he just didn't see it. He just wanted static displays. Dioramas! Really? I wanted more. I knew I could make his dinosaurs look real. Molded silicone skin with a special mixture of my own design that resembles the pebbled flesh of dinosaurs. Sculpted musculature on the bones to fill out that skin. So, it would not only look real, it would feel real. I mean, have you seen the claws?"

"Yes, covered with Dr. Darwyn's blood." Steel said.

Styles ignored the remark and crossed to the far wall. "For instance, look here." He shoved aside manuals and wires and pulled a small model of a dinosaur into view. It was about two feet tall. "This is a model of a Utahraptor. Not the same as Annieraptor, but it was a place for me to start with my modeling." The dinosaur seemed placid, standing with both feet firmly on the base of the display and its clawed upper arms held rigidly in front of it.

"Pretty boring, huh? I mean Morrant and Grant do all this three-dimensional work. We print out the components with a 3D printer and all the thing will do is just stand there like it's part of a wax museum. I mean, come on guys, let's make it live!"

He reached and retrieved another model. It was of the same dinosaur but the difference was remarkable. One leg was planted firmly on the display base and the other was extended forward with its claws visible. The upper arms were raised in what had to be an attack posture. The thing's head was tilted and its mouth was opened exposing needle sharp teeth. Ruth gasped as Styles shoved it at her.

"Imaging this thing coming after you! Pretty scary, huh? See what a difference my artistic side can make to their pure science? See?"

"What did Dr. Darwyn say to this model?" Ruth asked as she stepped back from the hideous thing.

Styles put the model behind him and it fell over into a nest of wires. "Too scary. Too frightening. Bad for customers and potential investors. The man has no sense of drama."

"So you built a static model?" Steel asked.

Something flickered behind Styles' eyes and he shrugged. "Yeah. Darwyn was the boss. He signs my paycheck. But--" He paused and glanced back at the model and then fell silent. "Never mind."

"But, what?" Ruth asked.

"Nothing. I was going to surprise the old man at the party but Miller got to him first and caused such a ruckus I backed off."

"What kind of surprise?"

"That last pose? The one with the claws extended? Probably not a good idea in retrospect. But, I gave the man his feathers! Feathers! Man, was that a mistake. Now, Miller was a piece of work. That man is crazy. Always spouting his religious nutcake spew. I was there at the party taking pictures for the big unveiling and then Miller goes ballistic. They went after it pretty heavy and Frank threatened the old man and stalked off."

"Threatened him how?" Steel asked.

"Said he would show him who was right. And, that he would win because he had God on his side." Styles grimaced. "I told Darwyn hiring Miller was a mistake. The man is unstable. Now, if you'll excuse me, I have to find my Feldercarb 360."

Ruth looked at the green rod. "That's not it?"

Styles picked up the green rod and bent the end at an angle. He lowered it down over his shoulder and began to scratch his back. "No. This is my backscratcher."

10

———————

The Galleria was filled with kids. Ruth had forgotten the schools were out for Christmas break. On the fourth floor an outside seating area for a Chinese restaurant proved to be way too loud. She sat at a table overlooking the ice rink four floors below. Steel studied the menu on the other side of the table.

"Good Chinese food?" He asked.

"I come here often. It's usually not this crowded. Or loud."

A man brushed by her and paused to look down. He was bald and wore a three-piece suit stretched over his prominent abdomen. "Ruth Martinez? Is that you?"

Ruth looked up. "Hey, Steve."

"I heard you're representing Dr. Miller in the Darwyn murder." The man smiled as he wiped sweat from his forehead.

"That's right." Ruth tried to smile. "Uh, this is Jonathan Steel. He is our investigator."

"Steve Atchison, attorney at law. Mostly probate." Atchison extended his hand and Steel shook it. "I also heard Nicholas has joined the D.A.'s office. Is he leading the prosecution?"

Ruth nodded. "You heard right."

Atchison leaned forward, his mouth close to her ear. "He's going to eat you alive. And, you won't have a hail Mary pass like you did with Drake." He laughed and moved on to another table.

"Who was Drake?" Steel asked. Her face grew warm and she avoided his intense gaze.

"Not now. Back in the Institute what was that all about?"

"What was what all about?"

"Those questions. The confrontation."

"You needed help. I did my homework. I was the bad cop. You were the good cop." He studied the menu. "Are you always the good cop?"

Ruth opened her mouth to protest and then shut it in confusion. "I can be the bad cop."

"I don't believe you." Steel didn't look up. "Give me time and I'll have you whipped into shape."

"You'll have me whipped into shape?" She said out loud.

Steel looked up and a ghost of a smile fleeted across his lips. "See what I mean. I tend to rub people the wrong way. It's my gift. Let me be the sandpaper so you can see what lies beneath the pain."

Ruth sighed. "Who are you? What do you do?"

"I help people." Steel said, reaching into his shirt pocket to take out a card.

Ruth looked at it. 'A Help in the time of Need' was written on the card beneath his name, a phone number, and a web page address. "I thought you were a private investigator."

"I have a license. Don't carry a gun. Don't plan to." Steel said. The waiter appeared and they ordered.

Ruth handed him back the card. "So what do you do for defense?"

"I don't usually get involved in these kind of investigations."

"What kind of investigations do you get involved with?"

"When someone is oppressed by evil, I will help them."

"Evil?"

"Evil."

"Like, real evil?"

"Is there any other kind?"

"Some people say there is no good or evil."

"What do you say?"

"I've seen some pretty bad things in my career." Ruth said. Drake.

"So you believe in Satan?" Steel said quietly.

Ruth opened her mouth to answer and the waiter appeared, setting bowls of hot and sour soup before them. He stepped away and Ruth paused to study Steel's eyes. He was still waiting for an answer. "Look, I was raised in a good Southern Baptist church and I was taught all about the devil and hellfire and brimstone."

Steel waited and she popped a spoon of soup in her mouth. It was liquid fire. She sucked in air and took a sip of her water. Steel still waited.

"What is it with you?" She croaked.

"You didn't answer my question."

Ruth popped a couple of ice cubes from her water into the soup and stirred. "You're making me feel uncomfortable. I'm not so sure working on this case was such a good idea."

Steel pushed the soup aside and leaned across the table. "Someone killed Dr. Darwyn by running a steel replica of a dinosaur claw underneath his breastbone, piercing his heart and then ripping open his abdomen so that his intestines spilled out. Someone planned that. Someone thought up that attack. I would call any mind capable of those actions evil." He sat back and began to eat his soup.

Ruth blinked and laid her spoon on the table. "Look, I'm not very religious right now. I don't have time in my busy life to consider things about God and the devil. There was a time when I believed God was good and in control and the devil worked his hardest to oppose God. But, all you have to do is spend some time in the legal world to see that things aren't conveniently black and white. It's all shades of gray, gradations of relative good and evil." And, sometimes doing what seems to be good ends up being evil, she thought.

Steel finished his soup. "If there are shades of gray, they come from humans. Not God. I've looked into the face of evil and it is real."

Ruth finished her soup. What kind of a man was this Jonathan Steel? "How long have you been like this?"

"I don't know." Steel's averted his gaze.

"What kind of answer is that?"

Steel leaned back in his chair and his gaze turned to the ice rink below. "I suffer from amnesia. I don't remember anything about my past beyond the last year and a half. Except, I am looking for one particular force of evil. It killed someone I care about."

Ruth let her spoon clink into her empty soup dish. Something dark and shadowy clouded Steel's gaze. "Force? It? Is that why you're looking for this artifact?"

"Yes."

"That's how you met Grace Pennington?"

"Yes."

"Fine." Ruth pushed the bowl aside. "Tell me about it."

Steel's intense gaze focused on her and she refused to break the stare. "Okay."

I SHOWED up in Dallas two days before Christmas. The traffic was horrendous. The antique shop was little more than a junk shop just north of 635 in a run-down industrial area. The owner wasn't very helpful even after I told him I'd seen the mask on his website. Said he had sold the thing days before and forgot to take it off the Internet. He wouldn't tell me who had bought it. When I pressed him, he kept tapping his finger on a business card on his desk and babbling on about privacy. It was the buyer's card and twenty dollars later I had the name and number of the purchaser. Did I say the man sold junk?

Ms. Grace Pennington had purchased the artifact. I gave her a call the next morning on Christmas Eve. She was somewhat elusive, as I would have expected. She said it was to be her husband's Christmas present. Turns out he was a collector of odd artifacts like my mentor, Dr. Cephas Lawrence. I asked her if I could see it and when she pressed me for why, I told just a little of my story. I told her it might be attached to a criminal I was pursuing. She kindly ended the conversation and said she would get back to me.

Six hours later, I was pulling into the driveway of a huge mansion north of Dallas in one of the richest areas of town. A valet met me at the front door. Seems Ms. Pennington was having a Christmas party. Turns out she runs a law firm in Dallas; one of the largest and oldest. And, today was the annual Christmas party.

I was a little intimidated to show up at such a party in my jeans until Ms. Pennington met me in her foyer in that red cowboy shirt and her dark green jeans and high leather boots.

"Mr. Steel, I presume?" She smiled and took my hand. She was tall and willowy and moved with the grace after which she was named. "Won't you join me in my library?"

She led me through the boisterous partygoers and into a rich, mahogany paneled library. She pointed to a chair in front of a huge desk. "Won't you have a seat?"

I settled into the chair and a servant appeared beside me with a tray of drinks. I took a cup of spiced cider and watched as Ms. Pennington settled behind her desk.

"Now, Mr. Steel, just why should I give you my husband's Christmas present?"

I sipped the cider. It was hot and spicy. "I just want to see it. I need to find out if it is connected to my adversary."

Ms. Pennington sat back in her chair and nodded. "Cephas seems to think so."

I choked on the cider. "You know Cephas?"

"We represented him a few years ago. He came to Dallas for one of his, shall we say, interventions? The family was less than pleased and filed a lawsuit against him." She sat forward. "Of course, I'm not at liberty to divulge information, Mr. Steel, but Dr. Lawrence did save the girl's life. And, he thinks very highly of you. He said you have become a top notch investigator."

I sat the cider cup on a nearby coffee table. "I have a license, but I really just try to help people in trouble. Because, where there's trouble, there's usually evil. And, one day, it will lead me to the thing I search for."

She frowned and leaned forward on the desk. "You speak of it in such inhuman terms."

"It is inhuman." I said.

"Evil, you mean?"

"Yes. Do you believe there is true evil in this world?"

Ms. Pennington touched her chin with her steepled hands as she considered her answer. She reached forward and retrieved a folder. She opened it and slid it across the desk toward me. "Yes, I do, Mr. Steel."

I leaned over the desk and studied the folder contents. Photographs spilled out. My hair stood on end. My fury built. My righteous indignation burned within me. "What is this?"

"One of my dear friends has gotten himself into some trouble. He is innocent and one of my associates is in danger of leaving the firm. She is up for a partnership slot along with another associate and the other full partners have decided the two should go head to head over this case to decide who gets the next slot. I'm pulling for Ruth Martinez and she will need all the help she can get." Ms. Pennington leaned forward and her gaze burned into mine. "I don't want to lose her, Mr. Steel. And, even more importantly, I don't want to see my dear friend convicted for a murder he did not commit." Ms. Pennington closed the folder. "You may see the artifact on one condition."

I felt the anger seep away as the photographs disappeared. "What is that?"

"That you help Ruth Martinez with her investigation. I will pay your expenses, of course. And, you may find some lead to this creature you seek."

This is not what I had expected when I had walked into the mansion belonging to Ms. Grace Pennington. But, a common theme in my life was finding myself in places I never expected and discovering that God had something there that I must do. It was becoming a practice I was increasingly uncomfortable with. It was as if God were saying He would help me if I would help Him. I felt the inevitable settle over me like a cloud of cold mist. I shivered. Maybe I could get out of this. "I'm not much of an investigator."

"Dr. Lawrence tells me otherwise. He suggested I ask you." Ms.

Pennington tilted her head as she studied me. "You help people, Mr. Steel. My friend and my associate need all the help they can get. Will you please help them?"

I relaxed into the chair and felt the answer form on my lips. "I can consider it."

Ms. Pennington sat back and smiled. "Mr. Steel, I use my maiden name because of my law firm, but my friends call me Grace. I would be honored if you would call me by that name. Would you like to join my party?"

I opened my mouth to turn down the request when the doors to the library slid open and this small, agitated woman rushed in. That is when you came into the picture.

THE WAITER ARRIVED with their entrees and Ruth watched Jonathan Steel's gaze fade into the distance. She ate in silence for a while until he seemed to return from some far, distant land. He picked at his food and then looked at her.

"That is why I am here, Ms. Martinez. I'm here to help you fight this evil that has entered the lives of Ms. Grace and Frank Miller."

Ruth sipped at her iced tea. "You must have cared a great deal about your friend who died."

Steel's eyes burrowed into hers and for a second she thought she saw a tear glisten in the corner of his eye. He reached to his neck and pulled a gold chain into view. A small cross hung on the chain. "This was hers. It reminds me every day of my mission. I will stop at nothing to track it down."

Ruth shuddered and wanted to ask more but to prod open Pandora's box was to invite danger and destructive evil into the world. Some things were better left untouched. She looked away and he continued to speak.

"Ms. Martinez, if you want to save Dr. Miller, you're going to have to find a deeper motive than just to save your career. The man is innocent and there is someone evil out there who killed Dr. Darwyn and framed Dr. Miller. He deserves the best you can give him. And, for the right reason." Steel's turquoise eyes glowed with ferocity and he tucked the cross back into his shirt.

Ruth looked out over the vast open mall. Below them, ice skaters laughed and squealed with delight. Shoppers bent on spending their Christmas gift cards swirled along the walkways. Normal, happy people who had no idea that Steel's "evil" dwelled among them. She toyed with her fried rice. "I've looked into the face of evil, Mr. Steel. And, I was so self-centered, I let that evil back out into the world."

"Tell me about it." Steel said.

Ruth shook her head. "I don't like talking about it."

Steel nodded. "Neither do I. But, if this affects your ability to defend Dr. Miller, I need to know."

Ruth sat back and sighed. "Okay, it was January of this year and I was assigned to one of my bosses, Robert Birmingham to help defend Reginald Drake. He was a snarky, young spoiled brat who was arrested for murdering an escort. His family was wealthy and tied to the law firm so we took the case. It wasn't going well. Birmingham was too lazy and the case got away from us. Just two hours before closing arguments, everything changed."

11

"This is a disaster!" Bob Birmingham pounded the conference table.

Ruth flinched with each blow. Birmingham's face reddened, the crimson stain spilling up into his bare scalp. One of his double chins wobbled with each blow and his eyes narrowed as he glared at her.

"Grace promised me you would deliver, Ms. Martinez. She promised me you could handle this case! We have nothing left!"

"This case wasn't defensible to begin with." Ruth said.

Birmingham glared at her and shuddered with anger. "Why did Bryan Nicholas have to get appendicitis days before this trial? Huh? If he were here, well, if he were here." He paused and fell silent.

"Nothing would be different." Ruth finished quietly.

A shadow fell over her. Reginald Drake stood behind her. She turned slowly in her chair to face him. As always, his eyes shocked her. His right eye was a pale, icy blue and his left eye a deep chocolate brown. His handsome face was framed by silver hair making him look much older than his age of 20. He wore a shiny, silver Armani suit with a burgundy tie held back by a tie tack shaped like a scorpion.

"Mr. Birmingham, as the senior partner in this endeavor, I place the blame solely on you. Ms. Martinez is an associate and it is you who have let her down." He straightened his tie with his long fingered hands and his perfectly manicured nails. "Now, my father retained this firm for his oil company and I believe you earned millions off of his oil deals before his untimely death. Those millions he paid to you came from his hundreds of millions of dollars now tied up in my trust fund. While I do not yet have control over that fund, I assure you there are numerous skeletons in the closet guarding those funds and you do not want those skeletons exposed to the public." He sniffed and paced along the length of the conference table.

"Sir, we still have closing arguments and, at best, the evidence is circumstantial." Ruth managed to say. She shivered as Drake turned to study her with those unsettling eyes.

"Ms. Martinez, I will not go to prison for this murder. I am innocent of these charges and you will do whatever it takes to postpone closing statements until you have a better defense." He suddenly rushed toward her, leaned down and pressed his face close to hers. Ruth gasped and tried to pull away but was pinned against the table. His breath smelled of boiled eggs and vinegar. "Do you understand?"

Ruth swallowed and managed to spin the chair and pull away from the man. Birmingham stood up and buttoned his coat over his generous abdomen. "Well, I for one don't hold out much hope for your acquittal, Mr. Drake and your skeletons will just have to be exposed for the world to see. I'm going across the street for a drink. And, Ms. Martinez, I suggest you take the next two hours to find a way to close out this trial with the most impressive closing argument you will ever make."

As he headed for the doors Ruth stood up. "Me? I'm making the closing argument?"

Birmingham never paused as he shouted, "Yes."

The doors slammed behind him leaving her alone in the room with a monster. She heard Drake breathing heavily behind her and felt the heat of his body as he stepped closer to her. Is this what Maria Zuniga had felt just moments before her death?

"He's throwing you to the wolves." Drake said.

"What?"

Drake shook his head in disgust. "You're so weak. He knows it. He wants this Bryan Nicholas to move forward and not you. Can't you see it?"

Ruth tried to lean away from his voice. "No, Bryan was in the hospital."

"Oh, wake up, Ruth!" Drake said. "Birmingham knows this is a hopeless case. He knows he would ultimately fail. So, you'll take the fall. You will bear the brunt of this and he'll get you fired."

Ruth stood up. Was it true? What had she gotten herself into? "I don't know."

"Ruth, darling." He whispered and he grabbed her right arm. His face was just inches from hers. "Must I do everything for you?"

"You're hurting me." Ruth hissed and jerked her arm from his grasp. "Is that how you hurt Maria?"

Drake raised an eyebrow and massaged his hand. "Now, now, Ms. Martinez. You represent me and you must assume I am innocent. It's what you are well paid for. You don't want to disappoint me." He moved closer and she stepped back, stumbling on the chair and falling back into it.

"Don't threaten me, Drake. I'm your attorney and I am the only one who can get you acquitted. You don't want to make me mad." Ruth said.

Drake laughed and whirled around, walking along the length of the conference table. He spun chairs as he circled the table, his laughter echoing in the room. "You? Mad?" He stopped and leaned against the head of the table. "You little cow! You're nothing but an herbivore in the midst of predators. You can't get any angrier than a heifer who has lost her cud."

Ruth's face warmed with anger that quickly became fear. The man was insane. "Fine, what would you have me say? What can I possibly do to convince the jury that a monster like you is innocent?"

Drake straightened and nodded. "It would seem that I will have to do your work for you. Save my neck and save your career. I'm afraid Birmingham won't like it. Not at all. You'll make him look like a drunken snit." Drake raised an eyebrow and smiled. "I'd rather like that, come to think of it. Now, listen carefully. Louisiana's exception to the UDDA. Dr. White's testimony and his white paper on the issue. You'll find it on the Internet. But, best hurry." He glanced at his watch. "You have an hour and forty-seven minutes until court reconvenes." He opened the door and gestured outside. "Bailiff, you can take me back to my holding cell. I need to work on my anger management."

Drake cast one last long look at her and pursed his lips in a kiss. "Mooooo!" He said as the bailiff led him away. Ruth fought back the cold nausea of panic and gasped for breath. She pressed her hands against her mouth and suppressed the tears. What was she to do? If she failed, her career was over. If she succeeded, that creature would walk.

Ruth opened her tablet and entered the parameters for a search. She clicked on the first heading and began to read. A few times in her professional career Ruth experienced an almost transcendental experience when things seemed to click; when the stars lined up; when the puzzle pieces fit perfectly. She called that moment her "aha" experience. As she read the testimony of Dr. Alba, all the fear and worry melted away under the sublime power of a paradigm shift. She saw it. She had it! Reginald Drake would soon receive his acquittal.

"Ms. Martinez, before the prosecution delivers its closing statement, does the defense have anything further to add." Judge Marshall Tucker said as he slumped behind his desk. His heavy Texan drawl perfectly matched his handlebar mustache. All that was missing was a cowboy hat.

"Your honor, before the defense rests, I would like to recall a witness from earlier in the trial." Ruth said. Drake smiled and tried to pat her hand. She pulled it away. She couldn't let him distract her. If she was going to make this work, she had to put the man's alien eyes out of her mind.

"The prosecution, of course, objects." Katrina Patrick stood up. "The defense has had ample opportunity to question all of my witnesses."

Ruth swallowed and kept her eyes on Tucker. "Your honor, I am sure the prosecution doesn't want the jury to think that Mr. Drake has not had the full extent of the law's protection. One is innocent until proven guilty. I merely want to clarify some facts from an earlier line of testimony. It won't take much time away from the prosecution's rush to deliver Mr. Drake his final fate."

Out of the corner of her eye she saw Patrick stiffen. The look on her face was priceless. Patrick sat back down. "Well, far be it from me to deny Mr. Drake ample opportunity to continue to convince this jury of his guilt. I withdraw my objection."

Tucker sniffed and massaged his mustache. "Well, I'm glad that little tiff worked itself out without my intervention. If ya'll want me to, I'll just mosey on to my chambers and let the two of you work out the great mystery of our legal system. Ms. Martinez, let's get this show on the road, shall we?"

"Yes, sir. I'd like to recall the medical examiner to the witness stand."

Ruth drew a deep breath and tried to calm her trembling hands as she followed Dr. McCormack to the stand. He was a walrus of a man with dark hair pulled back in a ponytail and tiny wire rimmed glasses. He settled into the seat and sighed. "I don't know what I can add to this charade, Marshall, but I'm like you. Get on with the rat killing."

Tucker pounded the gavel weakly. "Now, Rupert, no need for those snide comments. I might have to consider leveling contempt of court on you. Now, you behave for Ms. Martinez."

Ruth felt her cheeks warm and she swallowed again, trying to work up some spit. She was so nervous; she couldn't even find a shred of contempt for the way these two men were treating her. Instead, she funneled that contempt into a growing energy that fueled the battle that was about to begin. A battle she would win.

Ruth retrieved a folder from the witness table and placed it on the edge of the witness stand. "Dr. McCormack, this is your final autopsy report on the victim, correct?"

"Well, I prefer a PDF, but some of us are old school." He nodded toward Judge Tucker. The jury chuckled and Ruth waited for the gavel to rap in vain. The laughter died down.

"You may laugh at death, Dr. McCormack. But, I do not." Ruth said quietly. "Would you turn to page 135 for me, please."

McCormack sighed and grabbed the folder with meaty hands. He licked his finger as he thumbed through the pages. "Page 135. You want me to read the whole page?"

"No, just the final cause of death, please."

McCormack shrugged. "I can tell you what she died of."

"I don't want you tell me anything, Dr. McCormack." Ruth said loudly. "I want you to read what you put in the official record as the cause of death. That is all that matters right now. This folder has been placed into evidence by the prosecution and I could care less what you think. I want to know what you wrote down. So read the last entry! Now!"

Ruth was startled at the ferocity of her own voice. McCormack's face grew red and he smacked his lips. "I don't like being talked to that way, young lady."

"I am not a young lady, Dr. McCormack." Ruth stepped closer. "And, while you and the judge play glad hands with each other, I can easily file an injunction for a mistrial. I have an entire room full of witnesses to your harassment of this attorney and your scorn and disregard for this court of law. Now, read the entry!"

Ruth's voice echoed around the chamber and she waited for the gavel to fall. She was met with only silence. McCormack glared at her and looked down at the page. "Cardiorespiratory arrest."

"Thank you." Ruth reached forward and took the folder from him. "Now, I will ask you to please, in layman terms, tell this jury what that phrase actually means."

McCormack pursed his lips and crossed his arms. "It means the heart stopped and the victim died."

"The heart stopped. What about the brain?"

McCormack blinked. "What?"

"What about the brain? When did it die?" Ruth pressed on.

"Honey, the victim was beaten and suffered brain damage."

Ruth nodded and felt nausea creep up her throat. "Brain damage. But, when did the brain die?"

McCormack shrugged. "I'm not sure what you're getting at."

Ruth tossed the folder back onto the evidence table and retrieved another folder. "Are you familiar with the Unified Declaration of Death Act of 1981, the statute that established the medicolegal definition of death?"

McCormack uncrossed his arms and shook his head. "Of course, I am. I'm the coroner. I know death when I see it."

"So, isn't it true that statute established a bifurcated definition of death?"

"Bifurcated? What the heck do you mean by that?" McCormack said. "Marshall, stop this nonsense."

Ruth glanced at Tucker and he was leaning forward in his chair, his eyes narrowed. "I think you may be onto something, Ms. Martinez. Dr. McCormack answer the question."

"But, Marshall."

Tucker picked up his gavel. "Don't make me use it."

McCormack shrugged again. "I guess you mean the duel definition of death. Brain death versus cardiac death."

"Exactly, Dr. McCormack. Now, let me ask you something. In your professional opinion as a medical doctor and the medical examiner for this county, is it possible for the brain to still be alive after the heart stops beating?" Ruth moved across the floor toward the stand, the other folder in her hand.

"Well, sure. That is why we use cardiopulmonary resuscitation. Keep the circulation going to keep the brain alive."

"So, when the heart stops, the brain is still alive?"

"Technically, yes. But, the victim's brain was--"

"What?" Ruth was at the stand now.

"Damaged."

"But, was her brain dead?" Ruth asked.

McCormack opened his mouth and looked over her shoulder at Tucker. "Don't look to him for help. YOU are the expert. You said 'you know death'. Only YOU can answer this question. Was the victim's brain dead when her heart stopped?"

"No. Damaged but not dead." McCormack said.

Ruth plopped the folder in front of him. "You've read the hospital medical records of Miss Zuniga, correct?"

"Yes."

She opened the folder and pointed to a page. "I would like to remind you and the jury that this medical record was entered into evidence by the prosecution. Now, would you summarize for the jury, in layman's terms, what transpired during this surgical procedure?"

McCormack pushed his glasses back onto his sweating nose and studied the page. "Well, this is Doctor Broussard's record of her surgery to harvest the organs of Miss Zuniga after her death."

"Perhaps you could walk us through the procedure, Dr. McCormack." Ruth said firmly. Her heart was racing and her face was alive with fire, but she was in control. She had this! It was only a matter of time.

"Miss Zuniga was brought to the operating room."

"Alive?" Ruth interrupted him.

"Of course."

"So, she was alive when she was rolled into surgery, correct? Her heart was beating and her brain, though damaged, was still functioning."

"But functioning at a very primitive level. She was on a respirator to keep her breathing."

"But, you, the coroner of this county, had not declared her brain dead at this point, correct?"

McCormack looked like he had swallowed a bug. "No."

"So, being the well-respected medical examiner that you are, if you said this patient's brain was still alive when she rolled into surgery, it must be true."

"Objection, your honor. This is ludicrous." Patrick stood up and shouted.

Ruth spun and glared at her. "Don't you dare! Don't you dare stop this, Katrina. I have every right to ask these questions."

Tucker lowered his gavel and it pierced the sudden silence. "Objection overruled. But, Ms. Martinez get on with this. And, remember, I'm the boss around here."

Ruth ignored him and stared at McCormack. "I'm waiting for your answer. Was the victim alive when she entered surgery? Was she NOT 'brain dead'?"

"Yes, she was alive." McCormack mumbled.

"I'm sorry. I didn't hear that." Ruth said.

"I said her heart was beating and her brain, what was left of it, was alive."

Ruth nodded and swallowed, straightening her blazer and drawing a deep breath. She fought for calm and refused to look at Drake. She had to press on. She had started this and she would finish it. Out of the corner of her eye she saw Birmingham make his way from the back of the room to settle at the defense table. Now, the man decided to show up.

"Now, proceed with a summary of the procedure, please."

McCormack read the page and wiped his sweating lips. "Well, she was placed on the surgical table and her chest and abdomen were prepped with antiseptic. The surgeon's intention was to harvest the heart and lungs first followed by the liver and then the kidneys." He cleared his throat. "The incision was made and--"

"Stop!" Ruth said. "I believe you are leaving out something."

McCormack looked up at her with a forlorn and desperate expression. "Please, Miss Martinez, we don't want to go over this."

"Oh, I think we do, Dr. McCormack. I think the jury needs to know how this happened. What was done just prior to the incision?"

McCormack closed the folder. "The respirator was turned off."

"And, once the respirator was turned off, I assume the lungs no longer carried oxygen to the body, particularly the heart and brain, correct?"

"Yes." McCormack said stiffly.

"And, what exactly was the surgeon waiting for before making her incision?"

"For the cardiac activity to cease."

"Earlier, you said that the brain is still alive after the heart stops. For how long can the brain survive without circulation from the heart?"

"Three to five minutes." McCormack said.

"Three to five minutes? How long did Dr. Broussard wait after the heart ceased to beat?"

"The standard time."

Ruth turned and walked toward the jury. "The standard time? Now, I would assume that any surgeon would want to make sure that the brain, no matter how damaged, was dead before slicing open the chest and taking out the heart. After all, the patient was not under any general anesthesia. So, I would assume a standard waiting time would be, say, ten minutes? Maybe six?" She turned and looked at Dr. McCormack. "What is the standard time?"

McCormack was livid now, his face pale, his eyes wide in anger. "Ninety seconds."

Ruth shot across the room and stopped in front of the witness stand. "Ninety seconds? Ninety seconds? Given what you just told me, is it possible Miss Zuniga's brain, though damaged, was still functioning at ninety seconds?"

"Yes." McCormack said slumping into the chair.

Ruth paused and closed her eyes. Would she do this? Could she? She glanced at Drake. He sat smugly in his chair, his blue and brown eyes wide with fever, his lips quivering. She looked away shamefully. "Dr. McCormack, you said the cause of death was cardiorespiratory arrest. Who stopped Miss Sanchez's heart?"

"No!" Patrick shouted. "No, no, no! You are not going to go there."

The gavel pounded. "Miss Patrick, can it. I want to hear this."

Marshall said so fiercely, Patrick fell back into her seat. "Dr. McCormack, answer the question."

"Technically, the transplant assistant surgeon, Dr. Manning."

Ruth nodded and turned to the jury. "So, if the cause of death was cardiorespiratory arrest and if that cardiorespiratory arrest was caused by Dr. Manning, then we have the wrong man sitting at my defense table. Your honor, I move that all charges of murder be dropped as by the coroner's own admission, the person who murdered Maria Zuniga was Dr. Manning, not Reginald Drake."

The courtroom erupted into chaos and Ruth felt the bitter sting of tears as her moment of triumph quickly retreated in the face of the monstrous thing she had just done. She turned toward her table and through the prism of her tears watched as Reginald Drake threw her a kiss.

RUTH FINISHED her story and pushed the dish away and crossed her arms. She couldn't tell him the rest of the story. Not now. Not ever. "I wanted him to rot in prison. But, I had a job to do. Defend a monster. In the end, Tucker refused to dismiss the case but the jury found him not guilty. I was the star of the Texas legal profession for about thirty seconds until everyone realized a murderer was going to go free. But, they still pressed assault and battery charges on him. He's out on bail right now and going to trial for that in a month."

"Are you defending him again?"

Ruth choked and fell silent. She couldn't tell Steel the truth. She couldn't tell anyone. Ever. She looked away. "He hired another firm. After that case, I lost my mojo. I refused to take high profile cases where the client was obviously guilty. That's why this case is so hard for me."

"This is different. Dr. Miller is no Reginald Drake. He is innocent."

Ruth hugged herself and studied his intense gaze. "How can you be so sure?"

"He is not evil." Steel said simply.

"And, of course, you are the expert on evil, right?" Ruth barked. "Who made you God?"

Steel reached over the table and picked up the business card. "Ruth, I have looked into the face of pure evil. I have felt the slimy, fetid breath of a man possessed by naked, raw evil. I wish I did not have this gift, if that's what you want to call it. It's more like a curse. But, I embrace it wholeheartedly until the day I can find that thing of evil and end it. I know evil because I am familiar with it; felt its cold breath; seen its eyes shine with mad intent." He placed the card on the table and tapped it. "I know Dr. Miller is innocent. I promise it is true. And, I always keep my promises."

Ruth bit her lower lip and looked away. "I guess you see the good in Dr. Miller where I have to admit, I saw the evil in Drake. Drake deserved to die for his crime. Dr. Miller doesn't. I guess sometimes it's hard to understand why bad things happen to good people."

"Ruth, bad things don't happen to good people. Bad things happen to bad people. This idea that all people are basically good is wrong. We are capable of great deeds of goodness. But, every human being is capable of the most heinous, I can't believe I'm saying that, crimes imaginable. And, it all starts up here." He tapped his head. "And in here." He tapped his chest.

Ruth shivered at a distant memory of two differently colored eyes shining in the dark surrounded by drops of blood and a monstrous leer. Drake had no heart. Miller deserved something better. Maybe it was time she delivered. "We're going back to the Institute. I'm not done yet."

12

———————

"Why are you back?" Johnston met them as they entered the Institute foyer.

"We weren't finished." Ruth said.

"You interviewed all of the staff." Johnston blocked their way. "Dr. Morrant asked me to make sure you left. I don't think she wants you here."

"Too bad." Steel said. "We will decide when we are finished. Not Morrant."

Johnston looked away and seemed deep in thought. "Look, I want to help Dr. Miller. He is a good man and things aren't quite right around here."

"You said something earlier about secrets." Ruth prompted.

Johnston looked over his shoulder. "We all have secrets, Ms. Martinez. I don't know the secrets. I just know they are there. What else do you want to see?"

"I want to see the crime scene." Ruth said as she gazed up at the two fighting dinosaurs. "I want to see Annieraptor."

Johnston lowered his hands and sighed. "I can't deny you that, but it's still roped off by the police." He took them through the metal detectors and handed them their IDs again. "Just make it quick. I don't want Morrant to find out you're here."

Johnston led them from the foyer through a room filled with articulated skeletons of various dinosaurs. He paused before a huge set of wooden doors.

"Dr. Darwyn liked drama, you know." Johnston pointed to the doors. "Look familiar?"

"Like the gates in the movie. I get it." Ruth said.

"What movie?" Steel asked.

"The one about dinosaurs? Five movies and counting?" Ruth said.

"I don't do movies." Steel said. "And, if I did, I don't remember them."

"Right." Ruth nodded toward the doors. "What lies beyond these doors, Mr. Johnston?"

"The main exhibit. Annieraptor surrounded by a whole bunch of plants Dr. Miller came up with that are the closest thing to prehistoric foliage. Are you ready?" Johnston grabbed both door handles and pulled them open. Majestic music swelled from hidden speakers. The room beyond was dim and an illuminated path led the way through towering ferns and spiky plants.

"Welcome to the Cretaceous era." A voice echoed from hidden speakers.

"James Earl Jones." Johnston said.

"Darth Vader narrates a dinosaur display. I love it." Ruth headed down the path.

"Who is Darth Vader?" Steel asked as he followed her.

"Imagine walking through a humid, hot forest." The voice continued. "The sky is gray and the sun is hidden by swirling clouds. In the distance, volcanoes erupt, spewing ash and smoke into the sky to obscure the sun." The air shook with the sound of an explosion and Ruth stumbled. Steel caught her by the shoulders. She gently pulled away.

"Surround sound and a moving platform." Johnston said. "You hear and feel this exhibit."

Ruth drew a deep breath and pressed on down the winding path.

From around her, the narration continued interspersed with the exotic sounds of dinosaurs. She arrived at the center of the exhibit just as the narration concluded. "And now, prepare to meet Annieraptor."

The path took an abrupt turn and they stood at the top of a set of concentric rough stone steps leading down into the center of the chamber. Spotlights snapped on and bathed the exhibit in bright light. The drama of the moment was ruined by the yellow police tape draped around the diorama in the middle. Standing almost eight feet tall, Annieraptor towered over them. It reminded her of the velociraptors she had seen in the movies. But, this dinosaur was wildly colored in stripes of bright green and gray. It stood on one hind leg with another leg held in the air. The claws on the extended leg glittered in the spotlights. Two smaller forelimbs were raised in a posture of attack and were covered with gray and red feathers. The head was tilted and swiveled allowing one eye to glare down at her. The iris was a bright golden yellow. A spray of yellow and red short feathers crowned the back of its head and another spray of feathers sprang from the tip of its long, formidable tail.

"That posture." Ruth said.

"Yeah, Styles' surprise." Steel said.

Johnston led them down the steps to the center of the room and pointed up. "The second and third floor of the Institute have an open hallway that looks down on the exhibit. Up there is where the police think Dr. Darwyn fell over the railing and landed on the platform in front of Annieraptor."

"I want to walk through Dr. Darwyn's last moments." Ruth managed hoarsely. For a second a movement caught her eye and she glanced at Annieraptor. Had it moved?

"Of course. We'll take the maintenance elevator to Dr. Darwyn's office."

Johnston led them through the foliage to the back of the exhibit and onto an elevator. It took them to the third floor and opened on the walkway they had visited that morning. Johnston led them past Morrant and Grant's offices and stopped in front of Darwyn's office.

Dr. Morrant's desk and file cabinet were visible through the open door.

Johnston led them past Darwyn's office to the walkway overlooking the exhibit. A door to their left was closed and sealed with crime scene tape. Ruth glanced at the yellow crime scene tape and noticed something on the wall next to the door. Three deep gashes marred the wallpaper.

"Steel, look at this."

"Gashes. Like something gouged the wall. Maybe a claw?"

"That's the side door to Darwyn's office so he could, uh, leave without anyone knowing it. The boss' prerogative, I guess." Johnston said.

Ruth glanced down the walkway surrounding the lower exhibit chamber. The cleaning crew had come through after the crime but she could still see a crimson stain on the hardwood floors. "Blood."

"The wooden floors weren't sealed yet." Johnston said with a trembling voice. He cleared his throat. "The police report said he was first attacked here right outside his office. The trail leads to the stairway over there." He pointed a third of the way along the walkway. "Down the stairs to the second floor."

His cell phone chimed and Johnston studied the text. "Dr. Morrant needs me in her old office. Not good! You'd better head to the front entrance. As soon as I take care of Dr. Morrant, I'll meet you there and check you out of the security system."

"We can find our way back." Steel said. Johnston headed back toward the maintenance elevator.

"What now?" Ruth asked.

"We follow the blood trail." Steel said.

Ruth smiled. "You bet we do. After all, it is on the way back to the front of the Institute, right?"

"Right." Steel said and led them down the walkway, his gaze following the faint crimson stains. He paused in front of the stairwell. "Here. He went down the stairs."

"Wait." Ruth said. She pointed to the door handle. "Are those scratches?"

Steel squatted in front of the door and studied the handle. "Like the ones on the wall."

"I don't understand. If Dr. Miller was using the claw why would there be scratches?"

Steel stood up and opened the door. "The claw was in his hand. The killer scratched the door while opening it."

Ruth followed Steel into the stairwell. Here, the blood had soaked into the concrete stairs and had resisted cleaning. They made their way down to the second floor and out onto the walkway overlooking the display area. A large blood stain marred the floor just in front of the railing. Steel stopped and pointed to three huge gashes torn through the paint into the wood underneath. Four feet away, a second set of gashes were found.

"What do you make of this?" He asked.

Ruth looked at the gashes and then her eyes were drawn past the railing to the display below. Annieraptor looked even more formidable from this angle and she noticed the head had shifted position. The thing's gaze was aimed squarely at her. How? She found her breath coming quicker and she stepped back away from the railing. She thudded into Steel's chest and his hands came up to her arms.

"Are you okay?" He whispered.

She pulled away from him and rubbed her arms. "Yeah. It just doesn't make sense. These gashes on the railing."

"No, it doesn't. Darwyn fell from here and landed at the feet of Annieraptor." He said. "Or, he was pushed."

Steel gently pulled her away from the railing and pointed to another stairway that led to the display floor below. "Let's take the stairs. No more blood trail."

Ruth nodded and followed him down the stairs. They led to the side of the exhibit room and a narrow path of stone led them to the area behind Annieraptor. Ruth glanced at her watch as they stood in the shadow of the statue. "I'd really like to get a closer look at the base of Annieraptor where Darwyn died."

Steel shrugged and reached for the crime scene tape. "Wait!" Ruth shouted. "We don't want to give Bryan any ammunition. Let's wait for Johnston so we will have a witness that we didn't tamper with anything." She glanced again at her watch. It had been almost twenty minutes since Johnston had left. Was he expecting them at the front?

Steel studied the dinosaur. "I thought Styles said Darwyn didn't let him use this pose." He pointed to the forward foot. Three large claws extended from the forefoot with a huge claw from the heel. But, the foot in the air was missing the hind foot claw. It was the claw that was in the evidence box.

"That's where the claw came from. I've got to admit, it's mean and ugly. Go to the front and see if Johnston is waiting for us. I'm not leaving until I get a closer look." Ruth said.

"Good idea. I'll be right back." He headed off through the foliage and disappeared from sight.

Ruth hugged herself and turned her back on the dinosaur. It frightened her. Silly, she realized. It was just a statue. She tapped her foot. She checked her watch. Where was Steel and Johnston? To heck with this! Without hesitation, she ducked under the crime scene tape. She would be careful not to touch anything.

Ruth studied the fake grass, stone, and sand comprising the base of the display. A large area was stained with blood that had not been cleaned away. It must have been where Dr. Darwyn fell from the walkway. Maybe the fall killed him. If so, why bother with slashing him up? Such actions indicated rage. Ruth felt a cold chill come over her as she imagined the broken body of Dr. Darwyn crumpled across the rock, his chest ripped open. A shadow moved over the rock and she glanced up.

The skin crawled on her neck. Annieraptor was looking down at her. She backed away quickly. This couldn't be! The thing had been looking up at the second floor when they came down. Now, its head was pointed at her. And, was the mouth more open now? She glanced over her shoulder to see if Steel and Johnston had returned. All she saw were ferns and trees. Another shadow fell over her. She glanced up. Annieraptor's eye was only inches away. The iris contracted.

Ruth gasped and fell back as the thing moved. Its forward leg thudded down on the tile floor and it hopped through the air with one quick movement. She stumbled through the crime scene tape and fell up the stone stairs. She tried to scream, but the fall had stolen her breath. She rolled over and crawled off the path into the thick ferns.

Clack, clack, clack! Annieraptor tapped her claws against the stone pathway. Ruth stayed low and crawled through the rich top soil until she found a large group of false boulders. She reached into her purse for her phone. With each push of a button, the tones echoed around her. She almost had Steel's number in the phone when the foliage above her split aside. Annieraptor thrust her open mouth at Ruth and she jerked away from the boulders. She crawled around the rocks and her hand slid on the wet surface. She fell forward onto slick, wet rock and slid down into a pool of water. Her phone disappeared into the depths of the pond. Fish surrounded her and she slid deeper into mire and muck at the base of the pond. Her hands were stuck and she held her breath as she fought the thick mud. Finally, her hands tore away from the sucking mud and she lurched out of the water and gasped for breath. Annieraptor jumped through the thick trees and ferns and landed on the boulders above her. It turned its head sideways and studied her.

Ruth scuttled through the waste deep water, the mud sucking her feet. She reached the far side of the pond and crawled into the thick bushes. She glanced behind her and Annieraptor was gone! But, where? Her head thudded against a wall and she fell back into the ferns. Through the foliage, Annieraptor's head suddenly appeared, bobbing to and fro as if looking for her position. Its yellow eyes moved and the pupils constricted. It opened and closed its mouth.

Clack, clack, clack! And then, silence as it moved off the stone pathway into the soft earth. Why had it gone away? She didn't care. She needed help.

"Steel! Help me!" She screamed and at the sound, Annieraptor hopped forward out of the ferns and pinned her against the wall with its arms. It pressed its mouth close to her and swiveled its head so that its eye was only inches from her face.

Annieraptor shuddered as something heavy thudded against its head. It whirled and Jonathan Steel stood on the rocks beside the pond. He had thrown one of them at Annieraptor's head. Annieraptor moved with incredible speed, hopping across the distance in an instance. With a whirling movement, the dinosaur spun on its good foot and the long tail caught Steel in the chest. He hurtled across the pond and crashed into the trees.

"No!" Ruth screamed. Annieraptor spun to face her and in an instant hopped back and pinned her against the wall.

"Don't move!" She heard someone say.

Dr. Styles appeared through the ferns and paused behind the dinosaur. "Ms. Martinez, you have to remain absolutely still."

Ruth nodded and Annieraptor responded to the motion of her head and snapped its jaws just inches from her face. She closed her eyes and prayed. God, I need a little help. Please.

Styles slowly moved next to Annieraptor. He reached up quickly and popped open a door on Annieraptor's back. He punched at something, missed his target, and stumbled over a rock in the dirt.

Annieraptor's eye was right up next to Ruth's. Styles stabbed his hand toward the small open door and Annieraptor shivered. Its pupils contracted and then suddenly Annieraptor hopped away through the plants. Steel appeared from the trees. His long sleeve tee shirt was torn from shoulder to waist. Blood stained the bruise across his chest. He shoved Styles aside and pulled her up into his arms. She fell up against his bloody chest and sobbed.

"Are you okay?" His turquoise eyes burned with fury.

Ruth fought to control her trembling and realized where she was. She pushed away from Steel's bare chest and awkwardly wiped at her tears. Steel stiffened and stepped away.

"She'll be fine." Style said behind them.

Steel whirled and grabbed Styles by his lab coat. He drew back and punched him in the face. Styles stumbled back over the edge of the pond into the water. Steel stormed after him, wading into the muck and pulled Styles from the mud. He hit him again and Ruth ran after them.

"Steel. Stop!"

Steel paused with his clenched fist raised and let Styles fall back into the pond. "Why didn't you tell us that thing could move? It could have killed Ruth!"

Styles tried to stand up and his laughter echoed across the chamber. "You didn't ask."

"It's not funny!" Steel growled.

"Oh, no, it's not! Now, I'm going to press charges against you for attacking me." He wiped blood from his lip. "Security should be here any minute to throw you out of this building."

Ruth fought her shaking and trembling hands. "So that was the surprise you had planned for Dr. Darwyn. Annieraptor is some kind of robot."

Styles' eyes widened in anger. "Robot? My dear, Annieraptor is the next generation of organic cyborg. The advancements I've made alone will earn me the Nobel prize. Not to mention millions in patent payments."

Another man appeared on the far side of the pond. He wore a similar security uniform to Johnston's. Styles gestured to Steel and to Ruth. "Mr. Ramos, escort these two out of the building."

"Where's Johnston?" Steels asked.

"Dr. Morrant had to let him go. He was fired for letting the two of you back into the building. Mr. Ramos is our night security but he just got a promotion."

Ramos nodded. "Will you two come with me or do I call the police?"

Steel reached over and took Ruth by the arm. His grip was strong but not painful. "Let's get out of here." He hissed.

They followed Ramos through the trees and ferns. Ruth paused for a moment when she saw Annieraptor once again frozen on its stand. Ramos led them through the metal detectors and held out his hand. "Your ID's."

Ruth jerked her ID off her wet blouse and slapped it into the man's hands. Steel shook his head. "Mine is somewhere in the jungle." He pointed to his torn shirt. "Ruth, let's go."

Ruth blinked in the afternoon sunlight that seemed so much more welcoming than the shadowy exhibit hall. She slid into her car and handed Steel the keys. "I can't drive. Too shaky."

Steel sat behind the steering wheel and started the car. He turned the heater on high and reached over and took her hands. "Your hands are freezing."

"I'm soaked to the bone." Ruth's lips trembled. Steel rubbed her hands and she released the tension and the fear. She cried gently, her tears falling onto their hands. After a few minutes, she drew a shuddering breath and sat up straight. She pulled her hands from Steel's grasp and studied his intense eyes. Her gaze fell to his torn shirt and the bloody bruise across his chest.

"We need to get you to a doctor."

"I'll be fine." He said.

"I hate to be cold about this, but I want that bruise documented. You and I were attacked by a supposed statue. A thing that moved, Jonathan. A thing that was under some kind of control."

Steel nodded. "You're right. Dr. Miller didn't kill Dr. Darwyn. The claw was not the murder weapon. Annieraptor was."

13

Jonathan Steel

I DON'T BELIEVE in coincidence. Cephas taught me that. Not when there is something bigger and more powerful behind the curtain of reality. We don't dance to our DNA. We dance to the tune of the Creator of DNA. I drove to one of those quick medical care places and joined a dozen fellow sufferers in the waiting room.

The triage nurse took me back to a little cubicle and asked me what happened. I told her and she wasn't very happy. Seems she would have to notify the "authorities". Great! I held my breath for the X-ray machine and put on one of those backward dressing gowns and waited for my doctor to arrive. When the door opened, I was shocked to see Detective Nella Jones standing the door.

"You just can't keep your nose out of trouble, can you honey?"

"Why are you here?"

"Saving your butt." She closed the door behind her. "Your doctor will be here shortly but if you will cooperate and give me a statement about what happened at the Institute I can save you a trip to a holding cell."

"I thought you covered homicides. I didn't kill anyone. But, that dinosaur thing could have killed Ruth Martinez."

Jones sat on the stool. "Dinosaur? Dr. Morrant didn't mention anything about that."

"What did she mention?"

"That you attacked Dr. Styles and threw him in a pond. I've met the little jerk and I'm sure he deserved it. I overheard the phone call and told the patrol office I would handle it."

"You're doing me a favor? I didn't know you had it in you."

Jones shrugged. "I'm a sucker for pretty eyes. So, tell me what happened."

I did. She nodded and stood up. "I'll try and get the charges dropped."

"You don't seem too surprised about a walking, slashing dinosaur."

"Let's just say we've discovered some new evidence. Come down to the office in the morning once we've processed it and I'll let you check it out." She opened the door and a small, Asian woman stood in the hall holding a clipboard. "He's all yours, honey."

RUTH GLANCED AT HER WATCH. Where was Steel? She hadn't heard from him since the afternoon before. The law offices were back in full swing after the Christmas holidays and Bryan Nicholas was set to arrive in just ten minutes. He had asked for this conference meeting. Probably to offer some kind of deal. But, Ruth would have a surprise for him. After the attack yesterday by Annieraptor, everything had changed. The door opened and Jonathan Steel walked in.

"Sorry I'm late. I've been at the police station trying to find out about some kind of new evidence. They stonewalled me." He was dressed in jeans and a long sleeve denim shirt. His left arm hung in a black sling around his neck.

"What's wrong with your arm?"

Steel rounded the table and slid into a seat beside her. He groaned as he sat down. "Pulled a few muscles when that thing hit me with its tail. Cracked two ribs. The doctor said I was lucky not have dropped my lung."

Grace Pennington walked into the room dressed in a long, dark green dress with a maroon jacket. "I have just put the final touches on our complaint. We have every legal right to file a grievance against the Institute for endangering both of your lives." She tossed a folder on the table. "All you have to do is sign it."

"I'd wait on that if I were you."

Ruth looked past Grace as Bryan Nicholas hurried into the room trailed by three young interns, two women and a man. Grace rounded the table to sit by Ruth.

"You're late, Bryan."

"Well, some new developments from this morning had to be taken into consideration." He motioned to his interns to sit. He placed his briefcase on the table and popped it open. "The first thing being Dr. Styles' affidavit regarding his attack at the hands of your P.I. He has filed an assault and battery complaint with our office."

Ruth stood up and her face warmed with anger. "Dr. Styles' creation almost killed me and Jonathan Steel. We are the ones filing a complaint."

"Just a minute." Grace said loudly. "Let's put these two complaints aside, shall we? We have more important things to consider other than the two of you posturing for dominance."

Bryan chuckled. "Posturing for dominance? I will say that this is the most spunk I've seen from Ruth in months."

"Spunk!" Ruth shouted. "I'll show you spunk. How about the fact that Annieraptor is a fully functional robotic construct! How about the fact that the thing was controlled by somebody during the attack on Dr. Darwyn and the claw Dr. Miller pulled from Darwyn's chest was left by the attack from Annieraptor. Not, Dr. Miller. You need to drop this case Bryan before I bring you down in front of everyone."

Bryan raised an eyebrow and motioned to one of his interns. The man stood up and walked out of the room and returned with a large, plastic crate. The crate bore the stickers of the Dallas Police Crime Lab. "You might want to calm down, Ruth. I wouldn't want you to have an aneurysm when you learn what is in that crate."

Ruth blinked and fought for words. She looked at Grace and the woman shrugged. "What are you talking about?".

"First off, Ruth, I totally agree with you that Annieraptor is the murder weapon, not the claw. Secondly, I totally agree with you that someone was controlling Annieraptor and used it to kill Dr. Darwyn. You see, Grace, we can find common ground after all." He gestured to another intern. The woman stood up and opened the crate and took out a backpack. It was black and sleek. She took another object resembling an overgrown pair of goggles. Bryan adjusted his lavender tie and walked over to the two objects.

"What you see here, Ruth, is a backpack containing a modified gaming laptop with incredible computing power." He picked up the goggles. "And these are virtual reality goggles. They are connected to the laptop which in turn controls every movement of Annieraptor. Put on these goggles and it is as if you are Annieraptor. Sensors on the goggles, from what I understand, take into account your movement and control Annieraptor with a great deal of precision."

"And you know this how?" Ruth asked.

"Booted up the laptop and found the recording of the attack on Dr. Darwyn from a first person shooter point of view." Bryan said.

"Did you find that in Styles' office?" Steel asked. "Did he use it to attack us yesterday?"

Bryan placed the goggles next to the backpack. "Actually, no. From what Dr. Styles told me, and of course you can verify his account since you were both there, he was not wearing this device when Annieraptor attacked you. Correct?"

Ruth looked at Steel and watched the man's face redden with anger. "No." She said hurriedly. "He wasn't wearing a backpack."

"Right you are." Bryan smiled. "Because, my dear Ruth, this Feldercarb 360, as Dr. Styles calls it, has been missing for days. Until this morning. I sent an officer and a member of the crime lab to check out your story of being attacked by Annieraptor and they went through Dr. Miller's office once more. Now, his office has been sealed since the night of the murder, mind you. In a hidden compartment in the corner guess what we found?" He pointed to the backpack. "You guessed it, Ruth. A gold star for you. And guess whose fingerprints were all over the goggles? Care to guess again?"

"Enough, Bryan." Grace growled. "Get on with it."

Bryan frowned at being interrupted. Ruth slumped into her chair and put a restraining hand on Steel's arm. The muscles beneath his skin were tense with anger. "Dr. Miller's?"

"Yes." Bryan said quietly. He returned to his open briefcase and took out a folder. "What I have here is a deal that was finalized this morning. Before we found the backpack. With this new evidence, we really shouldn't put this forward, but murder is murder whether with a claw or with augmented reality." He slid the folder across the table. "Miller pleads guilty and we drop the death penalty. Life without parole. Best deal he can get."

Ruth stared at the folder as if it were a snake. She glanced at Grace and then at Steel. What did she think? Was Miller guilty? Had he used the goggles and laptop to kill Darwyn? If so, then why was he found hunched over the body holding the claw? Why wasn't he safely hidden in his office along with the backpack? Something didn't add up. She studied Bryan's smiling face. Their eyes met and locked. Trust your gut, she thought. No, trust that still small voice of truth that whispers in your soul. She closed her eyes and let Bryan have his false victory and she said a silent prayer for strength.

She laughed and sat back down, shoving the folder across the table. "Frank Miller is innocent. He is being framed by someone, Bryan, and you know it. You can take your deal and put it where the sun don't shine. We will see you in court." She pointed to the door. "You can leave now and take your evidence with you."

Bryan's smile slowly faded and his cheeks reddened. "You're making a big mistake, Ruth. Admit defeat and accept it now before I destroy you in court."

Steel stood up and slid his bad arm out of the sling. He grabbed his shirt and pulled it up. The huge, blood red bruise across his chest appeared. "Do you see what Annieraptor did to me? It did that while Dr. Miller was safely locked in his cell. We will find who did this, Mr. Nicholas. Ruth Martinez will expose the truth and you will go down in flames. Accept that!" He hissed and pounded the table with his good fist.

Bryan flinched and gathered the folders back into his briefcase. He motioned to the backpack and the female intern hurriedly returned it to the crate. "Fine! I'll see you and your terminator boyfriend in court. You will be the one going down in flames, Ruth. And, I will relish every moment of it. Just get ready to see my name on the placard out front because I will win." He stood up and paused. "But, I will throw you a bone." He reached into the plastic crate and took out an evidence bag. "The other hard drive from the security kiosk. We couldn't find anything of worth on it, but you're welcome to try." He tossed the hard drive on the table and stalked out of the room with his group behind him.

Ruth slumped into the chair and fought back tears. "What have I done?"

Grace put an arm around her shoulder. "My dear, you have risen to the occasion. I think you put the fear of God into Bryan Nicholas!"

Ruth felt little consolation in the remark. "Now, we have to find out why that laptop was in Dr. Miller's office. And, did he know anything about it?"

DR. FRANK MILLER ran his hands through his long, thick hair. He hadn't shaved since he'd been in prison. His eyes were sunken and haunted.

"How are you coping?" Ruth asked.

Miller laughed. "Coping? I'm just trying to keep a low profile. If the trial doesn't kill me, prison will."

"I need to ask you about this." She pushed a photograph of the backpack and goggles across the table.

Miller looked at it. "What about it?"

"We found it in your office." Steel said as he sat beside Ruth.

"Well it's not exactly mine but I use goggles for controlling my drones. I use drones to scout out forests for rare foliage. It's easier than trekking for miles through wilderness only to come back empty handed. But, this thing is not mine. I've never seen it before. What's in the backpack?"

"A high end laptop." Ruth said. She showed him another picture of the laptop. She had received more photos from Bryan after the meeting.

Miller nodded. "My goggles interface with a tablet, not a laptop. But," He studied the photograph. "This type of laptop is used by every staff member. We all have one of these. Not a Macintosh, mind you. It's a Linux based proprietary laptop that I helped to develop software for."

"Not good." Steel said.

"What?" Miller asked.

"Let me get this straight." Ruth tapped the photograph. "You wrote software for these laptops? Why?"

"Darwyn was paranoid. He didn't trust Macintosh or Windows software. He wanted something unique and secure. Why do you ask?"

"Who has a key to your office besides you?" Ruth took the photograph back.

"Security? The cleaning staff? We're not real compulsive about locking our offices. What is going on?"

"Did you know that Annieraptor could move?" Steel asked.

"Move? You mean can the display roll?"

"We mean move as in simulating a living dinosaur." Ruth said.

"Annieraptor can move?" Miller sounded confused. "You mean like some kind of robot or something?"

"Yes." Steel tapped the photograph. "And this laptop controls its every movement. The prosecution thinks that is how Darwyn was killed."

Miller blinked and stared off into space. "That explains a lot."

"What do you mean?" Ruth asked.

"Dr. Morrant had me tweak her programs to make the skeletal reconstruction more 'functional' as she said. I wasn't sure at the time, but with those modifications I made to her program and to Dr. Grant's program, it would be a simple step to produce a fully articulated model capable of realistic motion."

"Grant's program supplies the muscles." Steel said. "And, Styles has engineered the final synthesis of bone and flesh."

"Styles wouldn't let me touch his programs. I thought it was just arrogance. But, now I know it was to hide the fact he was going beyond an articulated model. But, synthetic muscles? We're years away from the kind of synthetic muscle that would allow this creature to stalk and attack like a real dinosaur. It would be more like something you'd see at a theme park."

"Dr. Miller, would such a product be of any use to anyone?" Ruth asked.

"Of course it would. Just the possibility of use in the entertainment industry boggles the mind. Think of all the creatures that could be created for movies alone. And then, you've got all the museums and science centers for hands on interaction with kids. If such a comprehensive product were available and financially feasible, the creator could make millions. Maybe even billions!"

"And, you had no knowledge of this?" Steel asked.

"None. Remember, my area is plant life. Not much future there for robotics!" He ran a hand through his unruly hair. "I'm such a fool. Grant's involvement would surprise me. He seems so genuine. But Morrant and Styles? They've already got a thing going on."

"A thing?" Ruth asked.

"Yeah, a physical relationship."

"Morrant said she was having a relationship with Darwyn."

"Your point is?" Miller smirked. "She would have a 'relationship' with whoever could advance her agenda. After my wife left me, she moved in for the kill. Now, I know why. She wanted my expertise in upgrading her program."

Ruth glanced at Steel. Where did this get them? How did it help?

She looked back at Miller. "What would Dr. Darwyn's interest have been in all this?"

Miller rubbed his bearded chin. "Good question. Did he know about Annieraptor's ability?"

"Styles said it was supposed to be a surprise." Steel said.

"Wallace would never have allowed someone to grandstand with his creation. You know he named it after his daughter who passed away some years ago. His Annieraptor was more precious to him than life itself. It was to be his crowning glory."

"So, Darwyn would have been upset with Styles' improvements?" Ruth asked.

"Definitely."

"Is that motive enough for murder?" Steel asked.

"Not really." Miller leaned forward. "I mean, Darwyn still controls the rights to all the programs developed at the Institute. He would have disapproved of the development but I don't think he would have stopped them from going forward. He loved money just like the rest of them did."

Ruth was deep in thought as she slid the picture back into her satchel. "Dr. Miller, who controls the money at the Institute?"

"I do."

Ruth drew a sharp breath. "You?"

"I'm the chief financial officer."

Ruth looked at Steel and his face flushed. "You might have told us that before now." He growled.

Miller shrugged. "What difference does it make?"

"With Darwyn out of the way, the financial officer controls the contracts and the flow of funds, Dr. Miller. That is motive for murder, particularly if this new development would mean more income for the Institute."

Miller's face paled and he licked his lips. "I never thought of that. I just assumed they were going after me because of the fight at the party."

Ruth closed her eyes and felt a headache coming on. Things couldn't get any worse. Or, could they? She stood up and leaned against the table. "Dr. Miller, we have three days until the trial begins. I want you to think very hard about what you've learned today and see if you can come up with any reason why someone else would want to kill Dr. Darwyn."

Miller laughed. "That's easy. Wallace was not a very friendly person. He constantly alienated and angered the people who worked for him. On any given day of the week, you could find at least one person who would want him dead. I was just in the wrong place at the wrong time."

14

J onathan Steel

I DIDN'T HAVE to be there for jury selection. My arm was feeling better. It seemed I heal very quickly. I have wondered why that is, but I'm afraid to keep asking. I took the hard drives and headed down to Austin on I-35. I hoped my encounter with Kristof would be better than the first time we met.

I first met Kristof McCoy back in October when he left a message on my website that he had an unnatural fear of the number thirteen. Not a surprising phobia, I thought. I almost didn't contact him until I checked out his website. He is a freelance computer security expert and his logo was a dot with a spiral around it. A spiral? Number thirteen? Could he have some knowledge of my adversary? I decided to contact him.

He lived in an apartment off Research Blvd. in northern Austin. I showed up at his door and stared at the red domed light in the center of the door. He was checking me out. Some kind of camera. I knew because I felt his gaze travel over me. A random memory surfaced of a computer on a spaceship. A red eye glaring at the crew. What movie? I couldn't remember the details. I heard the locks pop open and the door yawned into total darkness. I stepped into a metal cage just inside the door.

"Please stand on the yellow footprints." A mechanical voice said. I took two steps into the metal cage and the door closed behind me. A linear blue light played up and down my body. The far end of the cage popped inward. "You may enter."

The cage door led me into a small living room to my right and a dining room to my left separated from the kitchen by an island. The living room was filled from floor to ceiling with shelves stacked with all kinds of blinking electronics. The air was hot and dry and smelled of body odor, pizza, and ozone. A desk sat in the middle of the living room facing me.

"Yes, I'm paranoid." A squeaky voice came from the other side of a flat monitor. Kristof stood up and stepped into view. He wore a tank top and boxer shorts. He was short and thin with a sallow complexion and wild hair that stood on end. He had a week's worth of beard and pizza sauce dribbled down his chin. "I would shake your hand, but I'm a bit germaphobic."

"Jonathan Steel." I said. "You're a walking stereotype."

"I am what I am." Kristof glanced back at his keyboard. "No! No! NO!" He plopped back down into his chair and his hands danced over the keyboard. "Take that Darth Snyder." He slammed a finger on a key and stood up with arms raised in a victory stance. The body odor increased.

"You sent me a message on my website." I said.

He looked at me and his face was vacant for a second. "Oh, yes. You're still here. Steel, right? Message?" Suddenly his face paled and he dropped his hands. "Oh my! You're really here, aren't you?"

"Yes." My face grew warm with anger. This man couldn't possibly be in league with the thirteenth demon. "Thirteen? Fear? Evil?" I said.

"Yes, yes." Kirstof hurried over to a shelf. "I'm a man of science.

Pure science. I don't believe in the supernatural." He rifled through boxes of electronic junk. "But, quantum physics, now that's another slant on reality altogether. Explains a lot." He found some papers and shuffled through them. "Here." He handed a letter to Steel. "I received that a couple of weeks ago."

I looked at the letter. It was addressed to MythicDragon443. "You're MythicDragon443?"

"Yes. But read the body of the letter."

"Photons will flow more quickly in a world in which the sons of darkness channel the thirteen times thirteen spiral. When you see the mark of the dragon wolf and the soul of chaos sealed on the angel throne then you will know that I am coming and you will serve me for all eternity. Beware the tunnels you probe and the corridors you creep and the secrets you collect. I will find you and I will end you in the time of ultimate evil. Signed, ThirteenSpiral666." The words had the ring of evil to them. Too many references to thirteen. A connection to my adversary? "What have you gotten yourself into?"

Kristof jerked the letter from my hands. "My business is in security. I get hired by certain organizations to break into their servers and disclose their weaknesses."

"So you used to be a hacker but now you're legit?" I said. "How long were you in prison?"

Kristof put his hands up in defense. "Look, I never really got caught. But, I came close. Too close. So, I turned to the legitimate side of things. Only, my clients don't always operate in the light, if you catch my drift."

"Kristof, I'm looking for a thing that calls itself the thirteenth demon. My business is helping out someone who feels their lives are oppressed by evil, not the dark web." I turned toward the door.

"Wait!" Kristof shouted. "Don't leave! Two weeks ago, I was working on cracking a server for a certain business. I was tired, okay. I made a mistake in the code and must have hit the wrong letter or number, whatever. I ran the code and somehow ended up on a strange site. It wasn't the one I was trying to hack into." He started pacing and his face reddened with the effort. "It was strange. A graphic interface with all kinds of symbols and pictographs. I've never seen anything like it. And then," he paused and looked at me. "You're not going to believe what happened next. One of the symbols seemed to grow and expand and it was this face. This wicked, demon face with fangs and huge eyes and pointed ears and," He stopped and swallowed. "It came out of the screen. Came right out of the screen like some kind of three-dimensional projection. Not just an image. It was real! I could smell sulfur and ashes and then this forked tongue came out of its mouth and touched my cheek." His hand strayed to his cheek and he blinked. "I jerked the power switch on my computer. Lost everything I'd been working on, but I didn't care. The monitor died and it was like the face didn't want to leave. Like it was reluctant to be pulled back into the screen! Man, it was freaky!"

"What had you been smoking?" I asked.

"No! No, I don't do that, man! It messes with my mind. You can't do what I do when you're stoned. I put in the cage and the extra security after I got that letter."

The man was telling the truth. And, the problem was, I believed him. After what I had seen, a face coming to life out of thin air was not beyond the capabilities of my enemy. "Did you try and find the server again?"

"Are you kidding? No way! I'm telling you there are things going on outside of our reality."

"On that point, you are correct. A dimension of evil beings does exist right alongside our own. I've encountered them, too. My advice to you is to stay away from those websites. As long as you don't go looking for this ThirteenSpiral666, you'll be fine." I stepped closer and glared at him. "I've met the thing and it is deadly, Kristof. Forget about it. Don't go looking for it. And, get a Bible. Start reading it tonight. It'll help keep the demons at bay."

I thought he might laugh at me but he nodded. "Yeah! I thought about that. Been checking out sites like Reasons to Believe and GodandScience. Something is going on. I was hoping you might could help."

I drew a deep breath and regretted it. "Look, I'm not much of a religious man. But, there is protection from these things. I'm about to meet with a man who has more knowledge about this area than me. After we meet, I'll contact you and see if I can give you more advice. But, you have to understand something." I rested my hand on the metal cage. "These physical barriers mean nothing to the powers of darkness. They move in and out of our dimensions like a fish in water. Your only defense is to turn to the Bible." I jerked open the inner door to the cage with no effort. Kristof swore.

"It's not supposed to be that easy to open."

"If I can get through, so can they." I stepped through to his door. "If you do hear from this thing again, let me know."

"So, call you if it happens again?"

I glanced over my shoulder at the nervous man literally shaking in his boxer shorts. "Yes."

I TEXTED Kristof and he gave me a new address. The Domain was one of those shopping centers combined with upwardly trendy apartments. It was a mashup of consumerism and community. Ah, the future was so bright I had to wear shades. Mirrored shades.

I drove through the winding street surrounded by a Starbucks, an Apple store, a tea shop and a Sony store. I didn't see a person over the age of thirty. This was the new world. I found a parking spot next to a four-story building that looked like it was made out of metal Legos. I took the elevator to the fourth floor and was accosted by the stare of a skinny woman in tights who probably thought I had just ended the world by not taking the stairs.

I knocked on the door to apartment 433. No red eye staring at me. The door opened and I hardly recognized the man before me. Kristof had gained some weight and it was all muscle. His hair was cut short to the scalp.

"Mr. Steel!" He smiled and reached out to hug me. I stepped back. "Kristof?"

He paused. "Sorry. Come in, come in. I'm still moving in." He ushered me into an apartment vastly different from the last time I had seen him. Boxes sat around the room, but the furniture was new and trendy. The air smelled of cinnamon and spice. A Christmas tree sat in the corner.

"What happened to you?"

Kristof motioned to his kitchen, an open room with copper pots hanging over an island. Lots of glass and chrome. "Got into the Bible. Hey, I just got hired as the media minister of Grace Community Church. I'm also a worship leader." He stood before me, his face all smiles in his lose cardigan sweater and jeans. "You changed my life, man. Can I please get a hug?"

I stiffened as he hurled himself on me, squeezing me and patting my back. He pulled away and sniffed. "Well, that was like hugging a tree."

"I'm not a hugger." I said.

"Look, I'm just grateful for your advice. I got into the Bible. Got my relation with God right. And, no hint of demons, man. I keep them running!" He made a fist and tapped me on the shoulder. "Spiritual warfare? Heard of it?"

"Yes."

"Oh, man, you are a brick wall, aren't you? God's not finished with you, yet. I'd say He's barely started."

I cleared my throat and looked around his apartment. "I need some help."

"Anything for Jonathan Steel."

I took the hard drives out of my jacket pocket and handed it to him. "A hard drive from a security kiosk. It's supposed to be empty, but we're hoping you can find anything on it that might help identify a killer."

"We?" Kristof raised an eyebrow.

"I'm working with an attorney in Dallas. You may have heard of the murder of that dinosaur guy."

Kristof frowned. "Yeah, I heard something about it. You with the prosecution or the defense?"

"Defense."

"So, you think your man is innocent?"

"Yes."

Kristof nodded and put the hard drives on the island. "Jonathan, I will be glad to help you on this. No charge. You believed in me and if you believe in this man that he is innocent, then I will do everything I can to help him out."

He put out his hand and I shook it. "Now, how about lunch? You like TexMex?"

I glanced at my watch. "I suppose so."

"Then, let's go to Chuy's. Best TexMex in Austin."

He grabbed a jacket and shrugged into it. I paused in front of his door. "What happened to the cage?"

He put a hand on my shoulder. "God delivered me from it."

15

J ury selection went surprisingly well. Ruth anticipated Bryan
Nicholas objecting to anyone with a religious background, but
he didn't seem to care. By the time the jury was selected, ten
out of the twelve primary members were professed religious
people. This was, after all, the Bible belt.

Nicholas showed up with his young entourage and descended on
the prosecution table with glee. He was positively beaming. His suit
was perfect, his hair was perfect, well, Ruth knew the rest of it. He
wore a dark blue suit with a red tie. Red, the color of blood. It would
be a subtle reminder to the jury of the bloody nature of this case. In
contrast, Ruth wore a gray dress with black and white accents. This
case would be about the contrast between good and evil; black and
white. She used a soft perfume with an undercurrent of vanilla.
Warm, homey, comforting.

Grace Pennington sat in the audience section behind the defense
table leaving Ruth alone with Dr. Miller. She had instructed him to
get his hair cut and to shave off his beard. He looked ruggedly handsome in his suit although his face was pale.

Judge Preston Nettles presided over the trial. Ruth had appeared before him on one other occasion. He was a tough, law and order judge with a background in civil rights. His African American ancestors had been slaves and his father had been killed in the sixties while protesting the racism endemic in that era. He was a tall man with a shocking head of white hair. He arrived in the courtroom with a deliberate air of control and intolerance. He stood behind his desk for at least three minutes silently surveying the courtroom before he sat down.

"Let me get a few things straight, right off." Nettles glared at Ruth and then at Nicholas. "In my courtroom, I do not tolerate theatrics. In my courtroom, I do not stomach personal grudges or contests. I am well aware of the particulars of the relationship between the prosecution and the defense in this case. Bare that in mind. I will throw both of you out and assign new counsel for both sides if I see any personal abuse of the system. I hold the law above your petty agendas, and don't forget that. That being said, I would like to remind the jury that it is the job of the prosecution to convince you beyond any reasonable doubt of the guilt of the accused. And, the accused is innocent until proven otherwise. Now, I will hear opening statements from both sides."

Bryan Nicholas straightened his tie and stood before the jury. He studied them quietly and walked over to the bailiff's area and picked up the Bible. He brought it back to the jury and held it up. "When we swear in a witness, we require that witness to tell the truth, the whole truth, and nothing but the truth. So help me, God! Yes, so help me God! This book, for most of us, represents Truth with a capital T. It represents values and virtues that have shaped and molded this country for centuries."

He placed the Bible on the jury rail. "We all have strong beliefs. Every one of us. Every one of you. Those beliefs define our values. Those beliefs lie at the core of who and what we are. Many of you have particularly strong values that you cherish above any earthly standards. Our society has in the past few years tended to veer away from such core values. The ten commandments, for instance, have been attacked and demands have gone out to remove such images from our public buildings. But, I am here today to assert to you that the sixth commandment stands. Thou shalt not kill!"

Ruth sat forward. A cold chill ran down her spine. Several of the jury members were nodding in agreement with Bryan! How had she not seen this coming? No wonder Bryan hadn't protested the addition of religious leaning jury members. He was playing to their worldview. She closed her eyes and shook her head. He had done it to her again!

Nicholas fell silent and paced along the jury rail. He paused and leaned into the jury. "No matter who demands the removal of such values from our social consciousness, I believe that each and every one of you would agree it is wrong to take an innocent life. The prosecution will show beyond any reasonable doubt that Dr. Frank Miller felt betrayed by his mentor, Dr. Wallace Darwyn. We will prove that Dr. Frank Miller was angered when he saw the end result of Dr. Darwyn's life long desire to explore and display the wonders of nature. We will see that Dr. Frank Miller personally disagreed with Dr. Darwyn's interpretation of nature and in his anger and wrath, consciously planned a gruesome and heinous murder. We will show that Dr. Miller, like any violent religious fanatic who hijacks the goodness of a religion for his own nefarious purposes, betrayed the Truth that is God's Word when he chose to kill an innocent man. We will show that Dr. Frank Miller not only desired to kill his mentor, but to torture him; to tear his life from him and leave him displayed in a horrific posture for all the world to see. We will show that Dr. Miller betrayed the spirit of his own proclaimed values and deserves nothing more than to swiftly and decisively meet his Maker." He slammed his open hand down onto the Bible. He picked it up and took it back to the bailiff. He had delivered his opening statement with all the gusto of a traveling evangelist. He had decisively pulled them into his camp. She swallowed and glanced at Frank Miller. His face was red with anger and his fists were clinched. Bryan Nicholas walked quickly to his table and grinned at her.

"Ms. Martinez, we are waiting for your opening statement." Nettles interrupted the silence.

Miller tensed beside her, murmuring beneath his breath. "I told you he would go there!"

Ruth stood slowly and placed a restraining hand on Frank's arm. She needed him to calm down. She stepped around the table and stood before the jury.

"Our presiding judge today is the Honorable Preston Nettles. I have revered this man for many years. Do you know why? Years ago, Judge Nettles' father was falsely accused of a crime against a white girl in northeastern Texas. The local officials rushed to justice. The jury had decided his guilt before he was even led into the courtroom. In short, Judge Nettle's father was presumed guilty and died at the hands of a lynch mob. I do not use this example lightly for Judge Nettles has already informed you and the prosecution that like his father, my client should be presumed innocent until proven guilty beyond a shadow of a doubt. The defense will admit that Dr. Miller and Dr. Darwyn did have a public disagreement the night of the murder but this was in full view of the public and was predated by many such passionate disagreements. Such disagreements were common between Dr. Miller and his mentor and were typical of their professional relationship. They were fellow scientists who agreed to disagree on certain issues but continue to respect each other outside the arena of science." A thought ran through her mind and she paused, framing the words carefully. "Just as many of you have a strong faith in one God, but different denominations; so Dr. Miller and Dr. Darwyn had faith in science but different interpretations of the facts. He is no more guilty of killing Dr. Darwyn over such a disagreement as any of you would be over whether baptism is immersion versus sprinkling. Your devotion is still to the one true God. Dr. Miller and Dr. Darwyn's devotion was still to science, the search for truth."

She paused and let those words sink in. Some of the jury members nodded. "The defense intends to show you that the evidence is purely circumstantial. Dr. Miller was found over the body of Dr. Darwyn with the supposed murder weapon in his hand, but in fact, he was merely trying to come to the aid of his friend. He was in the wrong place at the wrong time and is certainly no more guilty of murder than Judge Nettle's father. We ask the jury to consider the evidence with this in mind and realize that Dr. Miller's guilt cannot be established beyond a reasonable doubt. Do not rush to judgment and end the life of an innocent man."

Ruth turned and headed back to her table, keeping her eyes away from Judge Nettle. There was a profound silence that stretched far too long. Ruth glanced up. Nettles face was inscrutable and he sighed as he leaned back in his chair. "Would both counsel approach the bench please."

Ruth followed Nicholas to the front of Nettle's bench. "Mr. Nicholas, I know that you have not experienced a religious conversion since we last met in this courtroom so I hope that you do not plan to conduct this trial like a tent revival. Do not touch my Bible, understand?"

"Yes sir. I will let the evidence speak for itself." Nicholas said quietly.

Nettles looked at Ruth. "Ms. Martinez, that was certainly a brave move on your part. But, I caution you to avoid using examples of the past that might prejudice me in my overseeing of this trial. I do not take lightly someone who might abuse my father's legacy. But, your words were both respectful and well put. Just don't go there again. Do we understand each other?"

"Yes, sir."

Nettles brushed them away with his hand. "Will the prosecution proceed, please?"

Ruth turned and Nicholas caught her eye. He leaned toward her. "Made out your resume, yet? Nice perfume. You smell like vanilla ice cream. Boring!"

She opened her mouth to respond and he adjusted his necktie and winked at her as he slid behind his table. Ruth settled into the seat beside Frank and he patted her hand.

"That was good." He whispered. She wanted to look over her shoulder at Grace, but couldn't handle what she might see.

16

———————

The prosecution began its case with the police report of the crime scene. Particular damning testimony came from photographs taken by Dr. Styles showing Dr. Miller crouched over the body with the claw in his hand. Ruth made a note. Why had Dr. Styles taken pictures? Why was he there at just the right time to catch Dr. Miller holding the claw in his hand? When it came her time for questions, she faced off against Detective Citronella Jones.

"Detective Jones, is it standard procedure for the homicide division to rely on the photographs performed by civilians?" She asked.

Jones shrugged. "Dr. Styles was there when the patrol office arrived. Claimed he had the camera for taking pictures of the party earlier. We confiscated the camera for evidence. It's been in our possession since that night."

"Your honor." Ruth turned to Nettles. "The defense moves that these photographs be stricken from the record. How can the prosecution be so certain they were not tampered with?"

Nicholas stood up. "Your honor, I would like to remind the defense that I will ask Dr. Styles to testify to this issue when I put him on the stand. I humbly request your patience with this issue. If the defense is not satisfied after his testimony, we will gladly remove the photographs from evidence. After all, the photographs performed by the crime unit are convincing enough."

Ruth opened her mouth to protest. She had fallen into Nicholas' little trap. Again. It no longer mattered if the photographs were in evidence. The jury had seen them and now, Styles would be a credible witness to the crime scene. "I withdraw my motion, your honor."

Ruth slumped into her chair and rubbed her eyes. This was not going well and they were just getting started. Then came the medical examiner's report on the injuries. Dr. McCormack arrived in the witness stand, still a walrus of a man. He hadn't lost weight since Ruth had faced off against him in the Drake trial. He frowned at her as he settled into his seat. During the prosecution's questions, he described in great detail, with pictures and diagrams, the multiple lacerations and injuries sustained by the victim. The final portion of his testimony was damaging.

"Dr. McCormack, you described the victim's final position as draped over a rock on the display floor. Is it your opinion he fell from the balcony and landed on the display?" Nicholas asked, his gaze straying to Ruth. He was gloating.

"Yes, there were fractures of the upper lumbar and lower thoracic vertebrae that could only have been sustained by a fall from the balcony. The fractures of the tenth and eleventh thoracic vertebrae drove bone fragments into the spinal canal thus paralyzing the victim." Dr. McCormack used a laser pointer to outline the images of the spine from a CAT scan projected on a large flat screen display.

"Was Dr. Darwyn still alive after he hit the rock?" Nicholas asked.

"Yes, there was considerable pulmonary contusion related to the fall and hemorrhaging into the lung tissue that could only have occurred if the victim was still alive." McCormack pushed up large black rimmed glasses onto his meaty face.

"What was the cause of death?" Nicholas asked.

"Exsanguination from the piercing of the heart by a sharp object and the bleeding from the eviscerated intestines." Dr. McCormack pushed a button on his remote and a picture of the victim's body draped over the display appeared in all its bloody glory. "And, these are my team's photographs, Ma'am." He nodded to Ruth.

"By exsanguinations, you mean he bled to death?" Nicholas asked.

"Yes."

"You said the heart was pierced by a sharp object?"

"Yes."

"Did you compare any of the evidence from the crime scene with the wound?"

"Yes. The metal claw recovered at the crime scene matched the torn heart muscle and abdominal tissue. In my opinion, it was the object that produced this damage." McCormack adjusted his glasses again and smiled at her.

"Your witness."

Ruth drew a deep breath and calmed her racing heart. Her last encounter with McCormack had not gone well. "Dr. McCormack." She said as she straightened her dress.

The man merely nodded and smiled at her. "We meet again."

Ruth watched his lips twist into a sneer. Why was she even intimidated by this man? She had bested him before and she would do it again. "Dr. McCormack, these wounds seem rather extreme. Have you determined the amount of force necessary to produce these wounds?"

"Amount of force?" McCormack frowned.

"Let me rephrase my question. How much force does it take to tear human flesh in this fashion with the murder weapon?" Ruth walked over to the evidence table and lifted the metal claw out of the box.

"Objection." Nicholas stood up.

Nettles looked at him over the top of his glasses. "Why?"

"The defense is asking the medical examiner a question that is outside his area of expertise." Nicholas said. His tone was halfhearted and he knew he had no grounds for the objection.

"Mr. Nicholas, I would hope a medical examiner and his crime investigation team would know precisely how much force would be necessary for such a wound. I will allow the question." Nettles turned back to McCormack.

Ruth rested the metal claw on the front edge of the witness box and waited. McCormack eyed it and shrugged. "A lot?"

"A lot? That's not very scientific. How much does this claw weigh?"

McCormack glanced at it and then looked over at Nicholas. "A couple of pounds?"

"You didn't weigh it?" Ruth raised an eyebrow.

"It's the murder weapon. What does it matter how much it weighs?" He shrugged and there was that smile again.

"Dr. McCormack, do you consider yourself a scientist?"

He blinked. "What?"

"A scientist? One who adheres to the discipline of the scientific method? You're an M.D., right?"

"Yes, I am little Missy." His face reddened. "I graduated in the top of my class."

Ruth ignored the remark. "Then, am I correct in assuming that you drew your conclusions about the victim's death based on objective, scientific facts?"

"Yes." He growled. "I didn't use a crystal ball or chicken guts."

The crowd chuckled behind her. "Thank you for that. I can sleep a little more easily at night knowing that this county's medical examiner doesn't use voodoo or tea leaves in its scientific determinations." Ruth said.

"Objection, you honor." Nicholas stood up. "Can we get on with it? The members of this court are well aware of Ms. Martinez's last encounter with the witness and we will not stand for her badgering a man of Dr. McCormack's expertise."

"Ms. Martinez, get on with it." Nettles said.

"I'm sorry, your honor. I've just never had a medical examiner talk about using chicken guts before. This jury has no idea how this man runs the medical examiner's office. I'm merely trying to establish the standard of his judgment." Ruth said.

Nettles crossed his arms. "I am satisfied that Dr. McCormack is the leading expert in this field at this time. Now, move on."

"He told you, didn't he, little Missy." McCormack said quietly. Ruth felt her heart race and she swallowed. Now was not the time to get into a childish fight with this man. Let the jury draw their own conclusions. They could see how condescending he was being. Stick to the facts, she reminded herself. Ruth turned and pointed to the evidence table. "Back to the question at hand, Dr. McCormack. I could kill someone with that table over there but if it's too heavy for me to lift, it wouldn't make a very effective weapon. Surely you weighed this claw, Dr. McCormack. You see, these injuries are quite extensive. You described over three dozen separate areas of trauma to the body that you claim came from this claw. Now, I am a very petite woman. In your professional opinion, could I have caused all of those wounds with this heavy claw?"

Nicholas stood up, opened his mouth, and then settled back in his chair. Ruth looked back at Dr. McCormack. He shook his head. "I don't think so."

Ruth returned to the evidence table and picked up a sheath of papers. She thumbed through them and then came back to the witness stand. "Do you recognize these reports by your crime investigation team, Dr. McCormack?"

"Yes."

"These are your initials right here, correct?" She pointed to the front page.

"Yes."

"Well, on page 135 there is a report by criminologist Williams regarding the weight and dimensions of the murder weapon. Would you kindly read these two paragraphs?" She handed him the papers.

McCormack frowned and pushed his glasses back up on his forehead. "The object in question is made of stainless steel with a ceramic coating and enamel paint. The enamel coating and paint have broken away from the underlying metal. The 'claw' weighs 6.6 pounds and is eight inches long in its greatest dimensions." McCormack blinked and looked up at Ruth. "Go on?"

"Please."

"The estimated force necessary to swing the claw and induce rib fracture and peritoneal evisceration is estimated at an equivalent to a 275 pound baseball player swinging his baseball bat at maximum speed for up to twenty minutes duration." McCormack handed the paper back to her.

"Dr. McCormack, you analyze human bodies all the time, correct?"

"Yes." He growled.

"I would like for Dr. Miller to stand up, please."

Frank looked around and stood up. "How much would you estimate Dr. Miller weighs?"

"Objection, you honor." Nicholas stood up. "The witness cannot be objective in his assessment of Dr. Miller."

"Of course I can." McCormack blurted out before anyone could stop him. Nettles tried to hide a smile and glanced at Nicholas.

"I think he answered your objection, counselor. The witness may answer the question." Nettles said.

"I pride myself on guessing weight and height of my subjects to within two pounds and a half an inch. Dr. Miller weights 187 pounds and is five foot 10 and a half inches tall." McCormack said and smiled with satisfaction.

"In your medical opinion, Dr. McCormack, after having read this assessment by your own team, could a person of Dr. Miller's size and strength have caused all of these injuries with this claw?" Ruth leaned against the witness box.

"No." McCormack said quietly.

Ruth walked over to the table and dropped the claw with a resounding thud onto the table. "Another question, Dr. McCormack. You've seen these photographs of Dr. Miller bent over Dr. Darwyn's body."

"Yes, I have."

"I understand from the police report some of these photographs were not taken by members of your crime lab. Why is that?"

"The crime investigation unit doesn't show up on the scene until the police call us. Some of these photographs were taken before the police arrived."

Ruth pointed to the screen. "How then can they be considered evidence in this trial? Isn't all evidence handled by the crime lab?"

"Objection, your honor." Bryan stood up. "We've been over this."

Ruth approached Nicholas' table. "You have damning photographs of my client that implicate him in this murder and those photographs were not taken by the crime lab. How do we know those photographs were not staged?"

"Excuse me, Miss Martinez." Nettles said. "I think I should have a say in these proceedings."

"Of course, your honor." Ruth said.

"We have established that you can question Dr. Styles about these photographs, have we not?"

"Yes, your honor."

"Besides." Dr. McCormack continued. Ruth spun around. Nettles raised his gavel but paused. "As always, you jump the gun, ma'am. Just like you did with Reginald Drake. Always rushing in where fools fear to tread."

Ruth gasped. "How dare you bring up another case. Your honor, this is highly inappropriate."

Nettles sighed. "McCormack, this is not about the past. This is about today's case."

Ruth watched the naked animosity pour forth from McCormack's gaze. "Sorry for that remark. Honey, the police confiscated Dr. Styles' camera the minute they arrived and it has been in the proper chain of custody since that time. I know that someone of your ilk wouldn't understand these matters, but it is impossible to fake photographs on such a digital camera. The best you can do is change their brightness and contrast."

"My ilk?" Ruth said as her face warmed. "My ilk, Dr. McCormack? What kind of 'ilk' is that?"

Nettles lowered his gavel. "That's enough from both of you. If you have no further substantive questions, Ms. Martinez, I suggest we dismiss for lunch"

Ruth frowned. "Very well, your honor. I guess a person of my ilk has no further questions."

17

———————

"I'm not sure that was the best approach with McCormack." Grace said.

Ruth looked up from her sandwich. "He got under my skin. Again."

Steel sat at the head of the conference room table, his sunglasses perched on his head. "At least he got a fire lit under you. No more Miss nice girl."

Ruth rolled her eyes. "He's a bully. The jury will pick up on that."

"And, you are level headed, kind, and compassionate." Grace leaned toward her. "Don't forget that. We don't want the jury to see you as an overbearing woman. Some of them still believe a woman should be submissive to her husband."

Ruth sighed. "Well, I can't be all things to all people all the time! Mr. Steel told me I had to step up my game. You're telling me to back off. Well, which is it?"

Grace nodded. "You're right. We're sending mixed messages."

"You said you trusted me. You gave me this case because you had faith in me." Ruth said. "Give me some of your namesake. Give me some grace. I have a strategy here, Grace, and I know what I'm doing."

"Well, your point about the weight of the claw will go away once Nicholas introduces the fact Annieraptor can move." Steel said.

Ruth couldn't eat her sandwich. "I know. But, if I can introduce the tiniest element of doubt about the evidence, it might make the difference with the jury. Besides, McCormack is such an arrogant jerk."

"And, you had to disgrace him." Grace sipped at her coffee. "Ruth, steer clear of personal vendettas. This trial is about Frank, not the past."

"I know." Ruth sat back in her chair. "I'm sure McCormack missed something in his rush to judgment, just like he has done before. I just don't know what it is. Yet."

Steel leaned forward from his chair and sipped at a bottled water. "Well, we should have something from the hard drives by tonight. And, I've been thinking. Something that bothers me is why Dr. Darwyn's cell phone was beneath him on the display."

"Maybe he was trying to make a call before he was pushed from the balcony and it fell beneath him." Ruth said.

"Exactly. He had it out of his pocket and he was trying to call someone. Who was he calling?"

"911?" Ruth answered.

"You were talking about getting lazy and not covering all the details." Grace said. "We didn't check Darwyn's telephone calls on his cell phone."

"I asked Jones about them and she said we had to subpoena the cell phone company." Steel said.

"Nonsense!" Grace picked up her phone. "I have some connections with the D.A.'s office. That's how I got Nicholas a temporary transfer there. The prosecution has those records. And, they haven't introduced them into evidence."

"Which means they may have something we overlooked." Ruth sat forward. Could this be a good break? She needed one.

"If you can arrange for Jones to give me the records, I'll gladly run them down this afternoon." Steel said. "Maybe we can catch a break."

Ruth frowned. "Where's your sling?"

Steel stood up and massaged his left arm. "I'm better. It was holding me back. I'll let you know something as soon as I get the phone records."

He walked out of the room and Ruth leaned back in her chair. "Grace, I'll have to admit Steel has been a big help. I wasn't sure at first."

Grace held her phone up to her ear waiting for an answer. "Well, just be careful around him. Dr. Cephas Lawrence tells me the man is good. But, he's a bit unstable. Avoid any personal entanglements." She started talking on the phone and Ruth took another bite of her tasteless sandwich.

"Dr. Styles, what is your position at the Institute?" Nicholas started out the afternoon by putting the scientist on the stand.

"I am the head of the biomechanical engineering division. Although it's not exactly a formal division. But, I take the skeletal models produced by Dr. Morrant and the muscle and soft tissue models produced by Dr. Grant and bring the dinosaur to life as a model."

Nicholas nodded. "Dr. Morrant and Dr. Grant are your colleagues?"

"Yes."

"Your statue of Annieraptor was to be the crowning glory for Dr. Darwyn?"

"Yes. I finished it in time for the party Dr. Darwyn held for the employees and staff to show off Annieraptor."

"Dr. Styles, do you recognize this item?" Nicholas held up the backpack and goggles.

"That is my Feldercarb 360."

"Feldercarb 360? Why do you call it that?"

"Just a name I made up. Most ordinary people wouldn't understand the real name. They tend to make up words for things they can't possibly understand like thingamabob or doohickey. So, I named it the Feldercarb 360." Styles grinned.

"I see. What does it do?"

"It controls Annieraptor."

"Controls?" Nicholas turned toward the jury giving them his best look of bewilderment. Ruth sighed. He was good at this. Very good. "I don't understand."

Styles laughed and leaned forward in the witness stand. "I'll let you in on a little secret. I was going to surprise everyone at the party. You see, Annieraptor is more than just a statue. It is a fully operational cybernetic organism." He raised his hands above his head and wiggled them. "It's alive! It's alive!"

The crowd murmured and Nettles pounded his gavel. "Enough of that, Dr. Frankenstein. Stick to the facts."

Styles shrugged. "For the layperson, it's sort of an animatronic, a robotic figure. But, it goes way beyond that. It has synthetic muscles that are ground breaking. It's a new technology that will win me the Nobel Peace Prize."

"So, Annieraptor comes alive?" Nicholas put on a shocked look.

"Yes, and the Feldercarb 360 is what controls it. I based it on the augmented reality goggles and program for drones like Dr. Miller uses in his search for prehistoric plant descendants." Styles nodded toward Miller. Ruth groaned. Here it comes. And, she couldn't think of a way to object to the line of questioning.

"So, this laptop in a backpack allows you to control the movements and actions of Annieraptor?" Nicholas held it up for the jury to see.

"Yes."

"Just what is Annieraptor capable of?"

"Walking, running, snapping her jaws, basically just about all baseline actions of a living dinosaur." Styles said. "I'm very proud of her."

"I bet you are. Can Annieraptor attack?"

"Objection." Ruth said, standing up. "Council is prejudicing the jury."

"Your honor, I am establishing a line of actions that leads inevitably to the use of Annieraptor as the murder weapon." Nicholas sounded wounded.

"I'll allow it. Proceed."

Ruth slumped into her chair. Her objection was feeble at best, but she had to try.

"You can combine certain actions into a sequence that would make Annieraptor emulate a stalking activity. I studied dinosaur behavior patterns and based her movement capabilities on what most paleontologists would agree are the actions of a predator of Annieraptor's abilities." Styles said.

"Such as chasing down the prey?" Nicholas asked.

"Yes, chasing the prey."

"What about harming the prey?"

"It is fully capable of such actions assuming the operator commands such actions." Styles pointed to the laptop.

"Could Annieraptor kill?" Nicholas said.

A tense silence fell over the courtroom and Ruth held her breath. This was it. And, she couldn't stop the train that was barreling toward Frank Miller.

"Yes." Styles said smugly. The courtroom erupted in a frenzy of voices. Nettles pounded his gavel and called for silence.

Nicholas paraded in front of the jury, holding the goggles for all to see. "Let me get this straight and be very clear about it, Dr. Styles. The person who wears these goggles controls Annieraptor. And, under the right commands, Annieraptor is capable of doing what any meat-eating dinosaur could do, slash and kill its prey. Correct?"

"Yes."

"Your honor, at this time, I would like to submit these items into evidence."

Ruth stood up to protest and Nettles pointed her down. "No, the defense cannot object to this. I will allow it."

"But!"

"No, buts, Ms. Martinez. I will allow them to be placed into evidence."

"Thank you, your honor." Nicholas smiled and placed the goggles and the laptop on the evidence table. He turned to Styles. "Dr. Styles, when was the last time you saw your Feldercarb 360?"

Styles rubbed his chin, deep in thought. "A couple of nights before the party. I was panicking because without it, all I could do was turn on Annieraptor for the party and she would do some basic movements such as blinking her eyes and tilting her head. Without the Feldercarb 360, I couldn't do much else with her."

"So, you lost it?"

"Or, it was taken." Styles said.

"Dr. Styles, are you aware that your Feldercarb 360 was found in Dr. Miller's office?" Nicholas asked.

"Objection, your honor." Ruth stood up. "The defense has not had time to consider the implications of this new evidence."

"Your honor, I met with Ms. Martinez a couple of days ago and informed her the police had found these items in Dr. Miller's office. We also informed her that the only fingerprints found on these items by the crime scene investigators were Dr. Miller's fingerprints. She is well aware of the importance of this evidence."

Ruth rolled her eyes. She had stepped right into Nicholas' trap. Now, he didn't have to call the police back to the stand. She had helped him establish the murder weapon was in Miller's possession.

"Overruled, Ms. Martinez. And, Mr. Nicholas, I will warn you again about these theatrics. If you want to introduce pertinent evidence in this courtroom, you will do so by calling the appropriate witnesses."

"I can certainly call the CSU team back to the stand, your honor. But, the jury now has access to the affidavit from the team regarding this item's discovery and the fingerprint evidence. The defense has every right to address this in their portion of the trial." Nicholas said.

"Just get on with this witness, please." Nettles sighed.

"Dr. Styles, how difficult is it to control Annieraptor with your Feldercarb 360?"

Styles shrugged. "Not too difficult for someone with programming knowledge or the ability to control remote objects."

"Such as drones?" Nicholas asked, turning to Ruth and waiting for an objection. She sat still and silent.

"Yes, like those that Dr. Miller uses."

"Dr. Styles, could you possibly turn on your Feldercarb 360 for us? We can interface the video output from the laptop over the jury's monitors."

"Certainly, if the batteries are still charged up. I put extra batteries in the lining of the backpack."

Nicholas pointed to the table. "Your honor, would you mind if Dr. Styles approaches the table and demonstrates the features of his laptop?"

"Not at all. I assume we are too far away from Annieraptor to actually control the thing?"

Styles hopped out of the witness stand. "Oh, yes, your honor. The Feldercarb 360 must be within about 100 feet of Annieraptor. I hope to improve the range with my upgrades." He opened the zipper of the backpack and snared a video cable. He plugged the cable into the laptop inside the backpack and turned it on. He donned the goggles and waited. A typical computer desktop appeared on the large screen monitor and was mirrored on the monitors mounted in the jury box.

"You probably won't recognize the interface. Dr. Miller is our programming assistant and he developed this program using Linux for security reasons. Now, what you are seeing on the monitor is what I am seeing in my goggles. The goggles have motion sensors mounted on the perimeter to pick up my hand and foot motion. When I activate the connection with Annieraptor, I am looking through her eyes. And, oh my!"

"What is it?" Nicholas asked.

"There seems to be a recording of the last session with Annieraptor."

The jury began to murmur and Ruth stood up. "Your honor, I strongly object to this process. We have not been apprised of this information. Nor, would it seem the prosecution." She glanced at Nicholas and he averted his gaze. The man knew exactly what would transpire. "You planned this!" She shouted at Nicholas.

Nettles pounded his gavel. "Stop it! Now!" He glared at Nicholas. "I warned you, Mr. Nicholas."

"Sir, if there is a record of the attack by Annieraptor, the jury has a right to see it. There are numerous precedents set regarding digital media."

"I am well aware of those precedents, Mr. Nicholas. Do not lecture me. Bailiff, clear the courtroom and sequester the jury while we watch this video. I will be the one to decide if the video is admissible as evidence."

Ruth collapsed into her chair and glanced at Miller. He was pale and sweating. "This is not good, is it?" He asked.

"No. Nicholas wouldn't allow this video to be seen if he wasn't convinced it would drive a nail in your coffin." She winced. "Sorry, I didn't mean that."

It took five minutes to clear the room and the jury. Once the room was clear, Nettles nodded to Styles. "Dr. Styles, you can play the video."

Ruth watched in absolute horror as the images played on the big screen monitor. Watching from Annieraptor's point of view, they followed its progress as it hopped off the display stage and jumped up to the third floor. They watched in horror as it opened the door to Darwyn's office. They watched Darwyn gasp in shock as Annieraptor attacked and ripped apart his lab coat. They followed along as Annieraptor chased Darwyn down the walkway and into the stairway and then watched him plummet to his death from the second floor. Then, Annieraptor hopped through the air and thudded onto the man's chest. At the last second, the claw from its left foot broke away in Darwyn's chest. Then, the point of view shifted, looking straight ahead into the ferns and foliage of the display room. For a second, silence filled the screen and then there was a sudden burst of static. The image cleared and the point of view was pointed down exposing someone's chest and body. The person was clad in a formless white lab coat and clearly seen in the lower corner was the ID bearing the name Dr. Frank Miller. The screen went blank.

Ruth gasped and slumped into her chair, her hands shaking.

Miller stood up. "That's impossible! I didn't do it! That's not me in the video!"

Nettles pounded his gavel. "Silence! I've seen enough, Dr. Miller. But, I don't think the jury has. I'll allow the video as evidence."

THE FOLLOWING hour was one of the worst of Ruth's career. The jury and crowd were allowed back in. Grace had left with the crowd and she listened to her gasp in horror as the video was played for the jury. Once the video was over and the mayhem was subdued by Nettles, Styles returned to the witness stand.

"Your honor, I have no further questions for Dr. Styles." Nicholas said. He smiled in her direction and settled back into his seat.

Ruth calmed her racing heart and slowly walked across to the witness stand. "Dr. Styles, the other day when I visited the Institute, Annieraptor came alive and stalked me. Do you recall that incident?"

"Yeah, I was on the second floor and heard your screams."

Ruth shuddered and nodded. "It was frightening, Dr. Styles. To be stalked and attacked by a dinosaur is not something I will ever forget."

"Getting beaten up by your assistant is something I will never forget."

"Let's stick to the current case, shall we?"

"But, I saved the day, didn't I?" Styles said. "I'm the hero. Not your investigator, Mr. Steel." Styles rubbed the bruise on his left cheek.

"Dr. Styles, just how did you stop Annieraptor?"

"There is a small access door on Annieraptor's back. I ran over to her, flipped open the door and pressed the reset button."

"There is a reset button?"

"Yes. It commands Annieraptor to return to her stand and assume her basic pose." Styles nodded. "She was scary, wasn't she? Had you going, didn't she?"

"I was frightened for my life, Dr. Styles."

"You should have been."

Ruth nodded and turned to the jury. "What if any member of this jury had been in my place that day? Would Annieraptor have stalked and attacked them?"

"Yes."

"Regardless of their identity?" Ruth turned.

Styles realized where she was going and sat there in silence.

"I asked you a question, Dr. Styles. Please answer me."

"Yes, it would have attacked them regardless of who they were."

Ruth hurried across the floor much like Annieraptor had come after her. "And, why was that, Dr. Styles? Your Feldercarb 360 was in the possession of the police by then. Why is it that Annieraptor attacked me when there was no one controlling her?"

Styles squirmed in his seat. "Probably because there were some remaining basic motions from whoever controlled her before."

"Perhaps you could be more specific."

"When you use the laptop to control Annieraptor, there is a buffer on the onboard CPU. The commands are very complex and in order to execute them in real time, the commands are saved in a buffer zone."

"Sort of a copy of what Annieraptor was told to do?"

"Yes."

"Then it is possible for Annieraptor to stalk and attack without anyone being in direct control at that time?" Ruth asked.

"Yes. And, no. The default for the controller is to return Annieraptor to her resting mode after any interaction. Once the final command is given and a certain amount of time elapses, the buffer is zeroed out and she returns to default mode." Styles said. "I know it's hard for you to understand being just a lawyer, but what you saw in the Institute was an echo of what Annieraptor was last made to do."

"Why wasn't the buffer zeroed out?" Ruth asked.

"I don't know. A glitch in the program? I haven't had my hands on the laptop since I lost it so I can't find out what happened." Styles said.

Ruth nodded. "So, let me get this straight. You tested out the stalking and attack mode sometime in the past, right? I mean after all, you had to make sure Annieraptor would do what you would claim it could do? Right?"

"Well, yes. But, I never told it to attack and kill. Never."

"But, if an echo of these commands remained and Annieraptor came to life the night of Dr. Darwyn's murder, isn't it possible she could have stalked him and killed him without anyone controlling her?" Ruth asked.

"Objection, your honor. Speculation." Nicholas said.

"Your honor, this is more than speculation. I am asking a question about the murder weapon from the very person who made it. I think we have a right to know what it is capable of doing." Ruth said quietly.

"Overruled. The witness will answer the question."

Ruth turned back to Styles. "Well?"

"Anything is possible, Ms. Martinez. It is possible you might win this case. But, that is unlikely given that the controller was in Dr. Miller's possession prior to Annieraptor's actions. If anyone tested out a stalking and killing set of motions, it would have been him. All you've proven is that someone took her through the actions before-hand. I've already told everyone I lost the controller days before the party. If there is an echo of a murder here, the original actions come from that man." He pointed to Dr. Miller. "And, you saw the video just like everyone did. You saw the name tag."

"Yes, it was very convenient that whoever controlled Annieraptor looked down at the ID at just the right moment to capture it in the images. Very convenient. You just told us it was possible anyone using the controller could have taken Annieraptor through those motions, correct?" Ruth asked.

Style's looked like he had swallowed a toad. "Yes."

"No further questions."

"Permission to re-direct." Nicholas stood up.

"Go ahead, counselor." Nettles sighed.

"Dr. Styles, let's get something straight. Can Annieraptor, on her own, by some mysterious programming, commit this stalking and attack behavior without the direct, hands on use of that controller?" He pointed to the evidence table.

"No. There is no way Annieraptor can be programmed to do something. Her actions are controlled live by the controller. What Ms. Martinez experienced is a glitch, a remnant of those commands still left in the buffer. If I had been able to merely turn on the controller, it would have connected with Annieraptor and made sure the buffer was zeroed out. What happened to Ms. Martinez was an anomaly. But, it was still an echo of the actions that led to the death of Dr. Darwyn. And, it proves that the last person who used that controller, used it to stalk and kill!" Styles said smugly.

"The last person who had possession of your Feldercarb 360 that was later found locked in Dr. Miller's desk drawer?"

"Right. Annieraptor didn't murder Dr. Darwyn. Dr. Miller did." Styles said.

Ruth rose to object and then stopped in utter exasperation and flopped back in her seat. Miller glanced at her with nothing buy misery on his face.

18

———————

Jonathan Steel

Detective Jones was still at the courthouse when I arrived at the police station. I had to talk to Destillo again to get a copy of the cell phone records. He never said a word as he handed them over and turned his back on me in disdain. I could care less.

The last two numbers on the record were placed at about the time of Darwyn's death. Someone had called him twice and he had not answered. Destillo had been thorough. He was an F.B.I. agent, after all. He had noted the numbers came from a cell phone purchased over the counter at a local convenience store.

I could barely understand the man's stilted English when I arrived at the store but he had a record of the purchase. The buyer had used a credit card to purchase the cell phone and he had to call in for confirmation of payment. He handed me a slip of paper with a name and an address on it. I looked at the name. Really? It was an obvious alias. But, when I looked up the address on my phone, it was a local motel.

The sun had set and the air was filled with a cold mist when I pulled up to the motel. Fire trucks blocked the driveway of a crescent shaped, two story motel probably built in the late 1960's. Three police cars sat on either side of the road. I recognized the bright, yellow hair of Detective Jones.

"Detective Jones." I said as I walked up to the yellow tape.

She turned and her eyes grew wide in surprise. "You? Again? Don't tell me you have something to do with this fire, honey child?"

I shrugged. "I'm chasing down a phone number from Darwyn's cell phone records. If you had given them to me the other day, I might have gotten here sooner. Wherever here is. The buyer was in room number 11A."

"Of course I should have known that the powerful and great Jonathan Steel could have prevented this murder. Forgive me for not utilizing your services." She lifted the yellow tape and nodded toward the motel. "Get in here! Now!"

I ducked under the tape. The air was filled with a freezing mist from the fire trucks undercut by the odor of wet burned wood and charred rubber. "What happened?"

Jones glared at me. "Why should I tell you?"

"Because we are working toward the same goal. You know Miller didn't kill Darwyn. The evidence points to a 'heinous' killer. Miller isn't that kind of person. And now, we both turn up at what I must assume is a murder since you are involved."

Jones closed her eyes and shook her head. "All right. Listen up, because I'll only say this once. And then, you're out of here. We got a bomb threat this afternoon. Bomb squad arrived and evacuated the motel. Only about ten occupants, most of them on the hourly plan." She led me across the debris littered parking lot toward the motel. The fire had demolished most of the structure leaving behind black spindles of wood and melted iron railings. Some of the rooms remained intact and Jones led me toward the room on the first floor near the center of the motel.

"When the firemen got to this room, number 11A I might add, they couldn't get the occupant to open the door. That's when the bomb went off. Incendiary bomb. Powerful accelerant I understand. Two firemen were hurt in the explosion. The only casualty was the woman in that room."

I pulled the slip of paper out of my pocket. "Janet Dough?"

Jones cocked her head and frowned. "Of course, you would know who was in the room? How?"

"Last two calls to Dr. Darwyn were from a cell phone purchased by a Janet Dough and her address was listed at this motel."

Jones' eyes narrowed and she turned toward the room. "Crime unit is in there right now after the fire department cleared them for entry. Let's see what happened."

"You're still letting me tag along?" I asked.

"Only because of your pretty eyes, honey child." She motioned me to follow her.

We stepped over the threshold of the splintered, charred door. The room beyond was barely intact. Two crime unit technicians took photographs of a black lump the size of a bed. "What do we have?" Jones asked.

I put my hand over my nose. The wet, charred wood odor was bad enough but the odor of burned flesh made me queasy. Couldn't let Jones know that.

A technician turned toward her. He wore a surgeon's mask over his face. "Looks like this is the center of the blast and the fire. There's a body here, but it's so badly burned we'll have to take it back to the lab to identify it."

I glanced around at the remnants of the room. Some of its contents had been blown up against the outer wall. I spied a half-burned book wedged in the corner beside the melted air conditioning unit. "Looks like a book." I pointed.

"Nope. Don't touch it, Steel." Jones fished a flashlight out of her jacket and pointed it toward the corner. The blackened leather cover bore the title, 'Holy Bible'. "Doesn't look like your typical Gideon's hotel Bible."

"It might have the woman's real name." I said.

Jones glanced at me. "Figured Janet Dough was an alias, did you?"

"I'm not stupid." I said.

"We'll find out more once the techs get all of the evidence gathered. Now, it's time for you to leave. We've got work to do." She motioned toward the door.

I pulled my hand away from my nose and grimaced at a strong, chemical odor. "What is that chemical?"

"Probably the accelerant." Jones said. "Now, scoot."

I left the room and made my way across the parking lot toward my car. Why had Janet Dough, whoever she was, called Dr. Darwyn near midnight? It was obvious the two knew each other. Or, did they? Maybe this woman was some kind of dinosaur groupie. Whatever the reason, I had to find out her real name and see if there was a connection. I studied the name and address again and then tucked the piece of paper into my jacket pocket and looked up. Someone stood on the other side of my car in shadows. The man wore a heavy overcoat and his face was shrouded in darkness. I stared at him and he stepped back out of the cone of light from an overhead street light. The hair stood on end on my neck. The air grew still and a new cold wave played over me. Evil! I sensed it. Whoever was standing on the other side of my car resonated with unspeakable evil! I hurried to my car and beyond it into the darkness. An alleyway led away from the street behind the destroyed motel. It was empty. The evil had gone, dissipating like the foul odor of a passing skunk. Who was the man? Why was he here? I did not know. But, I was now more certain than ever that this mysterious woman was the key to locating the real killer of Wallace Darwyn.

RUTH RUBBED the fatigue from her eyes and put her laptop aside. The early January winter had settled into Dallas. Some days promised bright sunshine and a high in the low seventies. But, the weather could just as easily degenerate into a raging ice storm. The temperature outside had dropped into the thirties and Ruth had built her a fire in her meager fireplace. She sipped a cup of spiced tea and studied the fire curling and dancing in the hearth.

If Frank had not killed Darwyn, then who had? Styles was right about one thing. Anybody on the staff with access to the program and the laptop could have used it to kill Darwyn. Of course, for all she knew some teenager with knowledge in building video avatars could have hacked into the system and took over Annieraptor just for fun.

The next day promised to introduce the particulars of what happened at the party. She looked forward to questioning everyone on the eyewitness accounts of the fight. She just wished she had the security video. The doorbell rang and she glanced across her den. She lived in a small, but tidy house in one of those upscale neighborhoods where all the houses were basically the same shape with very little yard. She wore her soft, cotton gown; a warm, cozy cocoon of comfort that for her was a refuge from the harsh world outside the door. She hurried across the room to the front door and glanced through the peephole. Jonathan Steel stood on the other side squinting in the sudden light of her front porch.

She opened the door slightly and hugged her gown to her chest. Her face burned with embarrassment. "Jonathan, it's nine o'clock."

His bright turquoise eyes shone in the porch light and he frowned. "Sorry. I lost track of time. I found out some things you need to know."

Ruth stepped back and motioned him into the den. "Come in. I'm not dressed."

"You look dressed to me." He glanced at her and then around the room as if searching for hidden danger. He carried a paper bag in one hand. He wore a long sleeve tee shirt and a pair of jeans. In spite of the frigid weather outside, he seemed to be warm and cozy himself. His left arm was not in a sling.

"What about your arm?" She motioned to his left side.

"It's better."

"Uh, let's go sit at the dining room table." Ruth motioned behind her as she eyed the sack. "Did you bring dinner?"

Steel's gaze returned from surveying the room and he looked down at the sack. "No. I don't have a briefcase." He walked over and poured out the contents of the bag onto the dining room table. A stack of papers slid across the shiny wooden surface of the table.

Ruth glanced at the papers and settled into a seat. "So, you're not very organized. I can get you a briefcase."

Steel shuffled through the papers. "A back pack would do. Here. Darwyn's cell phone records. Look at the last two calls."

Ruth looked down the list. "He received two calls at midnight?" She looked up at Steel.

"While he was being murdered. That is why he had the phone out. It was ringing and he was trying to answer it. He probably forgot he had the thing on him with Annieraptor chasing him down the hall."

Ruth looked at the numbers. "It's the same number. Twice. Who called him?"

Steel frowned. "The number came from a burner phone. I tracked it back to a convenience store. They had a record. Owner wanted to protect herself in case the phone was used by a criminal. The name is an alias."

"What was it?"

"Janet Dough."

Ruth sighed. "Jane Doe? Great!"

"But there was an address. A room at the Shangri-La Hotel in Rockwall."

"That's east of Dallas."

"I went there this evening. It burned to the ground and only one occupant was in the room at the time."

"Let me guess, Janet Dough?"

"Yes." Steel tapped the table. "Someone killed her, Ruth. I'm sure of it."

"How do you know?"

"Detective Jones was there. Turns out there was a bomb threat and it went off in her room. Jones is with homicide. Janet Dough is in the morgue. No identity. None so far." Steel leaned back from the table.

"What about the manager of the motel?"

"He was stoned at the time. He's now in jail for a parole violation. I can go talk to him tomorrow, but one of the patrol officers said the man had no recollection of the woman other than she paid in cash."

Ruth picked up the cell phone records. "A mysterious woman killed in a fire phones Darwyn twice the night he is murdered. It'll probably end up with all the other dead end cases. Another homeless nobody."

"Ruth, I'll keep digging. I'm not going to let Janet Dough get buried without a proper name attached. Somewhere, there is someone who knows her." He fell silent and Ruth watched a dark shadow cross his features. "I don't remember anything about my past. The only person that I am aware of who is alive and knows me is my father. I have vague memories of him. And, I have some vague memories of my mother somewhere in my past. I don't want to end up like Janet Dough."

Ruth blinked in surprise. The man didn't want to die and not know who his family was? She would have never guessed. "You will find out, Jonathan. I know you will."

The shadow passed and the fierce gaze returned. He focused his bright, turquoise eyes on the pieces of paper. "I got a message from my techie about the hard drives. The hard drives had been erased. Bad sectors or something like that. Did you know the cameras were still active until 1 A.M.?"

Ruth looked into his intense eyes. "That would mean the cameras in the display area would have recorded the murder."

Steel nodded. "Of course that wouldn't help us much even if we could find the footage. We're assuming somebody controlled Annieraptor and wouldn't be visible. We'd still see Dr. Miller discovering the body which proves nothing."

"Then why did somebody erase it? We've got to recover those images. How soon can we get this?"

"He's still working on it so I don't know. How much time before you go on the offensive?"

"I imagine the prosecution will take until Friday. Today's Monday. That means we'll have the weekend to chase down any loose ends before we get to present our case."

Steel stood up and hugged the paper bag under his arm. "I'll tell Kristof he has two days."

Ruth looked up and frowned. "Two days?"

"I'm not an attorney, Ruth. But, I get the distinct impression that Bryan Nicholas likes to throw you off. I wouldn't be surprised if he finished before Friday just to get your goat."

Ruth shivered. "Let's hope not."

19

"Mrs. Greely, what is your job with the Institute?" Nicholas asked the small framed woman sitting primly in the witness box. She wore a bright blue dress and pearls and her hair was teased out into a pale, blonde mass. She wore excessive mascara and a huge pair of white rimmed glasses covered with sequins that magnified her eyes.

"I am the executive secretary for the staff." She said. She turned and smiled at the jury.

"And, where do you work in the building?"

"My desk is immediately across from the elevators on the third floor. No one gets by me without an appointment. You might say I'm the watch dog for Dr. Darwyn and his staff." Her features suddenly clouded and she pulled a tissue from her purse and dabbed at her eyes while pulling off the large glasses. If her mascara started running, Ruth feared a flood of muddy, salt water.

"Were you present at the party on December fourteenth?" Nicholas asked.

"Of course. I handled all the catering and the decoration. I have a niece who owns her own catering service if anyone is interested."

Mrs. Greely seemed to perk up and tucked the stained tissue back in her purse.

"That's not what we're here to talk about, Mrs. Greely. I'd appreciate it if you would stick to the question. Was Dr. Darwyn present at the party?"

"Of course. He was the master of ceremonies. He was wearing his nicest pair of pants and that pretty paisley tie I gave him last Christmas." She raised an eyebrow. "He's not a snappy a dresser as you are. Love that tie."

"Thank you. Now, go on." Nicholas said.

"Well, I have to tell him how to dress sometimes. He can be a bit absent minded. One day he wore two different color socks. But, what was really bothersome was he had on two different shoes. I just don't know how he got through the day without me." Her faced twisted and she snatched the tissue from her purse.

Nicholas glanced over at Ruth and she grinned. After all, Mrs. Greely was his witness. Judge Nettles leaned toward him. "Mr. Nicholas, please instruct your witness to confine her remarks to the pertinent answer to your questions."

Nicholas nodded. "Mrs. Greely, I think the jury is now well aware of your devotion to your boss. You don't need to make any more comments about that. OK? Now, tell me what happened when Dr. Darwyn unveiled Annieraptor."

Mrs. Greely nodded and finished dabbing at her eyes. "Well, it was Wallace's big moment. It was the realization of a lifelong dream. He stood up beside the display and Annie was covered by a huge cloth and announced, 'Behold Annieraptor'. He pulled a rope and the drape just fell to the floor revealing that dinosaur. I must admit, even though I can't stand the sight of that monster, it was impressive standing up there for all to see. Everyone applauded and that's when Dr. Miller ran through the crowd and started shouting. He was screaming, 'Fraud! Fraud! Fraud!' Can you imagine accusing Dr. Darwyn of fraud? Why, I never!"

She drew a deep breath and glared at Dr. Miller. "He started shouting about the feathers, of all things. Saying the feathers weren't in the fossil record. That Wallace had added them. That he had committed scientific fraud. Dr. Darwyn tried his best to shut him up. But, no, Dr. Miller wouldn't back off. Wallace tried to calm him down and when he put a hand on Dr. Miller's shoulder, he slapped it away! And, then, he grabbed Wallace by the front of his coat and started to shake him and shoved him! It was horrible!"

Mrs. Greely started tearing up again. Nicholas patted her hand and tried to move on quickly. "Did Dr. Miller threaten Dr. Darwyn?"

Mrs. Greely looked over at the defense table and a twisted, evil grin came over her lips. "He said he would get even and show the world that Dr. Darwyn was a fraud. He said Wallace would pay for his crimes."

Nicholas nodded and backed away. "Your witness."

Ruth cleared her throat and stood up behind her table. "Mrs. Greely, are you married?"

"Objection." Nicholas said before he even reached his table. "Relevance, your honor."

"It's really a simple question." Ruth stepped around the table. "I would like to establish the type of relationship Mrs. Greely had with the victim."

Nettles nodded. "I will allow it, but within reason, Ms. Martinez."

Ruth came closer to the witness box. "Are you married, Mrs. Greely?"

Mrs. Greely's face turned a bright red and she looked away. "My late husband was a perfect man."

"I didn't know one existed." Ruth said.

Mrs. Greely glanced up at her and took the bait. "Then, you never knew Dr. Darwyn."

"You're right. I never knew him while he was alive. But, you did. You must have been very close to him to help him with his wardrobe." Ruth had arrived at the witness box and leaned against the front rail.

Mrs. Greely brought the tissue up to her mouth and gasped. "How dare you imply--"

"Imply what, Mrs. Greely?"

"Dr. Darwyn and I were professionals. I worked for him."

"And told him how to dress. And bought him a tie. And called him by his first name." Ruth said.

"Your honor, must we really go on with this?" Nicholas stood up.

Ruth turned to Nicholas. "I'm just trying to establish whether or not your witness has a close enough relationship to the victim that she would color her testimony to place him in the best light and my client in the worst light. Judging from her comments, I would think she would do anything for Dr. Darwyn."

"I would." Mrs. Greely quipped.

Ruth turned quickly and leaned into the witness box. "Even lie?"

"That is enough, Ms. Martinez." Nettles pounded his gavel. "The jury will disregard that last remark."

Ruth pushed away. "I'm sorry, your honor. I have no further questions."

~

BRYAN NICHOLAS PARADED a half a dozen other witnesses through the morning and into the afternoon testifying to the fight at the party. After a while, Ruth grew tired of it and stood up.

"Your honor, the defense concedes that the fight took place. Do we have to go through more witnesses? How many people were at the party?"

Nettles sat back. "I agree. Mr. Nicholas, do any more of these type of witnesses have anything else of substance to add?"

"Just one, your honor. I call Dr. Morrant to the stand."

Dr. Morrant was resplendent in a white pantsuit and her long, lustrous hair cascaded around her shoulders. She was sworn in and Nicholas smiled at her as she settled into the witness stand.

"Dr. Morrant, would you please tell the court your position at the Institute?"

"I am currently the acting director and financial officer. Prior to the death of Dr. Darwyn, I was a general staff member. My specialty is skeletal reconstruction."

"I understand you have developed a computer program for your specialty?"

"That is correct. I can scan images of the fossils into my program and develop a complete three-dimensional skeleton that can then be used for reconstruction of the dinosaur."

"Dr. Morrant, you've heard the testimony up to now of the developments at the party. Can you add anything to the accounts?" Nicholas turned and looked at Ruth. He winked. Ruth drew in a deep breath and looked over at Dr. Miller.

"What was that about?"

Miller paled. "I think I know."

Morrant shrugged. "On the surface, the fight seemed petty but you'd have to know what went on in my office before the party."

Ruth glanced at Miller and he lowered his head. She punched him. "Sit up straight. Don't act guilty."

Nicholas acted surprised. "In your office? Why don't you tell us what happened?"

FRANK KNOCKED on the door to Morrant's office. He was livid and he knew he had to control his temper. If what he suspected was true, then the Institute was in grave danger. The door opened and Dr. Darwyn stood there in front of him. His jaw fell.

"You're giving in to her?"

Darwyn looked past him out into the hall and pulled him into her office. He slammed the door behind them. Morrant stood behind her desk, biting on her thumbnail.

"What do you want, Frank?" Darwyn looked harried and upset.

"I just heard about the new grants we received. I heard that you gave her my money!"

"The grants went to the Institute, Frank."

"No, they went to the authors of the papers for the Institute, Wallace."

Darwyn looked over his shoulder at Morrant. "Frank, Dr. Morrant needs this grant to complete her work. She can't go any further with her program without additional funds."

"Which you can't give to her from the general fund because she's already exceeded her share, right? Am I right?" Frank pushed past Darwyn and leaned against the front of Morrant's desk. "What did you waste the money on this time? Was it that trip to Cabo San Lucas to look for more dinorithium bones?"

Morrant shook her head. "I couldn't complete the skeleton without that pelvis, and you know it. That trip was legitimate."

Frank turned and looked at Darwyn. "And, you didn't go by yourself, did you?"

Morrant turned away and swung her hands out in anger. "There you go, assuming something happened that didn't happen, Frank. Yes, Wallace accompanied me but he needed to be there to supervise the first portion of the dig. That is his area of expertise, remember? You know what is wrong with you, Frank? You have this exalted sense of moral superiority because you're a Christian. How arrogant of you to think that non-Christians can't possibly have those morals!"

Frank backed away and stumbled into Darwyn. "Don't change the subject. This isn't about Cabo San Lucas. This is about taking my grant money by slinking up to the boss."

Morrant stepped from behind the desk and slapped him across the face. His face stung and he glanced back at her in shock. "You just hit me."

"And, you deserved it, Frank. Get over it. Your contract is just like mine. Any money awarded by grant because of work done for the Institute can be taken by the Institute for its own purposes." Morrant's face was crimson.

Frank turned at glared at Dr. Darwyn. "I'll stop you, Wallace. I'll do whatever it takes to make sure that money stays in my account." He shoved the door open and stalked off to his office.

"I SHOULDN'T HAVE SLAPPED him, but his accusations were way off base." Morrant said.

"Before Dr. Darwyn's death, who was the financial officer of the Institute?" Nicholas asked.

"Dr. Miller." Morrant said.

"So, he could have stopped the transference of this money?"

"No. Dr. Darwyn has executive power to override any financial assignments as long as those decisions are consistent with the operating by-laws of the Institute. Our finances come from grants and donations. As long as Dr. Darwyn was alive, he could put the money wherever he wanted within reason. With him gone, the merging of the directorship and financial officer could be done on a temporary basis. That would have given that person unprecedented control over the purse strings."

Nicholas nodded. "And that person would have been Dr. Miller?"

"Yes."

Nicholas turned and smiled at Ruth in all his triumphant glory. "Your witness."

Ruth glanced once at Dr. Miller and looked back at the bench. "Your honor, the defense requests a short recess before cross."

Nettles rubbed his chin. "Denied. I think you need to proceed Ms. Martinez."

Ruth sighed and stepped around the table. She had planned a tack to take but what she had just heard had changed everything. She thought furiously as she approached the bench.

"Dr. Morrant, in your professional opinion, was the inclusion of feathers on Annieraptor scientifically ethical?"

Morrant blinked and chuckled. "Scientifically ethical? Isn't that a contradiction in terms?"

"What do you mean?"

"Ethics and morality have nothing to do with science. Science is a hard field of endeavor that is devoid of human emotion." Morrant said tersely.

"And you were not being emotional when you slapped Dr. Miller?"

"Objection!" Nicholas said.

Ruth put up a hand. "I retract my statement. Dr. Morrant, isn't the scientific method in place to assure total objectivity?" Ruth asked.

"Why, of course."

"And, how do you determine if total objectivity is achieved?"

"By testing the model. You see, a scientist looks at a given situation and develops a model that will explain the situation. This model makes certain assumptions we call hypotheses. Then, we test the model by experimentation and gathering of information. Upon analysis, we determine if the data gathered supports the hypothesis. If it does, then we have arrived at scientific truth. If not, then we change the model and start over."

"The combination of your program with the other computer modeling programs of the Institute are a part of this 'scientific model'?" Ruth began to feel her way through the complexities of the issues. She was beginning to have an idea.

"Yes, they are."

"But, the data that you speak of comes from the field, correct?"

"Of course. Without the fossil record to build the models upon, there would be no Institute." Morrant lifted an eyebrow. "That's why it should be funded and why it should continue the hard work that Dr. Darwyn began."

"Have you seen all the field data on Annieraptor?" Ruth asked.

"Yes."

"And, where in the field data did Dr. Darwyn make the determination that Annieraptor had feathers?"

Morrant opened her mouth and then closed it. She seemed deep in thought. "I wouldn't expect you to understand this, Ms. Martinez, but sometimes we have to fill in the gaps with assumptions. Those assumptions are based on our best guesses."

"So, you build a model and then test it. When the model doesn't fit your expectations, you keep the model and ignore the data and take your best guess?" Ruth leaned forward. "It sounds like you are departing from the scientific method and getting away from objectivity to subjectivity."

"We can't know everything, Ms. Martinez. Sometimes we have to guess."

"So, even in science you take some things on faith." Ruth said, turning to survey the jury.

"Well, I don't know if I would use that word."

"But, faith is a word that you don't particularly like. It smacks of religion."

"You're correct. I don't accept blind belief."

"Blind belief. Interesting you would say that. And yet, you make the blind leap of faith that Annieraptor had feathers because of your prejudged position that this dinosaur was a missing link between dinosaurs and birds."

"Objection, your honor." Nicholas stood up. "I'd like to know where this endless chain of questions is going"

Nettles looked at Ruth. "I would, too."

Ruth approached the bench. "Your honor, Mr. Nicholas has impugned my client with testimony that is hearsay and highly emotionally charged by a witness that admits slapping my client. I need to establish this witness' frame of mind for the jury before they can honestly and objectively accept her damaging testimony. Please indulge me for a few more minutes."

Nettles nodded. "Very well. But, wrap this up quickly, Ms. Martinez."

Ruth turned back to Dr. Morrant who wore a look of utter contempt. "You're just as high and mighty in your judgment as Dr. Miller is." She said.

Ruth opened her mouth and then closed it. She stepped closer. "Are you making a moral judgment about me, Dr. Morrant?"

"Yes."

"How can you pass judgment on me when you don't believe in a moral standard?"

Morrant looked like she swallowed a roach. "I have a moral standard."

"Based on what?"

"Human decency."

"So, as a human being, you have the right to decided what is right and wrong?"

"Yes."

"Then why are we in this courtroom? If Dr. Miller did murder the victim and thought it was right to do so, how can he be held guilty of a crime?" Ruth pointed to Dr. Miller.

"It's the law, Ms. Martinez."

"So, there is a standard outside our own personal human desires? You admit that."

"Of course. Where are you going with this?"

Ruth leaned in to her. "Whether it is feathers on a dinosaur or a slap of the face or taking a trip to Cabo San Lucas or transferring the money that was hard earned by a fellow colleague, you and you alone are wrong in your actions, Dr. Morrant and you know it. You admitted as much when you apologized for slapping the defendant. So, how can you sit here in judgment on him when you have no solid ground for judging? You put feathers on dinosaurs where they never existed. You're putting the impression of a murderer on my client where none existed so you can make sure you get your precious grant money and your precious control of your program and keep the directorship of the Institute. We don't know if my client committed a crime or not, but we for sure know that you did."

It was only when Ruth looked away from the red face of Dr. Morrant that she heard the pounding of Nettles' gavel and saw Nicholas as he towered over his table.

"Ms. Martinez, I said to stop or I will hold you in contempt." Nettles shouted.

Ruth looked at him and then at the jury. "I apologize. I took a leap of faith and I would ask the jury to disregard anything I said." She felt a stab of victory when at least half of the members of the jury smiled.

"I do have one other question." Ruth turned. "If your honor would allow it."

"One more." Nettles pointed the gavel at her.

"Dr. Morrant, you said that with Dr. Darwyn gone whoever takes the position of director and financial manager in the interim has total and complete control over the dispensation of funds and the fate of any programs developed at the Institute. Correct?"

Morrant paled. "Yes. But, it is only temporary until the Board of Directors can fill both positions."

"When will that be?"

"February."

"And, until then who is the director and chief financial officer?"

Morrant grimaced. "I am."

"Seems like Dr. Darwyn's loss is your gain. Thank you so much." Ruth turned and left the witch in the dust.

20

———————

"That was stupid." Dr. Miller said as he slumped into the chair in the courthouse interrogation room. He had been shackled when he was taken from the courtroom and looked out of place in his suit.

Ruth slammed her briefcase on the table. "Let's talk stupid! You withheld damaging information from me, Dr. Miller. You should have told me you threatened Dr. Darwyn over the grant money."

Miller paled and looked away. "I didn't exactly say that."

"Well, it doesn't matter now what you did. It matters what the jury thinks. And, they are thinking more and more surely that you are a murderer!" She crossed her arms over her chest and paced around the room. "This is hard enough as it is without you hiding things. Any other threats I need to know about?"

Miller shook his head. "No."

"Good!"

"Well, it looks like Grace was right to put faith in you. You've certainly risen to the occasion. If anyone is to blame now, it's me. I'm sorry you're going to lose your job with your law firm." He said quietly.

Ruth stopped in her pacing, her eyes glued to the wall. She

blushed and felt her heart race. It was true. She had been thinking about losing and what it would cost her. She had never thought that way before. Always, it had been about the issue she was defending. It was always about the client's guilt or innocence. That was why she wouldn't take certain cases and that behavior had led her to this dilemma. She dropped her arms and turned to the table. She pulled out a chair and sat across from Frank. Reaching out, she placed her hand on his. He looked up at her with his dark eyes.

"You're right." Ruth said. "I don't know if it's Bryan and his obnoxious ways or," she swallowed, "Jonathan Steel rubbing off on me but I've never acted like this before. I've become obsessed with winning for the wrong reasons. You're innocent and we need to clear your name. Unfortunately, the only way to do that is to find the real killer and right now it could be any of a number of people."

He nodded. "What do we do now?"

Ruth pulled away her hand and sighed. "Tomorrow's Wednesday and I think the prosecution will rest on Friday. That at least gives us the weekend to look for more evidence. I'm not giving up, yet."

"Then I won't either. I'll have faith." Frank smiled weakly.

RUTH SQUINTED into the driving sleet and locked her car door. She carefully made her way across the parking lot to the restaurant and stepped into the stifling hot interior. Outside, the temperature was dropping below thirty and the sleet would soon turn to freezing rain as the warm moist air from the Gulf of Mexico completed its journey on top of the cold front that had descended from the Arctic. Just that morning, the air had been cold and the sky was clear. She looked around the interior of the restaurant and spied Steel sitting in the back. A woman sat at the booth with him.

Ruth took off her coat and unwrapped her scarf as she dusted the sleet out of her hair. She stopped at the end of the booth and looked at Steel. "I hope you had a better day than I did."

"I heard." Steel motioned to the woman. She was small framed with short, red hair and creamy complexion. "Meet Mrs. Frank Miller."

Ruth's eyes widened and she shook the woman's hand. "Frank's wife?"

"That would be me." She nodded. "I called your office to speak to you and they couldn't find you. Something about your cell phone being off in the courtroom. I talked to Mr. Steel and he agreed to meet me."

Ruth heard Steel pat the seat next to him and she slid into the booth after hanging her coat on the end of the booth. A waitress appeared with a bowl of hot chips and salsa. After fussing around for a few minutes, she took their order and disappeared.

"Mrs. Miller what can we do for you?"

"Kate. Please call me Kate." She played with her napkin. "I just wanted to talk to you about Bryan Nicholas."

Ruth glanced at Steel. "What about him?"

"He's asked me to testify against Frank." Kate looked up at them. "I don't want to. We've had our differences but I don't think Frank is capable of murder."

"Then when you get on the stand, say that." Ruth sipped at her water. She was on dangerous ground here and didn't want to be accused of tampering with a witness. "Kate, I can't tell you what you should or shouldn't say. You will take an oath to be truthful."

"I know. It's just what I'll say about Dr. Grant that will hurt Frank." Kate wiped a tear from her eye.

"Dr. Grant?" Ruth's brow wrinkled. "You know Dr. Grant?"

"Of course, I do. I worked for the Institute up until two months ago."

Ruth felt like she had been kicked in the gut. Frank had not bothered to mention this. Neither had Grace. Kate's face blanched.

"No, wait! No one knew about it. Dr. Grant came to me and offered me a job working at home. He said it would help Frank if I helped Grant finish the project. You know, Annieraptor. We met a few times over lunch and Dr. Grant always passed a flash drive off to me with information that had to be manipulated and processed. It seemed he had run out of money to hire an assistant to help him so he asked me to help out on the side. But, I couldn't tell Frank. He was the chief financial officer, you know."

Ruth leaned back as their meals arrived. She was ravenous and she began picking away at her enchiladas as her mind raced with this new information. "I can't ask you what Bryan is planning on bringing up at the trial, Kate. But, you can tell me anything that might help Frank."

Kate played with her fork and pushed food around on her plate. "There were some files I found on Dr. Grant's disks. They weren't supposed to be there. I don't how they got there. So, I opened them. They were spread sheets of money transfers. Money had been sent to an offshore bank account. At first, I was stunned. I mean, who else but Frank would have access to those funds?"

"Dr. Darwyn." Steel said.

Kate glanced at him. "Okay, but you see what I thought? Here is my husband the chief financial officer at the Institute and I had just uncovered evidence of possible embezzlement. You see where I found myself, don't you?"

This is what Bryan had up his sleeve! First, Frank funnels money to a Caribbean bank. Then, he gets in a fight over losing his grant. Then, he kills Dr. Darwyn so he can have control over the purse strings. This information would be devastating. Ruth felt nauseous and placed her fork on the table.

"Kate, do you still have those files?"

Steel dropped his knife. Ruth looked at him. "What?"

"You're not supposed to do this."

"It's evidence. Bryan is supposed to disclose the list of his witnesses. I don't remember Mrs. Miller being on the list."

"I am supposed to be a surprise witness." Kate said. "I do have copies of the files with all the information on them including Dr. Grant's models. I always make backup information before I start working on anything on the computer."

"Can I have them? Tonight?" Ruth asked.

Kate leaned over in the booth and pulled her purse out from

under the table. She reached in and pulled out a small flash drive. "The information is all in here. I put together a compilation of all the financial information in one folder. When I saw the spreadsheets, I went to Frank and accused him of seeing another woman. It made sense that if he was funneling all this money into bank accounts and he wasn't telling me then he was seeing someone on the side with very expensive taste. He denied the whole thing and I was so strung out by then, I refused to believe him." Kate pushed the tiny flash drive across the table and picked up her napkin. She dabbed her nose. "Now I know better and any chance I may have had of reconciling our differences will go out the window when he sees me on the stand."

Ruth picked up the flash drive and sighed. "Kate, I wish I could tell you that Frank will be forgiving, but I don't know the two of you that well. If I were you, I would just tell the truth. When I get a chance to cross examine you, I will ask you where you received the files to begin with and I'll try and push the jury into considering that maybe the offshore accounts were Dr. Grant's."

"Oh, but they weren't." Kate placed her napkin on the table. "I can't prove it, but I'm pretty sure they were someone else's. You see, Dr. Grant had to undergo surgery a couple of months ago. I had just started working on his files. He had some complications from the procedure and he was in the intensive care unit for three days. There was a lot of activity on the accounts during those three days. I pretended to be a representative of the client on the accounts and called. Whoever manipulated the funds did so over the phone with the proper passwords and the woman I spoke to said they use voice recognition software as an added level of security. Dr. Grant couldn't have authorized those transfers. He had a tube down his throat for three days. It was someone else."

Ruth frowned. "Let me get this straight. Grant sent you files but never meant you to find out about the accounts?"

"Someone wanted her to find them." Steel said. "It fits. Whoever killed Darwyn is pinning it all on Dr. Miller and doing a good job of it."

Kate put her hand to her mouth. "Then he didn't open the accounts! He wasn't with another woman! Oh, what a fool I've been."

"You've been manipulated just like everyone else, Kate. This was a carefully thought out plan that has played out over months. I think the killer took advantage of the fight at the party to rush ahead with the plan. That would mean that somewhere in their careful plans, they may have missed something in the rush to take advantage of the situation. Let's hope they made a mistake. Kate, was the voice of the account owner male or female?"

"They wouldn't say. What will I do when I get on the stand?"

Ruth took the last bite of her enchilada. "You won't be put on the stand. I'll see to that."

21

———

Judge Nettles called the courtroom into order and before Bryan Nicholas could stand up, Ruth rushed around her table. "Your honor, I request a short recess in your chambers."

Nicholas walked up beside her. "Whatever for, Ruth? Feeling a little overwhelmed?"

Ruth glared at him. "I don't like surprise witnesses with a secret flash drive in their vault."

Ruth took great joy in watching Bryan pale. He lifted his eyebrows. "What have you done?"

She leaned in to him. "I found out about your surprise witness. You introduce those financial records, and I'll petition for a mistrial. My client will go free!"

"You can't do that!" Nicholas hissed.

"In my chambers. Now." Nettles interrupted them.

They followed him back behind his bench and into his office. It was huge and warm and filled with pictures of his family. Ruth noted a prominent picture of Nettles as a young boy with his father.

"Ms. Martinez, care to illuminate me on what this is all about?"

"Mr. Nicholas was going to introduce my client's wife as a surprise witness with damaging evidence of possible financial wrongdoing at the Institute."

"He embezzled money!" Nicholas shouted.

"Somebody put money in offshore accounts." Ruth glared at him. "We don't know it was Miller. It could have been Dr. Darwyn. You have no proof of who opened those accounts. And, I will call your hand on it, Bryan."

"Just a minute." Nettles interrupted them. "Mr. Nicholas, you have proof of offshore accounts?"

"Yes."

"That doesn't mean anything. Anyone can have an offshore account." Nettles said.

"But, this account was opened by a staff member of the Institute." Ruth pointed out.

"Means nothing unless you can show the funds are missing from the books." Nettles said.

"Books Miller had total control over." Nicholas said. "It's obvious"

"It's pure conjecture." Ruth said. "You just want to make Miller look bad because he was dumped by his wife. You want to make him look like a thief and an adulterer."

"Adulterer? What a quaint little term, Ruth."

"Enough!" Nettles slammed his fist on his desktop. "Mr. Nicholas, I will not allow this evidence to be presented in court without my first hearing it in chambers. If I decide it carries merit, then we will present it to the jury. Agreed?"

Nicholas bit back his comment and nodded. Ruth smiled. "See, that wasn't so bad."

NETTLES SETTLED back into his chair as Nicholas cast one glare at Ruth. He stopped behind his table and glanced up at Nettles. Ruth sat in her chair and waited. Nicholas shuffled some papers and seemed deep in thought.

"Mr. Nicholas, will the prosecution continue?" Nettles asked.

Nicholas stacked his papers and smiled at Ruth. "The prosecution rests, your honor."

Ruth felt like she had been doused in icy water. She swallowed and looked quickly away. She felt Nicholas' eyes on the side of her face. She thought she would have two more days!

"Ms. Martinez, the defense may now proceed." Nettles said.

She looked up at his face and stood up. "Well, your honor, I thought--"

"You thought many things, Ms. Martinez. I'd say after what just happened in chambers that you should begin. Right now." Nettles nodded toward her.

"Yes." Ruth thought furiously. Could she pull it off? "I call Kate Miller to the stand."

Nicholas bounded to his feet. "Objection, your honor. This is outrageous!"

"I agree." Nettles looked like he had swallowed a live toad.

"Your honor, the defense wishes to put my client's wife on the stand as a character witness." She felt a tug on her sleeve and looked down at Frank. His eyes were wide in shock and he was shaking his head.

"Your honor, we just had a conversation about this in your chambers." Nicholas was apoplectic.

"A conversation about the prosecution using Mrs. Miller as a witness. We did not discuss the defense using her as a witness." Ruth glared at Nicholas. His face was red as a beet and his jaw was clinched in anger.

"I agreed." Nettles said through clenched teeth.

"Yes, you did. But, your honor said nothing about me being able to call her as a witness."

"She's not on your list." Nicholas picked up his witness list.

"But, she wasn't on yours either, Mr. Nicholas. And, you rested your case." She looked back at Nettles.

His rigid face spoke volumes. "Approach the bench."

Ruth stepped around the table and walked across the floor and she felt Bryan fuming at her side. "I'll get you for this." He whispered.

"Can't take your own medicine, can you?"

Nettles leaned forward. "I told you two not to bring this cat fight into my courtroom."

"Your honor, Mr. Nicholas gets to cross examine my witness. If he wants to bring up the offshore accounts, I don't mind." Ruth said quietly.

"After you discredit anything she would say about them." Nicholas hissed.

"Then I won't bring it up if you won't bring it up, Bryan." Ruth glanced at him.

"That's enough. I will allow the witness to take the stand." Nettles tapped the desktop and his eyes grew large within the frames of his glasses. "But if either of you so much as hint at offshore bank accounts, I'm pulling the witness."

Ruth nodded and returned to her table. Nicholas stood at the desk for a few moments until Nettles shooed him away. He stalked back to his table.

Kate Miller came forward, took the oath, and settled into the witness box. Frank grew restless beside Ruth and leaned over to her. "Why are you doing this? Are you out of your mind?"

"Trust me, Frank." Ruth said and she stood up.

"Mrs. Miller, how long have you and my client been married?"

Kate sniffed and cast a long, baleful look at Frank. "Ten years."

"Is he an easy man to live with?"

Kate laughed. "What man is? He's a dedicated, self-absorbed scientist who cares more about his work than just about everything." Kate said and she looked down at her hands. "But, I knew that when I married him. There are times he is distant. But, he makes up for it."

"I understand that you recently underwent a separation?"

Kate looked up and a tear trickled down her cheek. "We did. But, it was a misunderstanding." She looked over at Frank. Ruth glanced back at the man and his mouth fell open.

"A misunderstanding?"

"Yes. I found out some damaging information about Frank that led me to believe that he might be seeing another woman. But, when

I investigated the information," she looked over at Nicholas. "I found out it was information about someone else that Frank works with. I just drew the wrong conclusion."

"So, someone else at the Institute had been involved in some kind of activity that you interpreted as your husband's infidelity?"

"Yes. That sums it up. But, he wasn't the person behind the activity. I don't know who the other person really was, but it wasn't Frank." Kate smiled. "Frank is a kind, sensitive person. He teaches the children in Sunday School, you know. He loves to finger paint with them and shows them how to build trees and plants with playdough. I don't know how I could ever have doubted him." She looked over at Frank and Ruth saw tears run down the man's cheek.

"Mrs. Miller, that is a very moving and touching story and I'm sure that the prosecution will try and rip it to shreds in a few minutes so I'd like to move on to other issues. I understand that recently you were asked to do some work for one of the staff members of the Institute?"

"That's right." Kate avoided looking at Frank. "Dr. Grant asked me to help with image rendering of some of his computer models."

"That's odd." Ruth walked toward the jury. "Isn't Dr. Grant the staff member who works with muscles and soft tissues?"

"Yes. He put together these three-dimensional models by building tissue onto the skeletal models."

"Are you an expert in computers, Mrs. Miller?"

"I taught computer animation at U. T. Austin for five years until we moved to Dallas." Kate sat up and wiped her face. "I met Frank in one of our post graduate computer programming classes. Dr. Grant knew this and needed some help."

"Why did he need help?"

"He had run out of funds. He wanted to hire an assistant at the Institute to perform the computer work late at night when the servers weren't busy but Dr. Darwyn had transferred his grant money into Dr. Morrant's account and left him without sufficient funds."

Ruth heard papers rattling behind her and glanced over her

shoulder at Bryan. He was searching through his notes. "How did you know this?"

"My husband was the chief financial officer. He told me about it. Dr. Grant confirmed it when he brought me the data files."

"Did you ever tell your husband you were helping Dr. Grant?"

Kate shook her head. "Dr. Grant is a very humble man. He didn't want Frank to find out about his funding shortcomings. He knew that it would only create more trouble so he asked me to do it on the side without telling Frank. In retrospect, that was a mistake."

"Is your husband violent?"

Kate blinked. "He has a bad temper. But, his bark is worse than his bite. He'd never hurt anybody."

"Thank you, Mrs. Miller. I have no further questions."

Nicholas glared at Ruth and stood up. He straightened his tie. "Hello, Kate. You remember me, don't you?"

"Yes. I was supposed to be your witness."

Nicholas froze and shook his head. "We can't talk about that, can we?"

"Objection." Ruth rose.

"Sustained. Mr. Nicholas, if you have questions, get on with it." Nettles said.

"Of course. I may have a couple of questions left to me." He walked up to the witness stand. "Mrs. Miller, I understand you were the one to initiate separation from you husband, correct?"

"Yes."

Nicholas interrupted her. "And why did you do so?"

"I thought he was, uh, putting away money for trips with another woman."

"And why did you think that?"

"I said so earlier. I had information that made him look guilty."

"Did you ask him about this information?" Nicholas asked.

"No. I was afraid he'd lie about it."

"Does he lie often?"

"No." Kate looked confused.

"Then why did you think he would lie to you?"

"Well, he was up to something. I thought he was doing something that made him act guilty." Kate glanced at Miller and Ruth reached under the table and patted his hand.

"Does it matter then that he really did anything?" Nicholas asked

Kate's forehead wrinkled in confusion. "Of course it does."

"Isn't the thought in a man's mind as bad as the action? Isn't that what Jesus said? If a man thinks of lust in his heart, it is just as bad as acting on it." Nicholas leaned toward her. "He is guilty no matter what. Isn't that what you thought?"

"Yes, at the time. But, I changed my mind."

"Love is blind, Mrs. Miller. No further questions." Nicholas walked away before she could register her objection. Ruth felt a hand on her arm and looked into the eyes of Frank Miller.

"Thank you, Ruth. No matter what happens, I thank you for what just happened." He looked once at Kate and their eyes locked on each other as she left the stand.

RUTH CALLED Dr. Grant to the stand. He settled into the chair and smiled at her warmly. "Dr. Grant, you work at the Institute with Drs. Miller, Morrant, and Styles, correct?"

"Yes. And, with the late Dr. Darwyn."

"Did you ask Mrs. Kate Miller to help with your work?"

"I did. I knew about her background in computer animation. I didn't want to worry Frank over Wallace's financial decisions. So, I got her to help finish the renderings for Annieraptor."

"I understand that Frank Miller was the financial officer of the Institute."

Grant shrugged. "Well, that was on paper only. We all understood that Dr. Darwyn was the ultimate authority. The position of CFO was supposed to be a check and balance kind of thing. But, the truth of the matter is, whatever Wallace wanted to do with the money, he did. The only way to override him was to go to the board of directors and they are his old friends."

"So, Frank really never had any control over funds and where they might be kept?" Ruth asked.

"No. Any fund transfers, deposits, and checks had to be co-signed by Wallace or they would never happen." Grant pushed his glasses back up on his nose. "We knew how to play the game. But, we also knew that the best way to get and keep you grant money was to stay on Wallace's good side."

"So, in your opinion, if you had a disagreement with Dr. Darwyn, particularly out in the open in front of dozens of people, then your chances of getting your money were vastly diminished?"

"I'd say so. You wanted to be Wallace's friend." Grant said.

"What can you tell me about your working relationship with Dr. Miller." Ruth smiled.

"I had a good relationship with Frank. We often went to lunch together. Neither one of us got along well with the other staff members. They seemed too pretentious. Frank is a genuine soul. We had rather lively discussions on science and faith and creation versus chance. You see, I am a practicing Jew and Frank and I loved to discuss and debate some of these issues."

"Did these discussions ever get violent?"

"Of course not. Frank is a man who respects anyone's point of view. I'd say he is very tolerant."

"Were you at the party on the night Dr. Darwyn died?"

"Yes."

"Were you witness to the disagreement between Dr. Miller and Dr. Darwyn?"

Grant frowned. "I was. And, Frank said what a lot of us wanted to say. Wallace is a brilliant man but he stepped outside the bounds of true science in putting feathers on Annieraptor. He could have suggested it in an illustration in a paper. But, instead, he declared it to be the fact when he had no evidence." Grant leaned forward. "It happens a lot in science. In fact, it happens more than we want to admit. If every scientist who fudged the data to support his philosophical or personal agenda were to kill the scientist who disagrees with him, we would have very few scientists left."

"Fudge the data? I thought such a thing would be unthinkable for a scientist." Ruth stated.

"Why, one of the greatest minds of the twentieth century fudged his data. Albert Einstein discovered that the universe was simultaneously expanding and decelerating back in 1905. At that time physicists thought the universe was infinite in size and eternal in age. In fact, it had to be to support evolution. Without infinite time, even Darwin admitted his theory wouldn't work. So, when Einstein discovered the expansion coefficient it meant he had discovered that the universe was expanding which meant it had a beginning. And, if the universe had a beginning then it was the result of a cause. That meant it had to have a cause outside the universe itself. And, the only thing that fits such an entity is a transcendent creator. So, Einstein realized he was looking at unequivocal evidence that the universe was created by God. What was he to do? Destroy all of modern science? Undercut the foundation of evolution? So, he introduced the cosmological constant. It perfectly offset the coefficient of expansion and brought the universe back to a nicely comfortable eternal and infinite condition that needed no beginner."

Dr. Grant sat forward as if he were conveying a secret. "But, the problem was the constant devised by Einstein was purely fictional. It had absolutely no basis in fact! He couldn't face the philosophical implications of his discovery so he created a fudge factor. In fact, later in his life he said that the cosmological constant was his biggest blunder. So, you can imagine that if Einstein fudged the data for personal reasons, can we here in the twenty first century be any better? My point is that it happens. Science is no longer as pure as the driven snow because it is increasingly uncovering the fingerprints of God all over the cosmos. And, scientists are now bickering not over this evidence, but over keeping the sciences pure from metaphysical and supernatural contamination. Such disagreements as Dr. Darwyn and Dr. Miller had were commonplace and certainly not worthy of consideration as motive for murder."

"Thank you, Dr. Grant for that illuminating lecture." Ruth smiled. "Your witness."

Nicholas cast a wary look at Nettles and crossed his arms as he studied Dr. Grant. He was silent, glaring at the man until Dr. Grant sunk back in his chair, an uncertain look on his face. Nicholas stood up and paced.

"You said you needed help with some data programming? How did you give the data to Kate Miller?"

"On a flash drive." Dr. Grant said.

"Is the data all that was on the flash drive" He turned and looked at Dr. Grant. The man seemed instantly uncomfortable.

"Well, no. But, that was not intentional."

"What else was on it?"

"Objection, your honor." Ruth stood up. "And, you know why."

Nicholas didn't wait and hurried to the bench with Ruth close behind him. "You said I couldn't allow Kate Miller to bring up the offshore accounts." Bryan said before Nettles opened his mouth. "This is a different witness."

Ruth shook her head. "Your honor, you said not to bring even a hint of this evidence out in the trial."

"No, he said not to allow Kate to bring out the evidence." Bryan shoved his red face into hers.

"You tried to bring her on as a surprise witness."

"And you called her to the stand."

"Enough!" Nettles pounded the gavel. Murmuring had come up in the crowd and Ruth pulled back away from Bryan's flushed face. Suddenly, his perfect hair and perfect features seemed sullen and childish.

"Ms. Martinez and Mr. Nicholas, I have seen the trail that is being painted here about money. Follow the money, they always say. I believe there has been enough of that waved and bandied about in the air already. I do not want to go in this direction, Mr. Nicholas. Move on without it."

"I can file a--"

Nettles stood up. "You will file nothing, Mr. Nicholas. I made it clear that this is my courtroom. We will proceed with this trial and if I hear another word from you, I will hold you in contempt." He gritted his teeth and leaned in on Nicholas. "Now, proceed!"

Ruth slipped back to her chair while Nicholas rubbed his face and studied the jury. He turned back to Dr. Grant. "Dr. Grant, were you aware of any illegal activity being perpetrated by anyone on the staff of the Institute?"

Ruth started to stand up but Nettles put out a restraining hand. She swallowed her objection. Dr. Grant looked over at Ruth and then down at his hands.

"Sir, I cannot prove anything. But, I found evidence that money was not being moved around like it should. I do not know if this activity was at the hands of Dr. Darwyn or some other staff. It was not me. And, I do not know the nature of such wrongdoings."

"So, there was something potentially illegal going on that someone would like to have kept secret?" Nicholas looked over his shoulder at Ruth as if daring her to object. She bit her tongue.

"That would be my conclusion." Dr. Grant sighed.

"Would someone want to keep a secret bad enough to commit murder?" Nicholas asked.

Before Ruth had risen to her feet, Nettles had pounded his gavel. "Mr. Nicholas, you know that is inappropriate. The jury will disregard that last remark."

Nicholas nodded. "You're right, your honor. I was out of line. No further questions."

22

"We've run out of time, Jonathan. I don't have that many witnesses to parade in front of the jury. I need to know more about that woman and we need to see if there is evidence from the security cameras." Ruth took a bite out of her sandwich. But, it tasted vile and her stomach churned with anxiety.

Steel paced around the conference room. "My expert has found some video footage on the hard drives. But, there is a problem. It'll take hours to sift through it and find anything useful. We're looking at tomorrow at the earliest." Steel said.

Grace grimaced. "Then, I suggest we pull a rabbit out of the hat. I was anticipating this." She glanced at her watch. "In fact, our rabbit should be here any minute."

Ruth glanced at Steel. "What are you talking about?"

Grace leaned back in her chair. "I know you didn't want to get into the creation/evolution conflict but just in case it surfaced, I obtained you an expert witness."

Ruth opened her mouth and her heart raced. "Grace, you know I didn't want to go there."

"You may have no choice." Grace said tersely. "Ruth, there are times we all need help. I told you I would be working from behind the scenes. You need to trust me on this. The issue will come up. Bryan has stacked the jury with religious conservatives. He wants them to turn against Frank Miller whose ideas on creation are more progressive."

Ruth looked up at Ms. Grace. "I didn't see that one coming."

"I know. That is why I had to act quickly when Bryan rested his case so quickly. We may not need his testimony, but in case we do, Dr. Cephas Lawrence should be walking in that door any minute."

Steel grew rigid and glanced at the door. "You brought in Cephas?"

Grace nodded. "Yes, Mr. Steel. I understand you haven't seen him since your trip to New York City."

Ruth watched Steel in amazement. The man actually seemed shaken. He moved slowly across the room and sat at the table. "It's just that the weather is not the best. You shouldn't have brought him on this." Steel whispered.

"Ruth. Mr. Steel. Let us not forget that your comfort and your needs are not important at the moment. Frank Miller is quickly going down for this murder and we have to pull something fast to save him." Grace said.

Ruth drew a deep breath and felt moisture in her eyes. "I thought you trusted me. I thought you had faith in me."

"I do, Ruth." Grace reached out and patted her hand. "But, sometimes you have to know when to ask for help. You're doing well. You've actually gotten quite spunky with Bryan. I'm proud of you."

"What about the witness list?" Ruth asked.

"I put Cephas' name on there right before it went to the judge. You just didn't bother to check it." Grace leaned back.

Ruth watched Steel pace and a worried look came over his face. "Steel? Jonathan? Who is this Cephas Lawrence? What does he mean to you?"

Steel paused and studied her with his intense gaze. "He is somewhat of a mentor."

"A mentor? Can you be more specific?"

Steel leaned against the table. "Why don't I tell you about the time we first met?"

JONATHAN STEEL

THE CAB SCREECHED to a halt in front of the old building and I slid out of the back seat. The driver snatched the money from my hand, threw the car into gear and roared off down the street. I drew in a deep breath of the smoky air filled with a smattering of fat late October snowflakes. Definitely pot and probably crack cocaine. Across the street, dirty, graffiti covered a housing project with gray walls and boarded up windows. There were people present, huddled on stoops, stairways, and fire escapes, all listless and insulated in their own world of pain and despair. No wonder the cabby wanted to get out of here.

The building behind me stretched upward for twenty stories and its old stone and brick façade displayed a 1930's deco motif. The bottom floor walls were marred with graffiti and obscenities. A stairway led up into an open foyer and the doors were ripped from their frames.

"Yo, dude, where you think you're going?"

Three men stood in the street and their heads were covered in do rags and backward baseball caps. They appeared to be a mixture of different racial origins. The largest strutted forward and raised his left hand holding a pistol held sideways.

"Now, you just give us whatever's in your pocket, dude and we might let you live." He laughed. The man's pupils were constricted from a narcotic glaze. The other two guys stood to the bigger one's side.

"I don't want to."

"Too bad, dude." The tall one cocked the pistol.

I snatched the pistol out of the big guy's hand just as he pulled the trigger. The bullet ripped through the end of my jacket sleeve and buried itself in the brick wall behind me. I caught the big guy in the temple with a left hook and then brought the pistol around. The handle smacked across the shorter companion's face. I dropped the pistol behind me and snared the tall skinny one by the throat even as the other two dropped to the pavement.

"You want more of what is in my pocket?" The tall, skinny guy squirmed in my grip. He mouthed the word, "No."

I shoved him across the pavement and stooped to retrieve the pistol, slid the clip from the gun and pocketed the bullets. "Get out of here and don't come back." The skinny one bolted to his feet and disappeared down the street.

The two unconscious men were still breathing. Nearby, a stripped car sat on cinder blocks. Its trunk was open and empty. I picked up the men and threw them into the trunk of the car, slammed the trunk and pulled a piece of wire from the open engine compartment. I wired the trunk shut.

The gun rested comfortably in my hand. I felt the familiarity, the comfort of its weight. I hadn't touched a gun since the day at the gun club.

"Well, are you going to use the gun, or what?" A short, bushy haired man stood in the open stairway of the building. Small glasses sat on the end of his nose and he wore a flannel shirt, khaki pants and a housecoat. "You could have shot them all and no one would have cared."

I tossed the gun into an open sewer drain. "I don't shoot people." Anymore, was my unspoken ending to that thought.

"Well, you certainly are equipped to shoot them. Your moves were very impressive. Very quick." The man rubbed a huge mustache that draped over his mouth and nodded.

"Are you Cephas Lawrence?"

The graying man sighed and pulled his housecoat around him as snowflakes settled on his stooped shoulders. "If I'm not are you going to lock me in a car trunk?"

"They tried to kill me."

"Of course they did. It is what they do here."

"I was only defending myself."

"I do not fault your actions." The man stepped down the stairs. "Just your motives. I assume you are Jonathan Steel."

"Yes."

"And why should I allow you into my home?" Lawrence raised a bushy eyebrow.

"I have an appointment with you."

"Yes, to talk about evil. And yet, you bring evil with you." He gestured toward the car trunk.

"What would you have done?"

Lawrence frowned. "I would have dropped dead of a heart attack. But, I have a truce with the people in this neighborhood. They leave me alone. Of course, now if I invite you into my home they will probably ignore the truce. I must at least give you a hard time, you understand. If I appear friendly to you in front of all of them, they will come after me."

I glanced around at the buildings surrounding them. The people were there huddled in snowy shadows, draped on stairs, silent but observant. "Why do you live in this neighborhood if it is so dangerous?"

"This building is my home. I own it. I leave the bottom floors to the homeless. Winter is coming and soon it will be very cold. They need a place to escape the elements. I give that to them. It is part of the compassion of our Lord that I show." He turned and started up the stairs. "Shall we?"

I followed the old man into the darkness of the foyer. The floor was caked with mud and debris. "Let's go on upstairs." The old man motioned to an elevator. He inserted a key into the external control panel and the doors slid open. I followed him inside and Lawrence inserted the key into the internal keypad and the door closed on the dark, shadowy world of despair. The elevator door opened into a small foyer and Lawrence motioned to his front door. He opened it with another key. Beyond, the entire floor was an open unfinished space interrupted in places by partial walls. Lawrence locked the door behind him and keyed in a security code on a keypad by the door.

"I keep myself locked away up here. I am no fool to think that those people you ran up against wouldn't break their truce. After all, the enemy is quite devious and we must never let down our guard. At the same time, we must extend to those children around us the love and compassion of our Savior."

Lawrence led him past a room with a sofa and chairs around a partition. A kitchen occupied the next space and Lawrence motioned to the antique table and chairs. "Why don't you sit down? I shall make us some tea. I hope you like tea?"

Two monitors on the kitchen counter showed a video feed of the exterior of the building. "That would be fine. You own the entire building and you live only on this floor?"

"Yes. I bought it in an auction years ago. The top floor was unfinished and used as storage so I am filling it up with my stuff." Lawrence filled a teakettle from a bottled water dispenser and placed it on the stove. "Come, while the water is heating and I will show you my world."

I followed him around the partition to a huge open space filled with tables and shelves. Books covered the tables, some open, some stacked and more books cluttered the shelves all around them. On the partitions hung suspended paintings surrounded by statues and tables covered with artifacts. "I have here one of the most exclusive antique book collections in the world. Behind that partition is a vault with temperature and humidity control to store the rarest of the books. Artifacts from around the world. Now, you would not recognize the names of many of these artists. I do not collect them for their fame. I collect art and books that open a window into the hearts and minds of the people of the past."

In the distance, the teakettle whistled and Lawrence motioned for me to follow him back to the kitchen.

"Why?" I asked as I sat at his table.

Lawrence poured the steaming water into two mugs and lowered tea bags into each. He came to the table and sat a mug before me.

"They are part of a time machine. A window into the past." Lawrence turned to his kitchen counter and retrieved a bowl of sugar cubes and a small container of cream. "The enemy cannot see the future. He has no power to predict the events that are to come. But, he reveals himself in the events of the past. The ways in which he has worked in people's lives before this time." He sat down and squinted at me. "You see, every twist and turn; every seemingly meaningless event is a part of a puzzle. When that puzzle is assembled it will reveal the enemy's plans."

The hot tea was pungent and spicy. "I read your book. You try to stop Satan's interventions into peoples' lives."

"Interventions?" Lawrence sniffed and rubbed his huge mustache before he slurped his tea. "You make it sound so clinical. Satan destroys lives, Steel."

"I know."

Lawrence studied him for a moment. "When you contacted me last week, I did my own research. You awoke on a beach with no memory months ago. You were hospitalized for a few months and then worked for a doctor and his daughter at their beach house until a madman took all of that away from you. Now, you come to me for advice concerning demons."

I pressed the hard, cold memories of that night away. "That's part of the story."

Lawrence leaned back in his chair and sipped at his tea. "What do you really want, Mr. Steel?"

"To understand how they work."

"Why?"

I saw her face. I heard her last words. "I made a promise."

"Tell me about it."

I had trusted no one since that day. As far as I was concerned, any person I meet on the street could be in league with my adversary. But, Cephas Lawrence was different. He felt different. No evil. No sense of deception. I decided to trust him. "OK."

The tea was cold when I finished and outside the windows the sun was setting behind the skyline of Manhattan and snow had settled along the ledge. Lawrence stood up and stretched his back as he put the mugs in his sink. He turned slowly and crossed his arms as he studied me through his precariously perched glasses. He massaged his huge mustache and then ran his hands through his unruly gray hair.

"Is that the cross?"

I pulled the chain up out of my shirt and let the cross dangle before me. "Yes. I wear it to remind me of my promise."

"To remind you of this demon that prompted this madman to kill?"

I grit my teeth and felt the old anger stoke and build. "Yes. I want to find it."

"What will you do when you find it?"

My anger boiled and my face grew warm. "I don't know. That's why I am here. What can you do to a being like a demon? How can you hurt it? How can you destroy it?"

"You might want to put that back where it belongs." Lawrence pointed to the cross. "Before you break the chain. You know, put it over your heart."

The tension broke and I released my held breath. With a trembling hand, I tucked the cross back into my shirt. "Sorry. I have a problem with my anger."

"Come with me." Lawrence headed into the library. He crossed to one of the tables and sifted through the open books. "Ah, here we are. You know your Bible?"

"I've been reading it some. While the doctor was in his vegetative state, I would read the Bible to him every day." I saw the frail, emaciated body of the man destroyed by our adversary; the man filled with physical and mental devastation at the hands of evil; the man who could live no longer after she had died.

Lawrence adjusted his glasses and lifted an old Bible into view. "Then you remember this account. 'Just as Jesus was climbing from the boat, a man possessed by an evil spirit ran out from a cemetery to meet him. This man lived among the tombs and could not be restrained, even with a chain. Whenever he was put into chains and shackles—as he often was—he snapped the chains from his wrists and smashed the shackles. No one was strong enough to control him. All day long and throughout the night, he would wander among the tombs and in the hills, screaming and hitting himself with stones. When Jesus was still some distance away, the man saw him. He ran to meet Jesus and fell down before him. He gave a terrible scream, shrieking, "Why are you bothering me, Jesus, Son of the Most High God? For God's sake, don't torture me!" For Jesus had already said to the spirit, "Come out of the man, you evil spirit."

Then Jesus asked, "What is your name?"

And the spirit replied, "Legion, because there are many of us here inside this man." Then the spirits begged him again and again not to send them to some distant place. There happened to be a large herd of pigs feeding on the hillside nearby. "Send us into those pigs," the evil spirits begged. Jesus gave them permission. So the evil spirits came out of the man and entered the pigs, and the entire herd of two thousand pigs plunged down the steep hillside into the lake, where they drowned.'"

Lawrence closed the Bible. "The demons begged Jesus not to send them to Tartarus."

"What is Tartarus?"

Lawrence rubbed his mustache. "I believe it is the deepest, darkest corner of hell where the worst demons are sent by God for punishment. Once there, they cannot leave hell. They cannot go about the Earth and work their wickedness."

"So I must send this demon to Tartarus?" I felt a tremor of hope.

"Yes. Since you can't kill it." Lawrence placed the Bible on the table. "But, it is not as simple as it sounds, Mr. Steel. I have participated in over twelve exorcisms in the past thirty years. Casting out the devil is not some cavalier action like dispatching the thugs you encountered this afternoon." Lawrence slumped into a chair and suddenly seemed old and feeble. "It takes something out of you. Each exorcism was long and tedious and a great work. And never have I been able to send a single demon to Tartarus." Lawrence looked up, his eyes haunted with the memories. "I have wanted to. I have wanted to hurt these heinous things that destroy human lives. To torture them. To destroy them. You see, I lost someone, too. And, over the decades I have tried to understand their minds. I have come to realize their agony and torture is worse than anything we can ever conceive."

"Jonathan," Lawrence whispered and leaned forward, his reading glasses held in his right hand like a pointer. "Imagine what it must have been like to be in the presence of God before he created this universe. To bask in his glory and light. To slide between the bonds of dimensions we cannot ever understand. Imagine what it was like to be at His beck and call. And then, imagine the delusion of Lucifer as you follow him into utter darkness. To have it all stripped away from you, to have God exile you from his presence into this imperfect universe. To never feel His love, His gratitude. To always be separated for all eternity from your Creator. When I think on this, I almost feel sorry for them. But, they made their choice. They rebelled against God and now their mere existence is the ultimate punishment. Until the day the Savior returns."

Lawrence stroked his mustache and nodded. "I have compiled years of research regarding one disturbing fact. Although Satan is the author of confusion, he nevertheless tries to maintain some semblance of order among his demons. Of course, the demons are so self-centered, so focused on destroying life it is hard for them to follow any reasonable orders. But, over the years, I have noticed something odd. There are patterns in history, arcs that play out over centuries that bear the mark of Satan. There is some attempt at some grand plan here that most theologians and Biblical historians have ignored. It is reasonable to think that the most intelligent of the angels, Lucifer, would try and construct some type of long term strategy. What this creature said to you suggests some type of plan. What was its name?"

"I don't know. It called itself the thirteenth demon."

Lawrence's eyes opened wide and he slumped into a chair. "What did you say?"

"The thirteenth demon."

Lawrence shook his head. "It can't be." He stood abruptly and hurried to another table. "God's fortune may have fallen on us, Jonathan. The enemy has revealed himself at last."

I followed him. "What are you talking about?"

Lawrence shuffled through books then tossed them aside. He hurried from the library into the artifact room. The old man threw aside drawings and paintings until he paused.

"Here! Come see, Jonathan."

I peered over the man's shoulder at an old hand drawn manuscript. It depicted an image similar to the spokes of a wheel. Roman numerals from one to twelve went around the circle, a number at the end of each "spoke". In the center of the image was a pentagram. "You see, here at the center is the symbol for Satan and at the end of each of these rays is a number from one to twelve. Do you see these symbols?"

Above each number was an obscure etching. Some appeared to be animals or insects. Others were indecipherable. "Each of these symbols represents one of the original disciples. For years, scholars have maintained this is a drawing of the disciples encircling Satan for his defeat. But, I have always maintained that the numbers represent not a disciple, but a demon."

"A demon?"

Lawrence's eyes grew wide with excitement. "Yes, a demon for each disciple. Doesn't it make sense? Satan brought forth his most powerful demons and assigned one to each disciple to counteract the work of the Lord. And, over the past two thousand years this Council of Darkness has worked to thwart the work of the apostles and the church."

"But what does this have to do with the thirteenth demon?"

Lawrence smiled and dropped the drawing. "Ah, there is a legend written by early Christians about a demon so vile, so evil, so contemptible that even Satan could not control it. This demon came to Satan and demanded to be on this council. But Satan feared this demon. He feared he could not control him. So, he gave him the rest of the unknown world outside the influence of the apostles. This, Jonathan, is the thirteenth demon."

"The most powerful of the demons?"

"Yes." Lawrence placed a hand on my chest. "And now, you see, Jonathan, that you must be very careful. This demon is outside the influence of his master. This demon has worked alone for centuries to destroy human lives and wreak havoc with civilizations. If you pursue this demon, it may lead to your death."

I looked down at the drawing and reached up to touch the cross beneath my shirt. "But, I made a promise. I can't ignore that."

"There is more here than your pursuit, Jonathan. They must have tried to stop you in the past. You just cannot remember it. They fear you. Why, this very amnesia may be their doing." He paused and wiped his lips with a trembling hand. He reached out and touched my arm. "Pursue him you must, Jonathan, but be careful. Keep your motives clear and uncluttered with person revenge. There lies the trap of the Prince of Darkness. Let your emotions rule, and the enemy will triumph."

Lawrence motioned me to follow him back into the kitchen. "What is your plan?"

I paced around the small kitchen, digesting what I had just learned. "I don't want to become an exorcist. I just want to find this demon and send it off to Tartarus. But, finding him is the challenge. Cephas, I've looked everywhere for hints of his presence. How do you track a demon?"

Lawrence put his reading glasses back on his nose. He picked up a laptop computer from the kitchen counter and opened in as he sat at the table. It came to life and he began to hit some keys. "Search the Internet. Look, here is a news item about a woman who claims a demon made her try and kill her boyfriend. Here is an account of a man who claims an evil presence lives in his attic and whispers in his ears each night. Ah, a computer geek who thinks the thirteenth demon has possessed his laptop."

"Cephas, this stuff is ridiculous."

"Of course it is. But, somewhere buried in all of these accounts is a person who is really oppressed by a demon. And, that is where you will find your adversary."

I ran a hand through my hair as my frustration built. "There must be hundreds of such stories in the news."

"21,342 according to this search engine." Lawrence leaned back in his chair. "Why don't you let these people come to you?"

"Come to me?"

"When you called and I did not know who you were, you said you helped people in trouble from evil. I guess you think that is a kind of calling card. But, why not make it your business? Why not make it your profession? Advertise on the Internet. If someone is indeed in trouble from evil because of a demon, they will find you. And, if you can find one demon, you can find your enemy."

"I had already thought of that. I got my private investigator's license. I listed myself as a P.I. Sort of. Only, I'm not very good at helping people. I'm not very personable."

"So I've noticed. But, I'll help you. I've spent my entire life fighting these horrid creatures and you're the first person I've met with enough dedication to equal my passion. You narrow down these people and their problems then you bring it to me. I'll do the research for you. I will mentor you in everything I've learned about the forces of evil in this world. We can become partners, of a sort, as you say. Together, we can find the thirteenth demon."

I slumped at the table. "Cephas, do you realize what you're getting yourself into? I'm not easy to get along with and I have a temper that I just can't seem to control."

"Then, I'll just treat you like I would any other demon." Lawrence smiled.

"That's how we started out together. Over the past couple of months, he has taught me so much. We've looked all over the Internet. That is how I found out about Grace's artifact and its possible link to my adversary." Steel said.

Ruth closed her eyes and sighed. "Grace, you actually expect me to put this Cephas Lawrence character on the stand? I mean, demons and devils and age old conspiracies?"

Grace patted her hand. "Bryan will play the religious fanatic card sometime soon. Especially if you put Frank on the stand. When he does, Cephas will be your secret weapon. Trust me, dear. I've known Cephas for a long time. I've heard his testimony in a dozen trials. He is cool and collected in the stand." Grace smiled. "Besides, who better to handle Bryan Nicholas than an exorcist?"

The door to the conference room opened and they all looked up in anticipation. If Albert Einstein had a twin brother, he would have been the man that walked into the conference room. He was short and slightly stooped with a wild mane of white hair. His mouth was hidden by a huge gray mustache and he wore a pair of black rimmed reading glasses as he studied the label on the door.

"I presume this is Conference Room D?" He looked away from the door and surveyed the room. He wore a seedy beige wool blazer over a red turtle neck shirt and black pants. He pulled a wheeled suitcase behind him. "Is that you, Jonathan?"

Steel stood up and walked across the room and embraced the man. He patted the old man's hair. "You're looking stronger, Cephas."

"I should. I took your advice and got those vitamins. They helped." He shuffled over to the table and smiled at Grace. "And, Gracie, how are you?"

Grace Pennington stood up and towered over the little man as she leaned down to embrace him. "I'm doing well, Cephas. Thank you for coming."

"Anything to help my Gracie." He turned his gaze toward Ruth. He took off his glasses and tucked them into his jacket. "And, this lovely young lady must be Ruth?" He held out his knobby hand and Ruth stood up as she shook it.

"Ruth Martinez."

"I'm Dr. Cephas Lawrence, my dear. I have heard great and wonderful things about you and I'm here to help you."

Grace motioned to a chair. "Please sit down, Cephas. We were just discussing you, and, uh, the case."

Lawrence slid into a chair and groaned in pain. "Ah, my back and this weather. I may need to use your massage therapist, Gracie." He cocked his head in Steel's direction. "I assume you told them about our first encounter? Hmm?"

"Yes." Steel sat down. "Yes, about your expertise in arcane knowledge."

"Arcane?" Lawrence chuckled. "Such big words." He turned to Ruth and raised an eyebrow. "He is a man of few words. It seems you have loosened his tongue. Now, continue on since you probably don't have much time left before court is back in session."

Grace tapped her fingernails on the tabletop. "One reason I asked you to come is because the prosecution will ask Frank about his beliefs."

"I'm not sure I am going to put Frank on the stand." Ruth said.

"I don't see how you're going to avoid it. Time is now short and you don't have that many witnesses." Grace sat forward. "Ruth, bait the trap for Bryan and then put Cephas on the stand."

Ruth felt everything slipping out of her control. She closed her eyes and sighed. "You're right. I can parade character witnesses until I'm blue in the face but the real issue is Frank. I'm going to put him on the stand."

"I'll be ready by tomorrow, Ruth." Cephas said. "We'll need to go over some basic information tonight so you'll know which questions to ask."

Ruth rubbed her face and massaged her eyes. "The truth is, Frank wants to tell his story. Ordinarily, I would never put him on the stand. But, we're caught with our pants down. Unless something comes up soon, we don't have anything other than sowing seeds of doubt about the motive and the evidence. Maybe you better say a little prayer for us."

"My dear, I've been doing that all day."

23

"I call Frank Miller to the stand." Ruth said. The crowd began to murmur and Nettles pounded his gavel. She glanced over at Nicholas, but the look of surprise she had hoped to see was not there. Instead, he merely smiled, pointed a finger at her and winked.

Miller was sworn in and settled into the chair. Ruth watched his eyes flicker past her to the audience where she knew Kate was sitting. He smiled weakly and then looked back at her.

"Dr. Miller, I do not often ask my clients to take the stand. But, you wanted to tell your side of the story. Let me start by asking you about your position at the Institute."

"I am the director of paleobotany which is the study of prehistoric plants. I am also designated the vice president of the Institute and the chief financial officer." Miller said calmly. So far, so good.

"And, what are your duties as Chief Financial Officer?" Ruth asked.

"In theory, I oversee the disbursement of funds. But, in reality all I do is sign the paychecks before payday."

"So, you have no authority to transfer funds?"

Miller shook his head. "Not on my own. All transfers must be co-signed by the president of the Institute which up until a few weeks ago was Dr. Darwyn."

"In his absence, could you transfer funds on your own discretion?"

"For a few days until the Board of Directors made the determination of who the next CFO would be." Miller said.

Ruth nodded and looked at the jury. "Who currently is the CFO?"

"Dr. Morrant."

"And, to your understanding, in the past few weeks has the Board designated a new CFO to share the financial duties with Dr. Morrant?" Ruth studied the jury.

"No." Miller said.

"Is that surprising to you?"

"Not really. Sylvia always gets her way. She is very persuasive."

Ruth watched the jury's reaction and waited for comments from Nicholas. He was silent so she pressed on. "Were you aware of any illegal activities at the Institute?"

"Not illegal but certainly immoral." Miller sat forward.

"Immoral in what way?" Ruth turned away from the jury.

"Denial of grant funds designated to the authors of certain papers. Transfers of those funds into a certain staff member's account." Miller grimaced and his grip on the arm chairs tightened.

"You're speaking of Dr. Morrant, correct?" Ruth wished she could see the woman's face.

"Yes. As I said, what Sylvia wants, Sylvia gets. She convinced Dr. Darwyn to take my grant money and Dr. Grant's grant money and give it to her to complete her modeling program." Miller was getting a little louder as he spoke and Ruth shook her head subtly. He calmed down. "Of course, Wallace was perfectly within his rights to do so. He had total and complete control of any funds coming into the Institute."

"But that didn't make you feel any better, did it?"

"No. I was very angry. But, my anger was with Sylvia, not Dr. Darwyn. Dr. Darwyn was always a bit naïve when it came to those who would try to manipulate him. I tried to talk to him about it many times and he just wouldn't see it." Miller eased back in his chair.

"Now, there has been a great deal of testimony about the fight you had with Dr. Darwyn. Why did you get so angry with him?"

Miller looked over at the jury as Ruth had instructed him and began to speak in their direction. "Science is a rigid field of endeavor. It has certain unshakable tenets one of which is adherence to the supremacy of the conclusion based on fact. Objectivity is the hallmark of a scientist. When we allow our own personal issues to intrude, we run the risk of perverting the data and coming up with conclusions that are not truthful. Wallace was obsessed with proving there is a definitive evolutionary link between the later dinosaurs who survived the Cretaceous asteroid collision and the appearance of birds. Annieraptor was discovered by Wallace ten years ago. It has been the backbone of his dream to build this Institute. But, Annieraptor let him down. There was no convincing evidence of this transitional state. The skeletal structure was similar to a bird, but then almost all of the later dinosaurs showed similarity. That does not imply a true transitional state. The Holy Grail would be the discovery of feathers. We know that feathers are seen in the fossil record. So, when Wallace unveiled his simulation of Annieraptor, an object that would be seen by millions, I was appalled to find it had feathers on it. He had taken the subjective step of adding what he could not prove existed. He faked the data. He violated every principal of objective science. He betrayed us all. I was angry and I called his hand on it in public."

"Did you threaten Dr. Darwyn?"

Miller shook his head. "No. Contrary to what you've heard today, I never touched him. We have had such disagreements before, usual over the designation of funds to one of his favorites. But, I never threatened him."

"Where did you go after you left the party?"

Miller looked down at his hands and swallowed. "I went up to my office to write a letter of protest to the journal of Nature. I knew that it would soon feature an article on Annieraptor. I also knew that illustrations sent to the journal by Wallace did not feature the feathers. I wanted to file a formal protest before the article would go to press. I stayed in my office after that. Since my wife and I separated, I had been living there. I fell asleep at my desk and around midnight, I thought I heard someone screaming. At first, I thought it was a nightmare. But, then I heard a crash and another scream. I ran down the corridor and took the elevator down to the display room. When the doors opened, I couldn't believe what I was seeing." Miller stopped as his voice filled with emotion. "Wallace was draped over that rock. Blood was everywhere. And that claw was sticking out of his chest. I rushed over and pulled the thing out of his chest and tried to get a pulse. I couldn't find one. There was so much blood. And then, Dr. Styles and the night security person showed up."

"This night security person, was it Mr. Johnston?"

"No. Mr. Johnston had gone home right after the party. There's a separate night security guard."

"And, Dr. Styles was there also?"

"Yes. And, then Drs. Morrant and Grant came down from their offices."

"The entire senior staff was present at midnight?"

"I guess the party ran late that night."

Ruth crossed to the evidence table and picked up the Feldercarb 360. "Have you ever seen this piece of equipment?"

"No. Never."

"Do you understand what it is?"

"From Dr. Styles' description, it controls Annieraptor. I had no idea it could move."

Ruth walked over and handed him the goggles. "These are virtual reality goggles according to Dr. Styles. Are they similar to the one you use to control your drones?"

"Well, sort of. Only, my goggles don't have these motion sensors on them. I use toggle switches on a handheld controller sort of like ones used for video games. This is far more sophisticated than my goggles." Miller handed the goggles back to Ruth.

"There is a laptop in a backpack, Dr. Miller. It has a program that Dr. Styles claims you developed to control your drones."

"Well, I would have to see the laptop and power it up to be sure. But, I can tell you that controlling a drone is vastly different from controlling a walking robotic figure. My drones have very limited movement due to their five propellers. There capabilities are not nearly as sophisticated as the movements of Annieraptor must be."

"Dr. Styles has made the claim that you should be fully capable of controlling Annieraptor because of your familiarity with the computer program and your experience with your drones." She paused and waited for Nicholas to object. He was quiet. "Could you learn how to control Annieraptor? And, if so, how long would it take you?"

Miller shrugged. "Look, think of it like this. Anyone in this room could load up a flight simulator on their laptop and play with it for a couple of hours. But, would that person really know how to take off in a fighter jet and engage the enemy? Would you sit in the second seat with such a pilot? There is no way I could have known how to control Annieraptor with the kind of precision and accuracy it took to chase down and maul Dr. Darwyn to death."

Ruth looked back at her table deep in thought. "Your honor, that is all the questions I have right now, but I reserved the right to ask more questions." She deposited the google on the evidence table and returned to her seat.

"Of course. Mr. Nicholas?" Nettles said.

Ruth settled behind her table and wished she had her cell phone. Who was the other security guard? She glanced over her shoulder. Steel was sitting two rows away and she met her gaze. He nodded as if reading her thoughts and slipped out to the aisle.

"Good afternoon, Dr. Miller." Nicholas said in a friendly tone of voice. "A simple question. How did the Feldercarb 360 end up in your desk drawer?"

"I have no idea."

"It was locked in one of the drawers of your desk."

"Well, that would have been impossible for me to do."

"Why is that?"

"I lost my keys two days before the party."

The crowd whispered and Nicholas snickered. "Really? That is your excuse?"

"What can I say. Ask the security people. I reported them lost and they couldn't find them."

"So, you expect us to believe that someone stole your keys, killed Dr. Darwyn, and then planted the Feldercarb 360 in your desk drawer to frame you?"

"Yes." Miller said.

Nicholas nodded and paced toward the jury as he spoke. "Are you a Christian, Dr. Miller?"

"Objection, your honor. Relevance?" Ruth stood up.

"State of mind." Nicholas said tersely.

Nettles glared at them both. "Do I need to leave or are you two going to let me do my job?"

Ruth grew silent and Nicholas looked away from her. "Sorry, your honor. I want to establish the defendant's state of mind that night and I believe it is directly related to his religious views."

Nettles nodded. "Very well, continue."

"Yes, I am a Christian." Miller answered.

"How do you reconcile your job as an expert on prehistoric plants with the creation story of the Bible? It would seem to me you would have to live a divided life, so to speak, between science and faith." Nicholas paused in front of the jury.

"I see no conflict between science and faith. The only perceived conflict comes from differing interpretations of the Scriptures." Miller answered.

Nicholas whirled and laughed. "You've got to be kidding me. You just said you got into a fight with Dr. Darwyn over evolution."

"We had a disagreement over science, not religion. The presence or absence of feathers on Annieraptor is not a faith issue. It is a matter of whether or not you are going to be true to the scientific facts."

"And, the facts are that the Earth was created in six days which is indeed in conflict with current scientific thought." Nicholas drew closer to Miller. "Do you believe in Biblical inerrancy?"

Miller looked at Ruth and she opened her mouth to object but could not think of any compelling reason. He sighed. "In 1979, the International Commission on Biblical Inerrancy concluded that interpreting the first chapter of Genesis as six 24 hour days or six long periods of time were both equally valid and neither interpretation produces a problem with Biblical inerrancy."

Nicholas raised an eyebrow. "Well, I wasn't expecting that answer." He turned to the jury as he asked the next question. "What do you think about the King James version of the Bible?"

Ruth stood up. "Objection. Really, Bryan?"

Nettles pounded his gavel. "Sit down, Ms. Martinez. I think in light of everything that has been said today, there really is no reason to not go on with this."

"Your honor, this trial is not about God. It is about Frank Miller."

"Now, Ms. Martinez! Sit!"

Ruth plopped into her chair, her face burning with fury. Nicholas just smiled in her direction. He waited patiently for Dr. Miller to answer.

"Why do you ask such a question?"

"Just wondering where you stood on Bibles, that's all." Nicholas kept his eyes on the jury.

"Just because there are different translations doesn't mean the individual Bibles aren't inerrant." Miller said quietly.

"But, surely the best-selling book of all time has to have some importance to you."

"Of course it does. But,"

"But, what, Dr. Miller?" Nicholas turned to glare at him.

"Well, it's not my preferred translation."

"Oh, why is that?"

Ruth paled and a cold wave of fear came over her. She glanced at the jury. Some of them were now turning red faced. Some were scribbling in their notebooks. This is why Nicholas had weighed the jury with religious fundamentalists. She thought back to his questions to the jury. Over and over again, he asked them their favorite version of the Bible. King James. King James! She stood up to object and Nettles stared her down. She sat and tried to catch Miller's attention but he was studying his hands, trying to find a way to answer the question.

"Why isn't the King James your preferred version, Dr. Miller?"

"Well, I think it's a bit stodgy and old fashioned. It's out of date."

A jury member actually gasped and placed a hand against her mouth. Ruth closed her eyes in resignation.

"No further questions, your honor." Nicholas said.

"Ms. Martinez?"

Ruth drew a deep breath. Any further questions would just dig a deeper hole. She would have to rely on Dr. Cephas Lawrence to save the day. "No, your honor."

"Then, we will recess until tomorrow morning." Nettles stood and the courtroom descended into chaos. At the center of it all, Ruth felt her world slipping away as Dr. Miller was escorted from the chamber in his chains. She looked over at Nicholas.

"Gotcha!" He mouthed.

24

―――――――

J onathan Steel

IT TOOK me almost four hours to get through downtown Dallas and past I-20 on I-35 south before the ice began to clear up. What normally would have taken an hour at most was now a freezing nightmare with a wreck every couple of miles. Texas might have a four-wheel drive SUV and big trucks for every person but all that meant was they could spin out of control on four-wheel drive as easily as on two-wheel drive. Mercifully, the interstate cleared as I headed south for Austin. The sleet and freezing rain transitioned to a thunderstorm. By the time I reached Austin, it was late afternoon. The air was warm and balmy ahead of the cold front that loomed behind me like dark purple bruise on the horizon. I pulled into the Domain and found a spot near Kristof's apartment. Young millennials ran around in tank tops and shorts while Dallas was iced in just three hours' drive north of us.

"Hey, Jonathan." I heard as I got out of the car. Already, I was sweating beneath my jacket. Kristof hurried toward me from across the street. He carried a Starbuck's coffee cup. "Are you out of your mind, dude?"

"What do you mean?"

Kristof wiped sweat from his brow. He wore a tee shirt and jeans and flip flops. "I heard there's a freaky ice storm coming this way. You drove down in that?"

He led me up to his apartment as I shrugged out of my jacket. "Yes. I don't have time for ice storms."

Kristof headed into his apartment and motioned to his couch. "Well, take a load off. You must be pretty tense after driving in that stuff."

I sat stiffly on the couch. "I'm always tense."

Kristof sipped his coffee and laughed at me. He froze and frowned. "You're not kidding, are you?"

"The video?" I glanced at my watch. "I need to get back tonight."

Kristof slid into the chair behind his computer desk. "Well, I hate to tell you this, bro, but I was watching the news over at the coffee shop and they've closed I-35. You're not going anywhere tonight."

I gritted my teeth. "I'll make it."

Kristof leaned sideways to look past his monitor at me. "Really? What are you? A man of steel? Got a cape?"

So much for finding the other security guard. "Ruth is counting on me. Assuming you found something on the hard drives, I need to get it to her by morning."

Kristof motioned over the monitor with his right hand. "Well, come here and I'll show you what I found."

I hurried around his desk and sat next to him in a folding chair. Kristof finished off his coffee. "I stayed up most of the night working on this. I found some footage. Not much. I don't know if it will help."

"What happened to the hard drives?" I asked.

Kristof glanced at me. "I don't know what you've gotten yourself into, but someone pretty smart got their hands on these hard drives. They used some serious shake and bake software to erase as many sectors as possible. These hard drives are not SSD like you thought, but an older hybrid drive."

"You're talking Greek, Kristof."

He turned in his chair and his gaze was intense. "Jonathan, someone put an older hard drive in an SSD case and passed it off as a solid state drive. Want to know why? Because they planned from the start to erase this drive and corrupt the data."

That got my attention. "This was planned?"

"Whoever designed this so-called security system either substituted the hard drives themselves or someone came along afterward and replaced them. Probably the latter. Whoever did that wanted to make sure they could get rid of this data. But, they didn't reckon on me getting ahold of them." He turned back to his keyboard and monitor. "The only way these drives could have been erased in such a way as to elude the computer genius of Kristof would have been to toss the thing into a high field MRI."

"What?"

"MRI? Magnetic field?" Kristof glanced at me. "Never mind. Bottom line is I was able to find some corrupted data and rebuild it. I'd bore you with the specifics but they would only get me excited and leave you frustrated." He tapped on his keyboard.

"Can you just show me what you got?" I said.

"Sure. I've put the footage in a chronological timeline but it's very choppy."

A window on the desktop of his monitor opened and a static background played for a moment. "There's no sound. If you could read lips, we'd be golden."

He tapped away at his keys and the image cleared. The vantage point was from an angle pointing down on the security kiosk. Mr. Johnston, the security guard, stood beside the metal detector and greeted people as they streamed in. The footage was jerky and over a dozen people appeared dressed in festive clothing. They went through the same routine, dropping off items from their pockets and then retrieving them as they passed through the detector.

"Does any of this help?"

I sighed. "Not really. I was hoping we might find some footage of the actual party."

"I hate to disappoint you but all we have is this one camera. And, there's not much more of it. Unless you can identify each person that came through, it might not do you any good to see this."

I leaned forward onto the desk and tried to loosen my tight muscles. "We already have a guest list from those who signed in and received an ID. No surprises so far."

The line of people cleared out and Johnston stood quietly by the kiosk. He glanced at his watch and was about to walk out of the field of view of the camera when he stopped. He turned back toward the door. He stepped between the security kiosk and the entrance and held up his hand to stop someone.

The woman came into view slowly in an obvious painful hobble. She was an older woman in a long, seedy coat buttoned up to her neck. She wore a rain bonnet over her hair and carried a large purse. I sat forward.

"Now, who is this?" Kristof asked. "I've looked at this a dozen times and I can tell you I don't think she was invited."

Johnston stopped the woman and held out his hand. He was asking for her invitation and she shook her head. She opened her purse and pulled out a large, brown envelope stuck into the pages of a Bible. The hair stood on the back of my neck. Was it the same Bible?

Johnston shook his head and pointed toward the door. For a second, the woman tried to get past him and he blocked her way. She tensed and wiped at her eyes. Was she crying? She seemed to be pleading with Johnston, her hands animated after putting the envelope and Bible back into her purse. He took her by the shoulders and turned her toward the entrance and gently pushed her away. She paused after taking a few steps and stopped to look right at the security camera before disappearing from sight. The image faded away to an electronic snowstorm.

I sat back, my heart racing. What had just happened?

"Well, that's it." Kristof put his hands on his head. Outside his windows lightning flashed and deep, rolling thunder shook the windows. "And, there comes your storm. Have any idea who that woman was?"

I did. I just met Janet Dough. But, what did it mean? How did it help our case? "She's dead."

Kristof froze and slowly looked at me. "What?"

"I'm pretty sure that was a woman who later died in a fire at a Dallas motel. But, I have no idea what she has to do with the Institute." Could the Bible I saw in the motel room be the same one in her purse?

Thunder shook the walls again. "Well, if you could get your hands on that envelope, it might help." Kristof stood up. "Look, my couch is pretty comfy. I don't think you're getting out of Austin tonight so you might as well settle in until morning."

I pulled out my cell phone and dialed Ruth's number. A series of tones sounded. "All circuits are busy." A mechanical voice said. Had the storm knocked out cell towers?

"Can I send an email?"

Kristof had disappeared into his bedroom and returned with a pillow and a blanket. "Sure, I'll send one for you." That was when the lights went out. I looked around at the dark room.

"No!" Kristof dropped the pillow and blanket. "This city is not prepared for any kind of natural disaster!" He ran to his computer desk and I stood up out of his way. An alarm began to beep. "I've got to shut down this computer before the UPS runs out."

"UPS?"

"Uninterrupted power source. A battery but it'll only last about thirty minutes."

"What about my video?"

He snatched a flash drive from his computer tower and handed it to me. "It's on there. Now, shut up and let me think." His fingers raced over the keyboard and I went to the window in his dining room and opened a sliding door. I stepped out onto a balcony. The wind whipped down the narrow streets of the Domain chasing dust and leaves ahead of it. To the north, the cold front lurched toward us, dark and brooding and filled with lightning. How was I going to get in touch with Ruth? How was I going to get back to Dallas?

Rain hit me in the face like pellets of glass. In seconds, I was drenched from the onslaught before I could back into the apartment and shut the door against the storm. Water dripped onto Kristof's floor. I looked at the flash drive. I wasn't going anywhere tonight.

"You got a dryer?" I asked then shook my head. No electricity. No dryer. No washer. I just hoped we didn't have to bundle up together to get through this cold night.

25

———————

The next morning, Ruth arrived bleary eyed and tired at the courtroom clutching the list of questions Dr. Lawrence suggested she asked. She'd tried to call Steel's phone and got a busy signal. On the late news she heard the news about the storm closing the roads in and out of Dallas. And, the front had moved across south Texas with alarming speed. Steel was trapped in Austin for now. She had spent the evening reviewing Dr. Lawrence's questions and never had the opportunity to prep him. She could only put faith in Grace.

Ruth stood up as Judge Nettles sat in his chair and proceeded around the table. "Your honor, it is my intention to call a witness to testify to Dr. Miller's character. I was hoping the defense would not object." She smiled.

"Counsels, approach the bench."

Bryan appeared beside her and grinned. "Your honor, I have no objection to defense calling a character witness."

Something was wrong. She felt it. What did Bryan know? He was way too confident. "Thank you." She said. "I'd like to call Dr. Cephas Lawrence to the stand."

Dr. Lawrence hobbled to the stand and settled into his seat after being sworn in. Ruth retrieved her list of questions. "Dr. Lawrence, would you tell the jury a little bit about yourself?"

"Well, I was hoping it would be warmer here than in New York City." He rubbed his huge mustache. "Didn't know you folks would be having an ice storm. Right now, it's a balmy 50 degrees on the street where I live."

"I'm sorry for the cold weather." Ruth smiled. He was warming up to the jury.

"Now, about me. I'm retired from NYU. I taught there for a number of years in history, philosophy, and biology. I have three Ph. D.'s to my name. Don't mean to brag. Just never got tired of learning."

"And, how do you know Dr. Frank Miller?"

Dr. Lawrence leaned to the side to see around her and waved at Miller. "He was my student. A pretty good student, at that. I introduced him to his future wife. I taught him for two years right before I retired."

"I called you as a witness to testify to the character of Dr. Miller. What kind of person was he?"

"A bit obsessive compulsive you might say. A stickler for details. I remember once he showed up in my office after night class and we argued for four hours about the level of serotonin in the average goldfish gill mitochondria. Turns out my data was wrong and he had read a report somewhere. I made him track it down and prove it to me."

"In the years that you knew Dr. Miller, did he ever display any tendency toward violent behavior?"

Lawrence chuckled. "He crushed a Styrofoam coffee cup once. Lost a debate in my class. But, no, I wouldn't call Dr. Miller a violent man. Passionate, yes. Determined, yes. But not violent."

"I have no further questions." Ruth nodded and returned to her seat.

Nicholas stood up slowly and straightened his suit. He picked up a book from his table and faced the jury. "Dr. Lawrence, I'm showing this book to the jury." He paraded across the jury railing holding up the book. When he finished, he turned to Lawrence and studied the cover of the book. "This book is by Dr. Cephas Lawrence. Did you write this book?"

Lawrence reached into his shirt pocket and pulled out his reading glasses. "If you'll let me take a look at the title, I can give you an educated answer."

Nicholas strode confidently across the space between them and handed the book to Lawrence. He took it in his hands and read the title out loud. "The Devil Made Me Do It."

"Would you read the subtitle, please." Nicholas asked.

"Encounters with Lucifer and his Minions. Yes, I wrote this book. Have you read it?" He handed it back to Nicholas. "It might help you understand your clients much better." He paused. "And, your colleagues."

Someone in the jury laughed and a few chuckles came from the audience. Nicholas nodded and opened the book. "There can be no doubt that this world and its four dimensions of space and time are but one of many realities." He turned to the jury. "I'm reading from the book, by the way." He looked back at the page and turned to Lawrence. "Our purely physical existence, as claimed by the current scientific paradigm, is purely material. The possibility of a spiritual dimension inhabited by beings who can move in and out of our dimensions is dismissed by many scientists. Yet, in my encounters with these creatures of light and dark, I have looked into the face of pure, distilled evil and watched the light of goodness triumph over the forces of Lucifer and his fallen angels." Nicholas closed the book. "Do you believe the Devil made Dr. Miller murder Dr. Darwyn?"

"Objection." Ruth said.

"Counsel, rephrase that question." Nettles said.

"Yes, please rephrase it." Dr. Lawrence said. "Your question is a nonsense question. It would be like me asking you, 'Does your mother know you're stupid?'. A ploy commonly utilized in personal debates that descend into ad hominin attacks."

Nicholas blinked in momentary confusion. "What kind of attacks?"

"Ad hominin. When you cannot argue with the facts, you attack the person making the claims. Thereby, you hope to discredit the person's argument and its associated facts by tying it to the personality behind the argument." Lawrence rubbed his mustache and pointed a crooked finger at Nicholas. "No matter how I answer your question, I admit that Dr. Miller is a murderer. Very clever of you but I think the jury can see through your mechanics."

Nicholas froze. Ruth smiled. Now she knew why Grace had brought this man to the stand. "Dr. Lawrence, it seems to me that your book would lay down a firm foundation for the argument that a religious man like Dr. Miller could be subject to these dangerous, demonic forces and could resort to violent actions." Nicholas said.

"Look, Mr. Nicholas." Lawrence rubbed his hands together. "There are many who claim Christianity is a dangerous religion. They often cite the Salem witch trials and the Crusades and the Inquisitions. But, let me ask you one question. If you were arrested for murder, would that by association discredit all of the current status of the legal profession and its underlying principles? Of course not. It is not the system that is necessarily flawed in all of these cases. It is the person abusing the system. We are broken, Mr. Nicholas. Not the law. Not Christianity."

Nicholas shook his head. "I'm not interested in philosophy, Dr. Lawrence. I'm interested in your kooky ideas about angels and demons and the devil."

"Kooky? Is that a legal term?" Lawrence chuckled. "You think I'm wrong when I say there are angels and demons?"

"Any sane man would question your assertion."

"But, I asked you a simple question, young man. Many of the members of this jury believe in God. You yourself paraded the King James version of the Bible in this courtroom just to drive home that point. Some of them believe in the devil. So, answer my question please. Do you think that is wrong?"

"Yes."

"Ah!" Lawrence smiled. "So, you say there is a definite standard of right and wrong and I have violated that standard."

Nicholas turned and glanced at Ruth. Did he want her to object?

She shrugged. "He's your witness." She said. Members of the audience and jury laughed. She waited for Nettles to rap his gavel, but the man was enthralled by Dr. Cephas Lawrence.

"Dr. Lawrence, as fascinating at this discussion could be, we need to stick to the, uh, issue at hand." Bryan actually stuttered!

"Mr. Nicholas, you are the person who asked me about my book. You are the person who brought this issue to the attention of this courtroom. If you did not want to talk about good and evil; of Satan and God; of right and wrong then why did you introduce these ideas? I am merely the witness here. I am at your disposal." Dr. Lawrence smiled and pulled off his reading glasses.

"I want to ask you about Dr. Frank Miller, the accused."

"You already have. But, you can continue to ask me anything you want."

"Just a moment ago you so eloquently pointed out the flaws were not in a system but in the person who abuses that system. You also pointed out, correctly I might add, atrocities which were perpetrated in the name of Christianity. No one in this courtroom would deny that religious fanaticism has been at the root of horrific atrocities over the last few decades. So, my question to you is simple. Knowing Dr. Miller and knowing he is a professing Christian, is it possible that his devotion to the idea of God creating the universe in six days so conflicted with Dr. Darwyn's views that it led to an act of violence?" Nicholas turned and waited for Ruth to object. "No objection?"

"None." Ruth said quietly. She hoped the old man knew what he was doing. She glanced at Miller and the man was hiding a grin. She leaned over to him.

"What is he up to?"

"Dangling the carrot in front of the donkey." Miller whispered.

"Ah, so you think Dr. Miller's anger may have originated with an external conflict between the views of creationists?" Lawrence asked.

"Just answer the question, please." Nicholas said through tight lips. He wiped a bead of sweat from his temple.

"But, surely the jury has the right to know the context of your question. Wouldn't you agree, your honor?" Lawrence looked at Nettles.

"Oh, absolutely." Nettles leaned back in his chair. "When we get through with the lesson on theology, let me know."

"What do you presume is Dr. Darwyn's worldview?" Lawrence asked.

"World view?" Nicholas repeated. He shook his head. "I just want an answer to my question."

"A worldview is the sum total of all of your life's experiences, knowledge, education, internal conscious, etc. that combine to give you a perspective; an attitude toward the nature of reality as you understand it. For instance, Dr. Darwyn has been widely published and has, in the past, engaged in lively debates with proponents of young earth creationism. Some of those debates are available on the web and if you were to watch them you would be able to make a list of professionals who disagreed with him far more vehemently than Dr. Miller did." Lawrence sat forward. "To understand my answer, we must define Dr. Darwyn's worldview as he, himself, articulated it. It is known as naturalism. It is the idea that the sum total of reality can only be understood through the discipline of science. There can be no supernatural agency at work whatsoever. The idea of a Creator is anathema to a naturalist. In fact, I would wager that Dr. Darwyn's outrage over Dr. Miller's belief in a Creator God of the universe is far more emotional and far more violent than Dr. Miller's reaction could ever be over the issue of dinosaur feathers. I've seen the debates. If there is a fanatic in this setting, it would be Dr. Darwyn."

"That didn't answer my question, Dr. Lawrence."

"But, for the jury to understand Dr. Miller, they must understand these two competing world views. Creationism comes in several forms. There is young earth creationism. There is old earth creationism. There is theistic evolution. And, there is the Intelligent Design movement. Within these disciplines there are stark differences in interpretation of the Bible and interpretation of the facts of nature. This is so deeply emotional for many followers of these forms of creationism, the reactions rival that of your example of radical fanaticism used in the cause of terrorism."

Nicholas stepped closer to the witness stand. "And, which form of creationism would you say Dr. Miller ascribes to?"

"You should have asked him yourself when he was in the witness stand. Instead you asked him about the King James version of the Holy Bible, a translation that was written in 1611. Mr. Nicholas, you missed a golden opportunity to understand the mindset and the worldview of Dr. Miller."

Bryan opened his mouth and then closed it. He was speechless. He glanced at Ruth and the utter confusion on his face delighted her. Bryan cleared his throat and straightened his tie.

"Let's get back to the question at hand. Why don't you tell the members of the jury the differences between these forms of creationism?"

Lawrence smiled. "The Intelligent Design movement claims there is evidence for design within the cells of our body as well as in the structure of the universe. But, they do not take a stand on who or what that intelligence may be. The Theistic Evolutionist movement believes the process of neo-Darwinism is God's method for insuring the survival of His creation. They view evolution as God's 'gifted creation' and have nothing to argue with the science of evolution. The old earth creationists believe the creation account in the first chapter of Genesis outlines six creation 'days' that are, in fact, the day of the Lord. They believe these days are of unknown length and represent phases of creation. In fact, the order in which creation occurs in the first chapter perfectly parallels the record of nature." Lawrence paused and massaged his mustache. "Now, here is the final straw. The young earth creationists believe in a literal interpretation of the first chapter of Genesis. They believe each day was a literal 24 hours. That would place the age of the Earth between 6500 and 10000 years. And, this age of the Earth, and the universe I might add, conflict with the scientific record."

"And, there is enmity between these camps?" Nicholas asked.

"Oh, yes! Disagreements are very vocal. Very emotional."

"It seems to me that even with Intelligent Design, there is a tacit acceptance of the truthfulness of the Bible, correct?"

"Yes, although some of the camps belief in the inerrancy of the Bible more than others."

"So, each of these forms of creationism would accept the existence of God? Specifically, the God of the Bible."

"Well, the ID movement doesn't take an official stand on that. But, the others do."

"What about great scientists like Einstein?"

"I'm glad you asked." He fished in his jacket for his wallet. "There are some who say I resemble Einstein, but I assure you it is in appearance only. No man is as brilliant as Albert Einstein, wouldn't you agree?"

"Yes." Nicholas said impatiently.

Lawrence pulled a stained, folded piece of paper from his wallet. "I keep this with me all the time. It is a copy of a letter written to Albert Einstein about God and prayer. If I may read it, I think it will answer your question."

Nicholas threw up his hands. "By all means."

"The Riverside Church

January 19, 1936

My dear Dr. Einstein,

We have brought up the question: Do scientists pray? in our Sunday school class. It began by asking whether we could believe in both science and religion. We are writing to scientists and other important men, to try and have our own question answered.

We will feel greatly honored if you will answer our question: Do scientists pray, and what do they pray for?

We are in the sixth grade, Miss Ellis's class.

Respectfully yours,

Phyllis"

"Now, five days later, Einstein wrote back.

January 24, 1936

Dear Phyllis,

I will attempt to reply to your question as simply as I can. Here is my answer:

Scientists believe that every occurrence, including the affairs of human beings, is due to the laws of nature. Therefore a scientist cannot be inclined to believe that the course of events can be influenced by prayer, that is, by a supernaturally manifested wish.

However, we must concede that our actual knowledge of these forces is imperfect, so that in the end the belief in the existence of a final, ultimate spirit rests on a kind of faith. Such belief remains widespread even with the current achievements in science.

But also, everyone who is seriously involved in the pursuit of science becomes convinced that some spirit is manifest in the laws of the universe, one that is vastly superior to that of man. In this way the pursuit of science leads to a religious feeling of a special sort, which is surely quite different from the religiosity of someone more naive.

With cordial greetings,

your A. Einstein"

Lawrence placed the folded paper carefully back into his wallet. "My good man, if Einstein left room in this universe for the God of the Bible, then all of science should also."

Nicholas nodded and went back to his table to retrieve Lawrence's book. "Let's put all of this aside for the moment. Back to my original question. Is it possible for a man of God, a follower of the teachings of Jesus Christ to commit acts of evil?"

"Of course. All have sinned and come short of the glory of God. Paul wrote that and he was responsible for the death of many Christians before he met the resurrected Christ on the road to Damascus." Lawrence smiled at the jury. Some members nodded.

Nicholas opened the book. "I'd like to read a passage from your book. This comes from your own writings. 'I was stymied and dismayed at the events that took place that day. Who would have imagined that my friend, a devoted priest in the Church, would be so swayed by the powers of evil that he would be complicit in the death of an innocent child? Such is the overwhelming power of evil in our lives; an influence that burrows down to our very core; our essence. We are, at the base of it; at the heart of it; evil and vile creatures capable of the most heinous of crimes.'"

Nicholas closed the book with a snap and tossed it onto his table. Lawrence's face paled. "Why did you have to bring that up?"

"Answer the question, Dr. Lawrence. If you are a Christian, then do you maintain that we are all evil and sinful creatures and therefore capable of any type of crime?"

Lawrence blinked and looked away. He wiped at his mouth and stuttered as he talked. "He was my best friend. He was." Lawrence seemed confused, his eyes unfocused. "Why did you have to bring up the past?"

"We are waiting for your answer." Nicholas said firmly.

"Could you repeat the question?"

Ruth's heart raced. What had just happened?

"Yes, let me rephrase the question, Dr. Lawrence." Nicholas moved closer and leaned over the front edge of the witness stand. "Is it possible that Dr. Frank Miller, regardless of his world view, regardless of his devotion to Jesus Christ, could have been so consumed and influenced by evil that he was capable of cold blooded murder?"

Lawrence looked at Ruth helplessly. His gaze shifted to the audience and she realized he was looking for Steel. He wasn't there. He swallowed and replied. "Well, any of us could be."

Nicholas strode across the room to Judge Nettles' desk and snared the Bible. He brought it back to the witness stand and shoved it at Lawrence. "Go ahead. Find the passages in the Bible about David. A man after God's own heart, right? And yet, he had Bathsheba's husband murdered so he could marry her. And, what about Moses? Great man of God who delivered the children of Israel out of bondage. But, he murdered an Egyptian and was banished from his adopted father's court." Nicholas tried to shove the Bible into Lawrence's empty hands. "Go ahead and find the passage where Saul, a devout and upright Jew, held the cloak of Steven while he was stoned for his Christian belief. Saul who later became Paul and wrote that famous verse you just quoted, 'For all have sinned and come short of the Glory of God'. So, let me ask you again, Dr. Lawrence. Does 'all' include Dr. Frank Miller?"

Lawrence looked helplessly at Ruth and for a moment, there was pure confusion in his gaze. "Well, uh, you have to understand the context of those passages."

"No context, Dr. Lawrence. In view of your own Bible, your own 'world view' as you put it, is Dr. Miller no better or worse than David? Moses? Paul? Could someone like Dr. Miller have been influenced by his sinful nature to the extent he would be capable of murder? Yes, or no." Nicholas shouted.

"Yes." Lawrence whispered.

"Would you repeat your answer more loudly so that the jury may hear you?"

Nicholas turned and pointed the Bible at the jury like a loaded gun.

"Yes." Lawrence said. "But,"

"That is all of my questions."

"But!"

"Not another word, Dr. Lawrence." Nettles rapped his gavel. "Please exit the witness stand. Let's have a thirty-minute break, please."

Yes, let's do that, thought Ruth as Nicholas breezed past her table and dropped the Bible with a loud thump in the middle of her papers. He glared at her. "Don't get in the ring with the big boys unless you're ready, Ruth!"

26

Ruth stumbled through the afternoon calling a half dozen character witnesses before Judge Nettles mercifully adjourned for the day. Ruth glanced once at Grace in the audience as she hurried out of the courtroom.

"Thanks for the expert witness." She said as she hurried past Grace. She almost ran down the hallways and out of the building. She tossed her briefcase into her car and sat in the parking garage waiting for the inside to warm up.

Snow was falling and the air was bitterly cold. She shivered and felt tears trickle down her cheeks. What now? Where could she turn? Grace had let her down. Lawrence had let her down. Steel was nowhere to be found. And, Dr. Miller was headed for the injection table. She pulled out of the garage and headed into bumper to bumper traffic. By the time she pulled into her home, it was dark and the world was blanketed with a covering of white.

She slipped a couple of times on her walkway before making it into her house. She luxuriated in the long, hot shower before donning a pair of soft, flannel pajamas. She heated up a microwave dinner and built a fire in her fireplace for the first time in months.

She turned on her laptop and stared at the desktop trying to come with something, anything that would help.

A tone sounded and she had an incoming video message. She accepted and the face of Dr. Cephas Lawrence appeared.

"My dear, I wanted to apologize for my weakness today." He said.

"I was a fool!" She said quietly. "I didn't see it coming. Bryan weighted the jury with religious fundamentalists who worship the King James Bible. You tried but he managed to destroy your testimony with one question."

"It was not the question so much as the passage from my book."

"What happened?"

Lawrence sighed. "A very nasty event from my past. It was at a time when I did not believe in God. But, I met a mother and her daughter who believed they were being targeted by the eleventh demon."

"What?"

"Do not think any more on this. It is very complicated. Let's just say the events did not work out well. The only good thing that came out of it was I saw the reality of good and evil. I met God and it changed me forever." Lawrence ran his hand through his unruly hair.

"Is that the demon Steel is looking for?"

"Oh, no. He came to me for different reasons. I have experience with these matters. He does not. God is preparing him for a great spiritual battle."

"I am so confused with all of this talk of demons and angels and spiritual warfare." Ruth said. "What does any of this have to do with Jonathan Steel?"

Cephas wiped his mustache. "He does not even know it, yet, but Jonathan Steel has a long and arduous path ahead of him. God has chosen him to fight against the evil forces of this world. In fact, his journey has just begun. This is but a part of the winnowing away of all that is nonessential. In agreeing to help you, Ruth Martinez, he may seem to be only interested in possibly finding a clue to his elusive adversary. But, in fact, he saw that you and Frank Miller are up against something that is evil. Whoever killed Dr. Darwyn and made it look as if Dr. Miller committed the murder is a heinous, evil person. That person must be stopped and Jonathan Steel knew that. He may not have realized it on a conscious level, but he knew it almost intuitively. God speaks to him in that way. This is the first time he has helped someone knowing that the evil presence in the situation is possibly not the demon he seeks. He truly wants to do good. And, that is an encouraging development."

Ruth shook her head. "You're speaking nonsense. No one goes around helping others just because it's the right thing to do anymore."

"Now, Jonathan Steel does." Cephas stated quietly. "I was once like him. As I said, I let my own personal agenda get in the way of defeating evil. It cost me dearly."

Ruth nodded and sighed. "I understand more than you can know. Maybe we both have to stop blaming ourselves."

Cephas' tired eyes stared off into space. "All any good man has to do for evil to succeed is to start believing it doesn't exist. I know this is hard for you to accept, Ruth. You grapple with powers of the physical, the mental, and the law. We grapple with powers that are not of this realm. But, rest assured they overlap. Whoever killed Dr. Wallace Darwyn was a ruthless, evil hearted person with premeditation and planning. Only a person dedicated to great evil could have ripped that man apart like that. Focus on that, Ruth. In order to free Dr. Miller, you have to find the person who perpetrated that great evil."

The face with two different colored eyes flashed in her memory. The smell of blood. The madness behind that stare. She shook her head to clear the memory. "Get some sleep then, Dr. Lawrence."

Dr. Lawrence nodded. "I might be able to sleep, tonight."

"I doubt I will, Dr. Lawrence." Ruth said.

The old man smiled and his huge, bushy mustache twisted into a smile. "Call me Cephas, my dear." The call ended and the window disappeared.

She leaned back and sighed and ran her hands through her wet hair. Where to begin? Her cell phone rang. It was Steel.

"Where have you been?" She said.

"Sorry. Stuck in Austin. I started back this morning. Had to drive through a dozen out of the way little towns to get here. Where are you?"

"At home."

"I'll be there in twenty minutes. I have that video footage from the hard drive."

"Will it help?"

"If we can get a hold of Mr. Johnston."

"What happened to him?"

"He was fired that night." Steel said. "I think he knows something, Ruth. He couldn't tell us because he was an employee."

"But, now he's not!" Ruth's heart raced. "Call him. Go by and get him and bring him here, Jonathan."

"I've already thought of that. We'll be there within the hour. Have some coffee ready."

"I thought you didn't drink coffee?"

"I don't. Makes me irritable. But, I think we have a long night ahead of us."

RUTH CHANGED into a loose pink sweat shirt and warm jeans. Steel and Johnston arrived shortly after. She ushered them into her dining room and pointed to the table.

"This will be our work space."

Mr. Johnston placed a plastic bin on Ruth's dining room table. "This is everything I took from my office." He wore a brown flannel shirt and a cap peppered with snow. He smelled of fried chicken.

"I hope we didn't interrupt your meal."

"My wife had just finished when Mr. Steel called." He smiled. "She will be glad to get me out of the house."

Ruth glanced at Steel. He nodded. "Sorry I was late."

"You missed quite a show."

"I heard Cephas almost knocked it out of the park."

"Well, almost." Ruth pointed to a chair. "Have a seat, Mr. Johnston. I understand Dr. Morrant fired you the other night."

"The same night you were attacked. Yes."

Ruth nodded for Steel to take a seat. He paced for a moment and paused behind Johnston. "Why did she fire you?"

"I didn't get rid of the two of you fast enough. Being a security guard gives you some sense of permanence, but all it takes is one huge kick in the gut to make you humble."

"So, I take it you're no longer faithful to the Institute?"

"I was fired. I'm no longer bound by my contract. I can tell you anything."

"What we need is hard evidence that Dr. Miller did not kill Dr. Darwyn. I believe someone else killed him and made it look like Dr. Miller did. There are lots of possibilities. So, the first thing I would ask you." She leaned toward him. "Did you kill Dr. Miller?"

Johnston straightened and shook his head. "Why on God's green earth would I do that? Look, I left the party and I was asleep in my bed when he was killed. You can ask my wife. I handed off the security duties to the night guard halfway through the party."

"What about this guard?" Steel paused.

Johnston looked over his shoulder. "He started a couple of days before the murder. Moved here from California so his wife could go to SMU. I just don't see why he would do something like that."

"That leaves the other staff."

"And, Wallace's secretary. She did have a crush on Darwyn." Steel said. "Hell hath no fury like a woman spurned. Or, something like that."

"Well, there was another woman."

"Dr. Morrant?" Ruth asked.

"No."

Ruth blinked. "What do you mean?"

"A woman who came and visited Dr. Darwyn a few times. Her name was," he paused and reached for his bin. "I keep a written record of all visitors. Not required but I like to cover my butt." He pulled a spiral notebook from the bin and opened it. The pages were filled with hand written notes. "Let's see. Her name was Janet Dough."

Ruth stood up and Steel gasped. "What?"

"Janet Dough. Weird name."

Steel pulled the flash drive from his pocket. "And, we have a record of you stopping her from coming to the party."

Ruth glanced at the flash drive. "He did it?"

"Yes." Steel handed her the flash drive. "Pulled off a few minutes of footage at the beginning of the party. No other footage."

Ruth plugged the drive into her laptop and opened the file. They watched in silence as the scene played out until the woman walked into the frame."

"That's her." Johnston said.

"What did she want?"

"Wanted to see Dr. Darwyn. I told her she could only come in with an invitation. She argued with me that Darwyn had told her she was welcome anytime." Johnston said.

"She'd been there before?" Steel slid into a chair.

"Several times. She always came after hours and went straight up to his office. First visit was about a month before Darwyn died. I don't think Dr. Morrant liked her. She hired that P.I. to track her down."

"A private investigator? Why was Dr. Morrant hiring a P.I.?" Steel asked.

"Isn't it obvious? Jealousy!" Ruth said. "Mr. Johnston, do you remember the P.I.'s name?"

Johnston rifled through the box and pulled out a small notebook. "My personal notebook. I kept notes just for me. Let's see." He thumbed through the pages. "Festivan was his last name. I wrote down his number." He showed it to Ruth and Steel grabbed his phone.

"I'll call him right now. Maybe he will know why this woman was seeing Dr. Darwyn." He dialed the number and listened. A frown creased his lips. "Answering machine. But, it gave me his address."

"Go. Now!" Ruth said. "See if he is available to testify tomorrow if we need him."

"What about confidentiality?" Steel asked.

"That won't be a problem." Johnston tapped his notebook. "The last time I saw him Dr. Morrant had fired him. With Darwyn out of the picture, she was cleaning house. He's free to tell us anything he wants."

Steel actually smiled and headed out the door. Ruth sat back and sighed. "Now, we wait."

Johnston sat back in his chair. "Well, while we wait maybe I should tell you about the problem with the muscles."

Ruth raised an eyebrow. "What?"

27

Jonathan Steel

ROY FESTIVAN'S office address led me to a run-down strip mall in Mesquite, Texas. It sat just a block or two away from a huge shopping mall and housed a pawn shop, a sandwich shop and two deserted stores separating the small office of "Roy Festivan, P.I.". The snow had let up some as my car slushed through the empty parking lot. I parked in front of the office where the glass windows were covered with posters for local elections. Only the door was transparent with a "Closed for Business" sign dangling from a rusty chain.

I peered inside the office and made out an old wooden desk with a landline and a doorway leading to the rear of the office. I nudged the door with my foot and it swung inward, unlocked. The odor hit me full force and I choked. I used the flashlight setting on my phone and followed the foul odor down the hallway to the rear office.

The room was shrouded in shadows and I heard the buzz of flies.

Not good. A large glass and chrome desk sat beneath a rear window. Pale light cast shadows across the figure slumped over the desk.

"He just couldn't take it another moment." Someone said behind me.

I whirled and the man stepped out of the shadows. There are times in my life when I have felt the unmistakable brush of evil. It is like a powerful force that emanates from the darkest side of our human existence. But, the wave of pure evil that washed over me made me step back and reach for a gun I never had.

"What?"

The man stepped into the wan light from the window. "Sorry. Didn't mean to startle you. Reginald Drake." He held up his hands and I saw they were encased in blue latex gloves. His eyes were of different colors. So much for my eyes making people feel weird. His were downright creepy. "I'd shake your hand but we don't want to leave any evidence that we were here. I'm afraid Mr. Festivan ended his life a day or so ago." He pointed over my shoulder. "There's a note. He was in great despair after being fired by someone at the Institute."

"You are evil." I whispered hoarsely.

"Of course I am." Drake chuckled and his two disparate eyes glittered with malice. "I did not kill Mr. Festivan. But, we did harvest his soul."

"Who are you in league with?"

"Oh, just a minor bottom dweller demon. Something that can give me access to past memories and limited powers. It doesn't realize I'm using it, not the other way around. Now," He reached into his blazer pocket and retrieved a small object. "This is the flash drive Festivan tried to give to Dr. Morrant just moments before she fired him. Seems she was displeased with his progress and never looked at the images on here. I think Ruth will find them very helpful."

He held out the flash drive and I let him drop it in my hand. It was hot. "Why are you doing this?"

Drake shrugged. "Ruth was able to obtain my acquittal. I'm still facing minor charges, but I've got a connection I think that can get them dropped." He stepped toward me. "You see, I owe her. But, I

don't own her. Yet." He smiled and his perfect white teeth shone in
the weak light.

"I should call the police and report you."

"Oh, but you won't. You don't have time to go down to the department and fill out paperwork and make a statement, do you? Ruth
needs that flash drive now. So, run along and don't touch anything."

He stepped to the side and gestured toward the hallway. What to
do? I glanced once again at Festivan. The man was dead. His fate had
been sealed when he made a pact with the devil. I turned back and
Drake was mere inches away. He was studying my face, tilting his
head side to side like some reptile.

"You really do have the most striking turquoise eyes. Rocky
Braxton was right."

I flinched and stepped away. My hips banged against the edge of
the desk and stirred up a cloud of flies. Drake gestured to the flies and
they spun and danced in a sphere above his head until the sphere
formed into a perfect spiral.

"Braxton is dead." I hissed. "But, the thirteenth demon is out there
somewhere."

"I know." Drake swiped his hand through the air and the files fell
to the floor, dead. "You won't stop pursuing him, I know. But, far be it
from me to give you any hints as to his whereabouts." He stepped
around me and pressed the speakerphone button on the landline. He
dialed 911.

"911, state the nature of your emergency." A man's voice echoed
from the speaker.

"It stinks really, really bad!" Drake grinned. His voice sounded
like that of a teenage girl. "Like, I think something is dead in that
office. Maybe a possum or a raccoon." Before the voice could answer,
he killed the call.

"They'll be here in about five minutes so you best be hurrying on.
Give my best to Ruth." He saluted and disappeared from sight; just
disappeared, leaving behind empty air and a snap that made my ears
pop. I glanced around the office. Drake was gone. Like that. I had

forgotten about my phone light and I played it over the desk. Festivan's head was a sea of gore, and blood and brain splattered a hand written note on the desk. In the far distance I heard a siren. Without touching anything I hurried out and drove off from the office of death.

RUTH WAS on her third cup of coffee and over an hour had passed since Steel's departure. Johnston was asleep sitting on her couch. She sat beside him and he stirred.

"He back yet?"

"No." She sipped at her coffee. "Do you really think Dr. Morrant could have killed Darwyn?"

"I don't know. Why would she?" Johnston said.

"Love, money, or revenge. Three motives for murder. Jealousy could certainly be Morrant's motive." Ruth said.

Johnston shook his head. "They are all up to something, Ms. Martinez. Oh, there's a couple of other things you need to look at if you are tired of waiting."

"Sure."

Johnston reached into the box and took out a large, brown envelope. "That woman asked me to give this to Dr. Darwyn the night she came to the party."

"This is the envelope from her purse?"

"Just before she walked out, she asked me to take it. She was really nervous and asked me to keep an eye on this envelope. Said she wasn't sure if he would want what was in it."

He slid the envelope across to Ruth. She studied it and debated whether or not to open it. "If this is evidence, I could be accused of tampering with it." She hesitated for only a second and then ripped it open. "You're my witness." She glanced inside and poured the contents into her hand. Two keys slid out. "Looks like safety deposit box keys." She frowned and sighed. "Great! Keys to a safety deposit box and the bank will not be open until in the morning."

"I'm sure Mr. Steel can find the manager of the bank and have the contents before noon."

"How will we know which bank?"

"Look. It's engraved on the keys." He glanced at his watch. "It's getting late and the snow is picking up. I can't think of anything else to help out."

"I thought Steel gave you a ride."

"I followed him. Didn't want to be stranded. It's nasty out there."

Ruth patted his hand and placed the keys on the table. "You've been a great help. Maybe that P.I. will give us an angle. Go home and if you think of anything else, call me. I'm sure I'll be up all night."

Johnston stood up. "I was with the Dallas Police Department for fifteen years. Had back surgery and they told me I was disabled. I was a good detective, Ms. Martinez. You've got a mysterious woman showing up with a secret that needs to be tucked away in a safety deposit box. She's being tailed by a P.I. hired by a jealous woman. The only thing I know is that the two of them had something in common. All you have to do is connect the dots."

"Think that's why Morrant fired you?"

"Could be. Maybe she was afraid I'd connect the dots. Or, she's just cleaning out the debris left behind."

Ruth stood up and led him to the door. "Be careful. And, thank you again."

She opened the door and Jonathan Steel stood on the doorstep. The look in his eyes frightened her and she hurried Johnston down the walkway and pulled Steel inside. "You look like you saw a ghost." She wrinkled her nose. "And, you stink."

Steel looked away. "I probably stepped in something." He crossed to her table and opened her laptop. "I have a flash drive. Festivan was going to give it to Dr. Morrant. Claimed it had surveillance of the woman but she fired him before he told her." He slid the flash drive into a port. It began to blink. A message appeared on the screen. "It's compressed files. It will take a while to decompress and copy to your laptop."

Ruth sat slowly beside him. She noticed his hands were shaking.

"You didn't step in something. I recognize the odor of death." She reached out and took his face in her hands. His skin was ice cold. She turned his face toward her and his piercing eyes were moist. "Festivan is dead, isn't he?"

"Suicide." Steel mumbled. "Called 911 and left. Uh, read the notes in his notebook about the drive."

"Where's the notebook?"

Steel looked away, pulling his face out of her grasp. She placed a hand on his bad arm and he winced. "You're not a good liar, Mr. Steel."

"No, I'm not. I hate liars." He hissed.

"What happened at that office?"

He looked at her and the intensity of his gaze took her breath away. "Drake was there."

Ruth pushed back away from the table and her chair caught on the rug. She tumbled backward and fell against the end of the couch. She rolled over onto the cold, tile floor and nausea gripped her. Steel was over her immediately helping her up. She pulled out of his grasp and shoved him away.

"You talked to Reginald Drake at the scene of a suspicious death?" She punched his bad arm and he gasped in pain. "What is wrong with you? You should have called the police! He probably killed Festivan!" She was gasping for breath, her heart racing. "What was he doing there?"

Steel stood quietly while she began to shiver and shake. He took her gently and led her to the couch. She vaguely felt him put a comforter around her shoulders. "He said he was there to help you. He told me about the flash drive. Don't worry. I didn't touch anything."

"He's not there to help me!" She hissed. "Oh, God, help me!" She felt the pain blossom within, felt the guilt and shame take her. Darkness swam in her vision.

"Ruth? Ruth?" She felt a cold cloth on her face. "Are you okay?"

She felt woozy; dizzy. She looked up into the man's beautiful but dangerous eyes. "Your eyes. They're so nice." She mumbled. Where was she? Reality returned with a vengeance and she sat bolt upright on the couch.

"Drake! I should have known he had something to do with this."

"Do you think he's involved in the murder?" Steel asked.

Ruth took the cloth from Steel and pressed it against her eyes. "Of course not. He's a voyeur of sorts. He's obsessed with me."

Steel sat back on the couch. "What aren't you telling me?"

She froze. "What do you mean?"

"You told me about the trial. But, there's more, isn't there?"

Ruth stiffened and tried to stand up but she was still light headed. She fell back again on the couch. "Yes, there's more." She started to sob. So much more.

Steel's hands were on her face this time and he turned her to face him. His eyes were filled with something foreign, something that did not belong to this man; compassion; empathy; understanding. "Tell me." He whispered.

"I've never told anyone." She said, feeling his breath on her face. "Never."

"You're safe with me, Ruth. You can tell me." His lips moved. She blinked and gently pulled away.

"I can't."

"Something has been holding you back." His voice echoed in her ears. "Let it go. Tell me. I won't tell anyone, Ruth. You can trust me. I promise."

She turned and gazed into his eyes. They were moist and the pupils were dilated. What secret pains lived behind that gaze? "And, you always keep your promises."

"Yes." He whispered.

28

———————

A warm spring breeze swept through the parking garage chasing away the last vestiges of winter. The roads were choked with evening drivers and the sounds of traffic filled the parking garage with echoes. Ruth barely heard her cell phone ring and she paused at the bottom of the ramp to check the caller ID. Bryan Nicholas.

"Bryan? What is it this time?" She said as she walked on towards her car. She had to put a finger in one ear to hear him.

"Hey, don't be so hostile, Ruth." Bryan said. "Where are you? At the Hallsville races?"

"No, just the usual Dallas evening traffic jams. I just had a good day, Bryan. The sun is setting and its warm and the humidity is low and I'm looking forward to a weekend at Lake Travis. I have a three-hour drive to Austin in this traffic so don't ruin it for me."

"Look, Ruth, I know we haven't gotten along well since the Drake trial."

"Gotten along? You've been an insufferable bully." Ruth paused and leaned against her car. The concrete vibrated beneath her and she heard the distant sound of horns and metal on metal. Another traffic accident. What else was new? She pressed her hand and her phone tighter against her ears.

"I'm not calling you to fight, Ruth. Detective Jones from the DPD was just here. She's concerned about our safety."

Ruth stiffened. "What?"

"There's been a murder."

"Who?"

"No one we know. But, the victim was killed in a similar fashion to Zuniga."

"Drake!" Ruth hurriedly unlocked her car and slid beneath the steering wheel. She locked the doors.

"They aren't sure. But, the kicker, Ruth, is the victim was the man who received Zuniga's heart."

Ruth swallowed back nausea. "What?"

"They are contacting the other recipients to make sure they are okay. Just as a precaution." Nicholas said.

"I don't know what to say."

"You're to blame?" Nicholas said. "Was that what you were going to say?"

"Bryan!"

"Well, it's true. If you hadn't gotten that acquittal, that man might still be alive."

Ruth gasped. "How could you be so cruel, Bryan? You could have been handed that case."

"And, I would have gotten the man a deal. A win-win scenario, Ruth."

"I've heard enough, Bryan." She ended the call and threw her phone onto the passenger seat. Her hands were trembling as she tried to start the engine. A shadow passed over her and she looked through the driver window into the eyes of Reginald Drake.

"Help me!" He shouted, holding up his hands. They were covered in blood. She screamed and tried to start the engine and flooded it. She reached for her phone and it slid over the side of the passenger seat down to the floor by the door.

He banged even harder on the window, blood splattering on the glass. "Ruth, I need your help. She's hurt and I tried CPR and she's not breathing. You need to call 911."

Ruth slid from under the driver's seat onto the passenger's seat and rolled over to try and find her phone. More banging and the car shook. She looked up and Drake was on the passenger side. Blood dripped from his chin, beaded his hair. "Ruth! I'm not lying. She's going to die if you don't help."

Ruth found her phone and tried to pull back away from him and accidentally hit the recline lever. The seat back fell away from her and she tumbled into the back seat. Drake followed her, banging on the back window, screaming her name. She stabbed at the phone numbers and it took three tries to hit 911.

Silence fell as the operator answered. "I need help!" She shouted. "He's here. He's trying to kill me!"

Blue lights spun around her and she sat up. A police car whirled by her going up the ramp to the next level. That was fast! She ended the phone call and opened the door. Drake was nowhere to be seen. But, bloody footprints led up the ramp and around the turn. She dug in her purse until she found her mace and followed the footprints up the ramp.

When she made the turn, the scene was horrifying. Two cars had rammed into each other most likely during her conversation with Bryan. She had been so absorbed she hadn't heard it. Two police cars were parked with their lights whirling. Reginald Drake was pumping on the chest of a woman sprawled on the concrete. Another man hung out of the window of the other car.

A patrol officer ran toward her. "Ma'am, I need you to keep back. There's been an accident."

"But, he killed them!" She shouted. "Don't you see, he killed them!"

The officer took her by the shoulders. "Unless you witnessed the accident, I need you to go wait by your car."

She jerked out of his grasp and ran up the ramp. "Drake! What did you do? Huh? Couldn't stand it that you didn't get all of her the first time? Huh?"

Drake looked up from the blood covered body of the woman. "Officer, I think she's hysterical."

She felt the officer's hands on her shoulders and he pulled her back. She tried to pull away but an ambulance whirled around the turn and screeched to a halt between her and Drake. She jerked out of the officer's grasp. "Fine! If he gets away with it, you're to blame this time!" She screamed in his face and marched back down the ramp to her car.

She opened the driver door and sticky blood coated her hand. She sat down in the seat, her legs pointed out and put her face in her hands. Blood coated her eyebrows and she felt hot tears run down her cheeks.

"Don't worry. I didn't tell them who you were."

She looked up into the two strange eyes of Reginald Drake. Blood had dried in his hair and on his face. He smiled. "They won't even know you were here."

"What did you do?" She hissed.

"I tried to save that woman. The man was already dead. They were both texting, I supposed and driving a little too fast. Imagine dying in a car accident in a parking garage!" He rubbed his hands together and clotted blood rained onto her legs. She tried to pull them back.

"You did this. I know you did." She said. "Just like you killed the man with her heart. You couldn't stand it. Well, you won't get the rest of them. We're watching them, now."

Drake wore a wounded look. "I have no idea what you're talking about. But, I will tell you one thing, Ruth Martinez. I can tell the world how I called out to you for help. I can tell everyone how you refused to unlock your door and come to the aid of a dying woman. I can end your career, just remember that." He held up his phone and showed her the photo of her sitting sideways in her car with her hands and legs spotted with blood.

Ruth felt cold and icy inside and tried to back away. "What?"

"Or," he leaned in to her and his breath smelled of sulfur and blood. "you can drive away from here and never mention you saw me at this accident. Because if you ever do, I will destroy you." He blew her a kiss and walked away, whistling a happy tune.

RUTH FELT a hand on her arm. Steel's touch was warm and tender. "I'm sorry."

"I never told. What good would it do? It was freak accident. But, in a parking garage? I know he had to have something to do with. But, what could I prove? Drake disappeared so I never told anyone."

"And, the rest of the transplant recipients?"

"Fine. No threats. And, they couldn't tie Drake to the murder. He had an alibi that placed him in Las Vegas that day." She shuddered and leaned in to him. "I've been hiding that all this time. It's like he's had some kind of power over me. And, now he's helping me with this case. He'll never go away."

Steel's arm tightened around her shoulder and she felt the warmth of his chest, heard the slow, steady thump of his heart. She closed her eyes and let the tears flow, nuzzling into his chest until she heard him groan. This was his bad side, broken ribs and torn muscle, but she didn't care. She needed this. She needed the arm around her, the solace of his beating heart, the warmth of his presence. She looked up at his face through tear filled eyes. His lips were rigid and his eyes closed tightly as if he was fighting some great internal battle. Why didn't he give in? Why didn't he take her and sweep her off her feet and hold her and tell her it was going to be fine; that all the bad men would never find her because he would protect her? Why? She blinked and gently pulled away from his tense frame.

"I'm sorry." She whispered.

"I know. I can't." He said quietly. "I can't." He looked away and she saw moisture on his cheeks.

The laptop made a dinging sound. Steel stood up shakily and walked stiffly to the table. "The files are decompressed."

Ruth wiped her face with trembling hands and swallowed. She would face this. She would do this. She was strong and she didn't need Jonathan Steel to do what she knew she had to do. She shrugged off the comforter and came to the table. She sat beside Steel and avoided her shoulder touching his. He flipped through the images one by one. Most were of people leaving the Institute. Morrant. Grant. Darwyn. Mrs. Greely.

"You said he got fired on the last day of images and Morrant never saw them?" Ruth asked.

"Yeah."

"Let's look at the most recent." Ruth said.

Steel browsed through the list and clicked on the most recent images. The photo was of Janet Dough. She was an older woman, rather dumpy in a long, cotton dress covered by a raincoat. Her hair was grayish blonde and piled in a bun on top of her head. She carried a huge purse large enough to pack groceries in. Most of the images showed he at the hotel, at the Institute parking lot, at a discount store.

"So, Dr. Morrant never saw these photos of Janet Dough?" Ruth said.

"Apparently not."

Steel clicked on the next image and it shocked them both. Ruth studied the photo and felt that familiar realization; the dawning of truth accompanied by the sound of dominos falling. She looked at Steel and he grinned.

"Gotcha!" Ruth said.

29

R uth gulped her coffee and stood up hurriedly as Judge Nettles settled behind his bench. "Ms. Martinez, do you have anything else to add this morning?"

Ruth nodded. "Yes, sir. I'd like to recall Dr. Morrant to the stand."

She glanced over at Nicholas and his eyebrow lifted in surprise. She glared at him and dared him to object. He looked away.

Dr. Morrant stood up slowly from her seat and glared at Nicholas. She wore a silky, white dress and she smoothed out the wrinkles as she walked to the witness stand. She slid into the witness chair and the look on her face would have slain a dozen men.

"I'd like to remind the witness that you are still under oath." Nettles said.

"Yes, your honor." Morrant said.

Ruth straightened her blazer and drew a deep breath. She approached the witness stand and handed Morrant a file folder. "Dr. Morrant, would you please identify the contents of this file folder for us, please?"

Morrant glanced at her and accepted the folder. She opened it and her face paled. "Uh, where did you get this?"

"From the private investigator you hired to follow Dr. Darwyn."

"Objection!" Nicholas rocketed to his feet. "Counsel cannot introduce new evidence the prosecution has not seen."

Ruth turned slowly. "I think, your honor, that the prosecution has already violated that rule a dozen times. Besides, this is not evidence."

"Then what is the purpose of bringing up such a private, and may I add, confidential matter that has no relevance to these proceedings." Nicholas shouted, his face turning red.

"If your honor will indulge me, I will establish its relevance."

Nettles sighed. "I will allow this line of questioning. But, be careful Ms. Martinez."

Ruth smiled at Nicholas and he plopped back into his seat, leaning over to whisper to one of his associates. Ruth turned back to Dr. Morrant. "Now, Dr. Morrant, you can tell us all about this bill and why you retained a private investigator or I can call Mr. Festivan to the stand."

Morrant closed the file and tossed it on the floor. "He can't say a word. Our relationship is confidential."

Ruth picked up the file. "It would be if you had paid his bill. This file clearly shows you did not pay Mr. Festivan for his services and that nullified his relationship with you. He's free to testify to anything I can ask him regarding your cancelled employment of his services."

Morrant bit her lip and glanced at the judge. "Do I have to answer this?"

"Or course not, Dr. Morrant." Nettles massaged his mustache. "But, Ms. Martinez has established the right to call this Mr. Festivan as a witness if it is true you have severed your personal relationship. Have you?"

Morrant looked away. "The weasel stiffed me. I asked him to follow Dr. Darwyn and find out if he was seeing another woman. Instead, he took pictures of other people Darwyn met with."

"Other people? But, not with some mysterious woman Dr. Darwyn was supposedly meeting?" Ruth asked.

"No!" Morrant fought for calm. "Okay, so Wallace and I had a relationship. We've already talked about that. Then, this woman showed up at the Institute one afternoon. She kept trying to see him. When I confronted him about it, he lied to me. I know they met in his office more than once. But, Festivan never found out who she was. Kept calling her Janet Dough. Really? Jane Doe? He didn't have a decent enough imagination to make up another name? He was worthless."

"Your honor." Nicholas stood up. "What does this have to do with Dr. Darwyn's murder?"

Ruth spun and smiled at him. "I'm glad you asked, Mr. Nicholas. If your honor will allow me to follow my line of reasoning, I believe I can establish a reasonable doubt as to the circumstances around the murder of Dr. Darwyn established by the prosecution. After all, isn't that my job?"

"Yes, Ms. Martinez. It is." He held out his hand. "Let me see the file, please."

Ruth handed him the file folder and she smiled at Nicholas. His fists were clinched and his lips pressed together so tightly, they were a thin line. Careful, she thought. Don't let too much out of the bag. She looked away. Nettles placed the file folder on his desk. "I will allow this line of questioning if for no other reason than to see where you are going with this, Ms. Martinez."

"Thank you, your honor." She walked back to her table and picked up the flash drive. She held it up. "Mr. Johnston, the head of security, told us about Mr. Festivan's flash drive."

She walked over and handed it Morrant. She examined it. "Yes, he knew. How did you get it?"

"Mr. Festivan had it in his personal belongings. And, Mr. Johnston recognized it as the flash drive you gave to Mr. Festivan. You remember Mr. Johnston? You fired him and did not get him to sign a nondisclosure agreement before he walked out so he is under no obligation to withhold any information. He knows about your relationship with Mr. Festivan and his investigation."

"Okay, yes, he did. What of it?"

"What is on that flash drive?"

Morrant glanced at her. "All of the pictures Mr. Festivan took during his surveillance. But, it won't do you any good."

"Pardon me?" Ruth tilted her head in confusion.

"Not a single image of this mysterious woman is on this drive. She might not even exist." Morrant sneered and handed the flash drive back to Ruth.

"Then you don't mind if I introduce it into evidence?"

"Go right ahead."

"And, you've personally reviewed all of these images?"

"Yes. And, the woman's picture is not there." Morrant said smugly.

"At least not on the images you reviewed, correct?"

Morrant looked confused. "Well, yes."

"But, you fired Festivan before reviewing the latest images on the flash drive, right?" Ruth asked.

"So? It was obvious to me the man wasn't going to be able to help me. He was a buffoon stiffing me for more money." Morrant said.

"Your honor, I would like to enter this flash drive into evidence for the defense."

"Granted." Nettles said.

"No further questions." Ruth returned to her table.

Nicholas stood up and strode toward the witness stand. "Dr. Morrant, why did you hire a P.I. to follow this mysterious woman?"

"At first, I thought she had some kind of romantic interest in Dr. Darwyn."

"I believe you mentioned that. Were you jealous of the woman?"

Morrant snickered. "Hardly. She was old. I mean ancient. I couldn't see Wallace turning me down over her. But, I had to be sure."

Nicholas nodded. "You see, Dr. Morrant, what the defense is trying to imply here is that you might have been jealous enough of this woman to harm Dr. Darwyn. Is that true?" He glanced at Ruth.

Ruth shrugged. "If you're waiting for me to object Bryan, I'm not going to."

For a second, a look of confusion crossed his face.

"Why would I be jealous of a woman in her sixties?" Morrant laughed again.

Nicholas turned back to her. "Exactly. No further questions." He crossed to his table and slowly sat behind the desk. He looked at Ruth once and for the first time in the trial, he looked afraid.

Dr. Grant settled into the witness chair and Ruth smiled at him. "Dr. Grant, thank you for agreeing to allow me to ask a few more questions."

Grant nodded. "Of course."

"Now, do you see that man over there sitting at the end of the first row of spectators?" Ruth pointed behind her.

"You mean, Mr. Johnston?"

"Yes. Would you tell the jury what his responsibilities are," She paused and placed a hand on her mouth. "Ooops, I'm sorry. What his responsibilities were while he was employed by the Institute?"

"Henry was the head of security."

Ruth nodded. "Henry? Sounds like you knew him personally."

"We became friends. Sort of. He's a nice guy."

"Did you ever give him something to keep in confidence as Dr. Morrant did?"

"Objection!" Nicholas said. "Fail to see the relevance."

Ruth turned to Nettles. "Your honor, if the prosecution will be patient, I will establish relevance. My case, is, after all, evolving as we speak."

Some members of the jury chuckled and Ruth watched Nicholas' face pale.

"Proceed, Ms. Martinez." Nettles said.

"Now, Dr. Grant, did you ever give anything to Mr. Johnston for safe keeping?"

"No." Grant nodded.

"But, you called him by his first name. I take it you two became casual in your relationship?"

"Yes. We had coffee at times in the Institute coffee shop." Grant pushed his glasses up his nose.

"He's a very nice and capable man, is he not?"

"Yes."

"Can you tell us about your conversation regarding the problem with the muscles?" Ruth said.

"That's it!" Nicholas rocketed to his feet. "The prosecution has been more than patient, your honor. We don't have to hear about Dr. Grant's physical prowess. The defense is dragging these proceedings out."

"Your honor, if the prosecution thinks I'm dragging things out then he will certainly be uncomfortable if I have to call Mr. Johnston to the stand to recount conversations in detail he may have had with my witnesses." Ruth glared at Nicholas. "Or, is the prosecution in such a hurry to execute my client that he wants to waive my client's right to reasonable trial by his peers?"

Nettles pounded his gavel. "Enough! From both of you. Mr. Nicholas, I will allow this line of questioning and you will refrain from shouting 'objection' every time you feel threatened or uncomfortable. I know you are used to winning but please allow Ms. Martinez to present her defense!" He sighed and rubbed his face. "And, Ms. Martinez, get on with it!"

"Yes sir." She turned back to Grant and tried to hide her smile. "As the prosecution has helped me to point out, Dr. Grant, I can call Mr. Johnston to the stand. And, from the testimony just given by Dr. Morrant, the provisional director of the Institute regarding Mr. Johnston's employment status, he no longer is bound by his employment agreement with regard to confidentiality. Now, why don't you save us some time and recall for us what you told Mr. Johnston about the problems with the muscles."

Grant slumped back in his chair. He took off his glasses and rubbed his eyes. "They say confession is good for the soul." He whispered. He put his glasses back on and leaned forward in the witness stand. "As you pointed out earlier, my job is to reconstruct the musculature of our specimens based on the skeletal reconstructions from Dr. Morrant. When the recons from Annieraptor were sent to me, I ran into some problems."

"What kind of problems?"

Grant looked over at Morrant. "The skeletal recons were wrong. Inaccurate. I had Dr. Morrant redo them a dozen times."

"And that is why you were having problems with the muscles?"

"Yes. It's why I had to outsource some of the programming through Dr. Miller's wife. You see, the skeletal recons based on the fossil evidence supplied by Dr. Darwyn didn't match up. They didn't fit properly. And, when I tried to create musculature to fit the skeleton, I couldn't make it work." Grant leaned against the front of the witness stand. "I thought it might be a problem with the program, but it wasn't."

"Why didn't the skeletal recons work?" Ruth asked. "Were Dr. Morrant's recons flawed?"

"No." Grant paused. "The fossil record was flawed."

"Shut up!" Morrant screamed from the audience. She bounded to her feet and pointed her finger at Grant. "Don't say another word, Grant."

Nettles banged his gavel. "Enough, Dr. Morrant."

"Don't tell them, Grant. You'll ruin it all." She screamed.

"Bailiff, remove Dr. Morrant from the courtroom." Nettles shouted

Two security guards grabbed Morrant by the arms and she slapped at them with her purse. She bit one of the men on the arm as he tried to restrain her. They dragged her kicking and screaming out the back door. Nettles pounded his gavel some more and shouted for silence.

"I will have no further outbursts from the audience!" He shouted. "And, Mr. Nicholas don't even think of objecting. I want to hear what the witness has to say."

Nicholas threw up his hands and slumped back in his chair. Ruth suppressed the urge to do a victory dance. She drew a deep breath and turned back to Dr. Grant. "Go ahead, Dr. Grant. Tell us what Dr. Morrant did not want anyone to know."

Grant sighed and bowed his head. "Annieraptor is a fake."

Murmurs erupted from the crowd and Nettles pounded his gavel. When silence fell Grant looked up and turned his gaze on Styles sitting in the second row. "Dr. Styles knew it. Morrant knew it. We all knew the skeletal remains were pieced together from several different dinosaurs. It was the Piltdown man all over again. A fake. A forgery. But, by the time we found out, we had signed nondisclosure agreements."

"And, if you revealed Annieraptor was a fabrication, there goes your careers?" Ruth asked. "What you are really saying is that Darwyn had something to hold over your heads. In a way, he was blackmailing all of you."

"Yes. All of us were on our last legs. Our credibility was already in question or we wouldn't have been at the Institute."

Ruth smiled. She had it! She had him. "When I met you in your office for our first interview you told me a group of Japanese scientists were the only ones to perfect true artificial muscles. And, that they were not as effective as real muscles. And yet, when Annieraptor attacked me in the display garden, it seemed very adept and mobile. How do you account for this, Dr. Grant?"

Grant squirmed in his seat and frowned. "That help I received earlier? It was to help me finish my own proprietary versions of artificial muscles."

"I see. And, did Dr. Darwyn know about these new artificial muscles and their capabilities?"

Grant swallowed and glanced around the courtroom. "No. It was supposed to be a surprise."

"I see. What kind of surprise?"

"At the unveiling, Annieraptor was supposed to come down off the display and walk around."

Ruth glanced over her shoulder at Dr. Styles in the audience. "So, you and Dr. Styles planned this surprise together?"

"Yes. Dr. Morrant knew too."

Ruth stepped closer. "Dr. Grant, how did you think Dr. Darwyn would react when he found out about this new development?"

"Objection. Speculation." Nicholas said.

Nettles shook his head. "Overruled. I want to hear this. Continue."

Grant rubbed his face and seemed to slump in his chair. "We knew he would be furious."

"Why did you think that?" Ruth was getting closer.

"Because the artificial musculature I had developed up that point was for display only. It wasn't supposed to work."

"Why would the development of working artificial muscles anger Dr. Darwyn?"

Grant sat quietly and Ruth leaned into him. "I asked you a question, Dr. Grant. I want to know why these new artificial muscles would anger Dr. Darwyn?"

He slumped even further into the chair. "Because my contract with Darwyn only covered the first version of the muscles. It would mean that I, and I alone would own the patent for the new working artificial muscles."

Ruth paused. She could push on and back Grant into a corner. Did he have motive sufficient enough to arouse the suspicion of murder? Should she continue? Or, should she let Bryan do her job for her. Again.

"No further questions."

Nicholas slowly stood up and studied her as she walked to her table and sat down. She averted her eyes. He tapped his finger against his cheek.

"Dr. Grant," he walked toward the witness stand. "Would you say that finding out your entire career was about to end would make you a little angry at Dr. Darwyn?"

"Oh, yes. That's why I talked to Mr. Johnston. He was a good listener. I was able to talk through my anger."

"Well, we've seen how Dr. Morrant reacted. She must have been pretty angry, too." Nicholas said.

"Yes, she was."

"Angry enough to murder Dr. Darwyn?" Nicholas said. He glanced over his shoulder. Ruth bit her tongue. How she wanted to object! But, he was going for the bait. Nicholas paused, anticipating but not getting the objection.

"No, she loved Dr. Darwyn. She told me several times how much she loved him. She wanted to move in with him. She desperately wanted him to marry her. That's why she was so obsessed with her possible rival."

"And, as we have already heard, she wasn't angry enough to hurt Dr. Darwyn by the defense's own admission." Nicholas leaned forward and planted his hands on the front of the witness stand. "But, what about Dr. Miller?"

"What about him?"

"How did he react when he found about the fakery?"

Grant shrugged. "We never told him."

Nicholas stepped back. "But, he found out just before the party, right?"

"No, he never knew the fossils were fake. He never knew about the new artificial muscles. His area was botany. He was mad about the feathers, that's all."

Nicholas froze. "Mad enough to murder Dr. Darwyn?"

Grant laughed. "The issue of feathers was a purely academic disagreement. It would never have threatened Dr. Miller. He's a botanist. No, I can't imagine him wanting to kill Dr. Darwyn over that. Now, the rest of us? Maybe. But, Dr. Miller. No."

"In your opinion." Nicholas punched the air with his finger but the gesture was weak.

"Of course. But, you're the one who asked the question." Grant said. "No, if there was anyone in this whole affair who stayed above the immoral and unethical shenanigans behind the scenes it was Dr. Miller." Grant paused and smiled. "And, yes, Mr. Nicholas, that is my opinion."

30

D r. Styles wore a shiny white shirt with a psychedelic tie-dyed tie. His hair stood up on end and he was chewing gum as he settled into the witness stand. "Yeah, I know I'm still under oath. Yada, yada, yada."

"One more yada and I'll have you for contempt, Dr. Styles." Nettles growled. "Get rid of the gum."

Styles smiled like some slick, smart aleck high school kid. He spit the gum into his hand and stuck under his chair. "No problem. So, what do you need, sweetie?" He asked Ruth.

Her face burned with anger and she closed her eyes and took a deep breath. She opened her eyes and smiled. "Dr. Styles, do we need to consider you a hostile witness?"

"What?"

"A hostile witness. Let me see. If I remember correctly from my years in law school, a hostile witness is a witness whose testimony on direct examination is either openly antagonistic or appears to be contrary to the legal position of the party who called the witness."

"I'm here to help out however I can. For instance, you don't have to ask. Yes, I knew the bones were fake. Yes, I knew Grant and

Morrant's heads were spinning. But, none of that mattered to me. My job wasn't to recreate Annieraptor. Mine was to bring it to life. So, all I had to do was modify the bones and muscles with my own proprietary program, by the way, and the finished product came to life."

"Literally." Ruth said. "I'm glad we got that out of the way because I'm not going to ask you about the fake bones." Ruth crossed to her table and picked up a folder.

"What do you know about this mysterious woman who visited Dr. Darwyn?"

"Objection." Nicholas said.

"Overruled." Nettles said. "We've been over this, Mr. Nicholas. I am allowing this line of questioning so save your breath."

"I heard the rumors. That's all." Styles shrugged.

"So, you never actually saw her?"

"Nope."

"Never actually met her?"

"Nope."

Ruth nodded. "You were here earlier when Dr. Morrant testified about the private investigator and his flash drive?"

"Sure, I was here. Trying to take a nap! But Morrant kept yapping." He laughed and the crowd murmured. Nettles banged his gavel.

"Getting close to that line, Dr. Styles." He said.

"Sorry! What's your question, Ruth?"

"Ms. Martinez to you. If you recall, Dr. Morrant said there were no images on the flash drive of this mysterious woman. But, what she did not know is that according to Mr. Festivan, the final pictures he took the morning he was fired were placed on the flash drive. It was in those last few pictures that Mr. Festivan claims to have found the mysterious woman."

"Objection, your honor!" Nicholas shouted. "These questions should be directed to Dr. Morrant!"

"Who was escorted out of this courtroom this morning in contempt of this court." Ruth pointed out.

"Then what makes you think Dr. Styles would have knowledge of those photos?" Nicholas came from behind his desk. "Look, this entire line of questioning is absurd. You're taking us on a wild goose chase! Present Mr. Festivan. Have him verify these photos."

"I'd be glad to, Mr. Nicholas, but, like Janet Dough and Dr. Wallace Darwyn, he's dead. It seems anyone associated with this Institute turns up dead."

Nettles pounded his gavel and motioned to them. "Both of you. Up here. Now!"

Ruth approached the bench and Nicholas stood right beside her. She felt the heat roll off him and she kept her eyes straight ahead. "Ms. Martinez, where is this going?"

She opened the file folder and placed it in front of Nettles. His eyes widened and Nicholas stepped back, the air leaking from his balloon. Nettles closed the folder. "You may proceed."

Nicholas slunk back to his chair and Ruth smiled at Dr. Styles. "The reason I'm asking you these questions, Dr. Styles, is because of this photograph from the flash drive that Dr. Morrant testified came from Mr. Festivan's investigation." She pulled an 8 by 10 from the folder and placed in front of Styles. She nodded toward the table. Grace pressed a button on her laptop and the big screen lit up. Dr. Styles was standing on a sidewalk in a park. Directly in front of him was an elderly woman in a long skirt with her graying hair pulled up in a bun. She wore cat eye glasses and held her huge purse against her chest. Ruth leafed through more pictures placing each one before Styles. On the screen more photos flashed up showing Styles in a heated exchange with the elderly woman.

"I believe you know exactly who this mysterious woman was. I believe you know her name. And, I believe you know why she was trying to see Dr. Darwyn." Ruth said quietly. "Now, Dr. Styles, I think it's time for you to shove that cheeky attitude of yours up your nose and come clean with this court before you are charged with perjury."

Styles sat back in his seat and rubbed his face. "Her name was Naomi Wilberforce."

"Wilberforce?"

"I wouldn't expect you to know the name."

"Why is that, Dr. Styles?"

"The famous debate over evolution back in 1860? Come on! You Bible belters are so ignorant of evolution. You still cling to the fairy tale of creationism. Ruth, get over it! Wake up!" Styles shook his head in disgust.

"Well, Dr. Styles, it seems we superstitious and ignorant people," She glanced at the jury. Most of them were frowning. "need to come out of the dark ages. We have had a rather lengthy education during this trial about the conflict between creation and evolution. Why don't you continue our education in the foundational concepts of evolution? And, please, try and tell us why that pertains to our mysterious Janet Dough."

Styles sat forward. "Yeah, why not. Well, Samuel Wilberforce was a 'high churchman' in the mid 1800's. A religious man. His is best known for the famous 1860 debate with the naturalist, Thomas Huxley concerning evolution." Styles leaned forward and grinned. "He was way out of his league in that debate. He criticized Darwin's theory claiming it was not supported by the scientific facts. Something a lot of people today; stupid, uneducated people I might add; still maintain." He sat back and Ruth heard Nicholas groan. She wanted so badly to look at the jury for their reaction but she was afraid if she did, Styles would notice and he might stop digging the grave he was currently excavating for himself.

"So, most people today don't believe in evolution?" Ruth asked.

"Not here in the south, they don't. Ignorant, superstitious people. That's why I brought Annieraptor to life, to prove them wrong."

"So, that's the end of your story?"

"No way. You see, Wilberforce showed his ignorance by his question to Huxley. He asked the leading naturalist of the time, a man second only to Darwin, if it was through his grandmother or his grandfather that Huxley considered himself descended from a monkey." Styles laughed at his own statement but the courtroom was deathly quiet.

"How did Huxley respond?"

"He was one smart dude. He said that he would not be ashamed to have a monkey for his ancestor, but he would be ashamed to be connected with a man who used his great gifts to obscure the truth." Styles shook his head. "Wilberforce actually thought he won the debate. But, Ruth, let me tell you that debate is considered the turning point in modern man's acceptance of evolution. Wilberforce failed and he didn't even know it. Just like this woman failed. She was carrying on Wilberforce's legacy."

Ruth let the statement ride. For now. "So, in your opinion, Dr. Styles, the name Wilberforce would be repugnant to you, wouldn't you agree?" Ruth asked.

Styles nodded. "Yeah, it would be."

Ruth went over to her table and picked up a brown envelope and emptied the two keys into her hand. She held each one up with both hands. "Did you know about the safety deposit box?"

Styles flinched. His face grew pale. "What does that have to do with anything?"

"The contents belonged to the woman in the photograph. I guess you didn't know about the contents of the box. Or, do you know? You know Dr. Darwyn's secret? What was Ms. Wilberforce doing? Was she blackmailing Dr. Darwyn?" Ruth walked closer to Styles holding up the keys. "What do you think was in the box?"

The courtroom was silent. Styles seemed to deflate. "Yeah, maybe she was. Maybe there were pictures and a copy of a birth certificate in that box. Maybe she knew that Dr. Darwyn was hiding his real name."

Ruth nodded and lowered the keys. "What was his real name?"

"Richard Owen Wilberforce." Styles growled.

"A name he hated. So, he changed his name to Wallace Lyell Darwyn." Ruth stepped closer. "What I don't understand is why change the spelling?"

"Legal reasons, I guess. If anyone was looking for him they'd spell his last name like Charles Darwin. He got to use the name of two people he admired, Robert Owen and Charles Darwin." Styles said. "He chose the name Annie because that was the name of the daughter of Charles Darwin. You know, the daughter who died even though Darwin pleaded with your God over and over to heal her? Wallace never had a daughter named Annie."

"He told you this?"

"Yes."

"So, not only was his Annieraptor a fraud. But, his entire life was a lie." Ruth said. "And, Ms. Wilberforce discovered that and she was going to expose him, wasn't she?"

Styles sat quietly and glanced around at the room. "Well, not really."

Ruth stiffened. That wasn't the response she had expected. "Then, Dr. Styles tell me why?"

Styles looked at Nettles and shrugged. "She just wanted to get back with her long, lost brother. That's all."

The courtroom exploded in murmurs and Nettles banged his gavel. Ruth stumbled backwards. She had thought Ms. Wilberforce might have been a wife Darwyn had spurned. But, his sister? She shook her head in confusion. The room slowly settled down and she tried to think. The back door opened and Jonathan Steel walked in. She locked eyes with him and he nodded. So much for this setback. She turned to the bench.

"Your honor, I have one more piece of evidence I'd like to introduce and it may take a while. I suggest we have a short recess while we bring in the evidence."

Nicholas stood up slowly and began to clap. His claps echoed around the chamber. "Good show, your honor. But, everything we have heard up to now changes nothing. Nothing! And, to add another piece of so called evidence the prosecution has not seen? I think we've all had enough of Ms. Martinez's soap opera."

Nettles raised an eyebrow. "He has a point, Ms. Martinez."

Ruth walked over to Nicholas. She glared at him and he smirked. "So, am I to understand that the prosecution would not mind if I threw out the evidence I am about to admit?"

"Sure." Nicholas shrugged.

"Your honor, if we throw out this evidence, then my client must be freed."

"What?" Nicholas said. "That's absurd."

"Mr. Nicholas," Ruth fought for calm. "We wouldn't have a trial without the murder weapon." She motioned toward the back and both doors opened. Standing in the hallway surrounded by security guards was Annieraptor.

31

During the recess, Ruth bowed her head and prayed. Silently she pleaded for calm; for clear thoughts; for cunning. More than anything, she prayed for Frank Miller. She felt a hand on hers and glanced to her side. Dr. Miller was patting her hand.

"You're doing a great job, Ruth. No matter what happens, I trust you. I believe in you." He whispered.

Ruth drew a deep breath and calmed her racing heart. She tried to muster up enough spit to wet her mouth as they arose for Judge Nettles. He settled into his seat and glared at the monstrosity sitting beside the jury box. Annieraptor stood attached to a metal pole on a rolling platform. She was in the same pose from the Institute with one clawed foot raised before her in attack mode.

"Your mistake will be my victory." Nicholas whispered toward her. "You'll lose all sympathy from the jury. So, thanks for handing me the new partnership."

Just a meter away and she felt like he was breathing down her neck. She stood up and clasped her shaking hands. Dr. Styles had been returned to the witness box. She walked over to the evidence table and picked up the backpack with the laptop. She slid the laptop out of the bag.

"Dr. Styles, I hope you don't mind that I've brought your greatest creation for the world to see. I know you were hoping to hold off until the Institute's big unveiling, but I want the jury to understand Annieraptor and how she functions. Can you help us with that?"

Styles seemed to relax. "Of course."

"Now, this is the laptop."

"Yeah, my Feldercarb 360 they found in Dr. Miller's office." He said.

"And, the goggles." She picked them up and walked to the witness stand with both objects. "You said these two items allow you to control Annieraptor like one would control an aerial drone."

"Like the ones Dr. Miller uses." Styles said.

"Yes, we've established that. So, Annieraptor is little more than a sophisticated drone?" Ruth said meekly.

Styles' face twisted. "Ruthie, she's far more sophisticated than that. Annieraptor is much more than a drone."

"Of course she is. She is both beautiful and terrible at the same time." Ruth handed the laptop to Styles. "Maybe you could just point out how the controls work. I've attached the laptop video out to our big screen television." Ruth rolled her eyes. "Well, I had the technical guys do that. After all, I'm a lawyer not an engineer. So, maybe you can show us how you control Annieraptor. Without turning her on, of course. We wouldn't want her stalking the jury, now would we."

"Ruthie, as I told you before, Annieraptor's default mode is never to stalk."

"Of course. The controls?"

The laptop beeped as it came to life and the desktop appeared on the big screen television. The desktop was covered with a dozen toggle like switches and sliding control levers. In a frame to the side of the toggles, an animatic of Annieraptor stood motionless. "The laptop has a touch screen. If we had a tablet with the computing power, you could use that for control. But, the idiots in Silicon Valley haven't created one yet. If they would just have listened to me, we'd be a decade ahead of where we are."

"Yes, you are so smart, Dr. Styles." Ruth said with a smile.

Styles seemed confused as if he couldn't decide if she was joking or not. "Well, we have toggles for leg and arm motion forward and backwards." He slid his fingers over the laptop screen and the toggles moved on the big screen. The animatic of Annieraptor responded moving through each maneuver. "Dials for eye movement and mouth movement. Even a control for the tongue." Styles played with some of the switches and Ruth turned to watch the terrified jury members eying the possible monster that could rip their heart out with one swipe.

"And, you can transfer some of the major controls to the goggle motion receptors. You can control Annieraptor through virtual reality, actually augmented reality." Styles said.

"It seems very, very complicated."

"Not if you've played video games."

"How many people at the Institute could control Annieraptor?"

"We went over that the other day. Any of the staff could become an expert in a few short hours."

"How long was the Feldercarb 360 missing from your office?"

"A couple of days. Long enough for Dr. Miller to learn how to control Annieraptor."

Ruth nodded. "Or Dr. Grant. Or Dr. Morrant."

"But, the controls were found in Dr. Miller's office, remember? Locked in his desk, remember? And, only he had a key to his desk, remember?" Styles said.

"Dr. Styles, what is this slot for?" Ruth ignored his remarks and pointed to a slit like opening at the side of the laptop.

"What?"

"This." Ruth came closer. "This small slit?"

"Oh, that is for, well, you know a memory card. It's a standard feature of laptops, Ruthie."

"A memory card? Why would you need a memory card?"

Styles shrugged. "You could store information on it."

"I see. There isn't a card in here, right now."

"Well, to be honest, I've never used that feature."

Ruth nodded. "Oh, so the program can access a memory card if it needed to?"

Styles blinked. "Well, yes and no. I mean."

"You just said you never used the feature but if you wanted to, you could. Does your program access the memory card for storage?"

"To be honest, I don't know. It was just a standard feature I might have used in the future." Styles said.

"Okay." Ruth took the laptop and goggles and returned them to the table. She picked up the blood stained claw and studied it for a moment allowing the jury to get a good look before she put it back in the evidence box. She picked up a camera.

"Dr. Styles, is this your digital camera?" She brought it over to the witness stand.

"Yes."

"Earlier, we had testimony that photographs you took showed Dr. Miller in a heated confrontation with Dr. Darwyn. You took those photos, right?"

"Yeah, I said I did."

"This digital camera looks pretty sophisticated. Why didn't you use your smartphone?"

"Smartphones are good, but that camera is much better. 30 megapixels per image. Able to shoot 3D video. When you are recording something important, don't use a smartphone." Styles said.

"And, you knew the party was very important, didn't you?"

"Yes. It was everyone's first real look at Annieraptor since I finished her. I wanted to capture their reaction." Styles said.

Ruth played with the camera for a moment and opened a slot on the side. "Does this camera use internal memory or one of those storage cards?"

"Both." Styles said.

"That's right. I remember now, Dr. Styles, that earlier testimony established your pictures came from a storage card." She walked over to the table and dropped the camera abruptly. It bounced on the table and she caught it before it could hit the floor.

"Hey, be careful with that thing. It cost plenty." Styles said.

"Sorry." Ruth said rummaging through the evidence on the table. She picked up a small plastic bag and brought it over to Styles. "Now, this looks like the memory card from your camera. I think it's labeled as such." She held it up.

Styles nodded. "Yeah, that's it."

"It's so small. Smaller than my pinkie fingernail."

"And it holds over 500 gigabytes." Styles boasted.

"Would you mind if I take it out of the bag?"

"No. Go ahead."

Ruth took the tiny chip from the bag and held it up. "It's amazing that such a small thing could be the evidence that convicts a killer. Such a small thing."

"Good things come in small packages." Styles said. "One of those old school sayings you probably understand better than me."

Ruth raised an eyebrow. "You're very amusing, Dr. Styles."

"Your honor." Nicholas stood up. "I don't know what is going on here with Ms. Martinez's grandstanding. Can we hurry this up? She's has all but proven the evidence convicts her client. She's doing my job for me."

Ruth planted her hand on a hip. "Are you talking about me? This helpless little attorney that can't seem to understand technology? Why, Mr. Nicholas are you afraid of this little bitty chip?"

Nicholas frowned at her and shook his head in confusion. "Afraid? That chip proves your client had a fight with the deceased."

"Yes, about feathers. Not faked bones or faked muscles, right? Isn't that what Dr. Grant said?"

"Motive is motive."

"Enough, both of you. Ms. Martinez, get on with it."

Ruth nodded. "If you insist." She walked over to Annieraptor and paused, glancing up warily at the clawed hands and the sharp teeth. "You see, the other night when I was at the Institute, Annieraptor came to life and stalked me. Why was that again, Dr. Styles?"

Styles shrugged. "It was the echo of a previous session. We've been over that."

Ruth turned slowly. "So, we presume this 'echo' was of a session where the killer used movement of the dinosaur like a cat playing with a mouse."

"Yes."

She walked over to the evidence table and picked up a white coat. "Is this Dr. Miller's lab coat?" She held it up. Streaks of blood covered the front of the coat and had dried to a rusty brown.

"Yes."

"Now, the night that you saved me from Annieraptor, you wore a lab coat just like this." She walked over to Dr. Styles. "Would you mind putting this on, Dr. Styles?"

"Why?"

"I want you to demonstrate how Annieraptor works. I want to recreate your appearance on the night she came after me. I want to show the jury that Annieraptor chose me over you because you were the operator. Isn't that valid?"

Styles stood up and took the coat. "Sure." He shrugged into it, avoiding the blood stains. Ruth went back to the table. "Let's see. Oh yes, the name badges. Mr. Johnston testified that every visitor had to wear a name badge and we have them all right here. Well, all of them but yours."

"I lost mine a few days before the party." Styles said. "In the confusion afterwards, we never made me a new one."

Ruth turned around and held up two badges. "Funny, both of these have Dr. Darwyn's name on them. And, there is a badge in the evidence box with blood all over it. Why does he have so many?"

"He's the boss." Style shrugged. "When he forgets his badge, he gets an extra."

"Are these badges any different from the one he wore that night? I mean do they look any different?" She walked over and pinned one of them on Styles' lab coat lapel. He tried to pull back but she hung onto the edge of his coat.

"Uh, no. They all have the same RFID chip to track us wherever we are in the Institute."

"Too bad Dr. Miller wasn't wearing his ID the night of the murder." Ruth stepped back, placing a name badge on her lapel. "I believe they found it in his office."

"Yeah, he probably took it off so he couldn't be tracked while he killed Dr. Darwyn." Styles said.

"But, he killed Dr. Darwyn from his office while wearing the goggles, right? We saw his name tag. Oh, never mind. Now, we have created the same circumstances of the night I visited the Institute. You have on a white lab coat and an ID. I have on an ID and a business suit." She studied Styles. "I'm a bit confused. Was Annieraptor under a program as you stated or under manual control?"

Styles sat down in the witness box. "An echo of a program, like I said. Uh, I used the manual reset switch to turn her off."

"If someone had put a memory chip in the controller while running Annieraptor through the motions of stalking and attacking would the controller store those movements?" She didn't allow him to answer and hurried to the evidence table. She picked up the laptop and pointed to the slit in the top. "A program that was stored on a chip like this one from your camera? I noticed something, Dr. Styles." She didn't allow him to answer and turned to Annieraptor. She flipped open the tiny door on the thing's back. "When you opened the access panel on Anniraptor's back you pushed a reset button, right?"

Styles nodded and wiped sweat from his forehead. "Yes. I saved your life."

"Oh, that's right. An echo can kill. Interesting." She pointed to the open door. "There's a slot on Annieraptor just like the one on your controller. What would happen if I put this chip in that slot?" She said and popped the storage chip into the slot.

Two things happened at once. Styles screamed "No! Stop!" and Annieraptor sprang to life. It lowered the clawed foot to the floor and swept Ruth away with a vicious swipe. She tumbled across the floor as Annieraptor tore away from the pole. She thudded to the floor and bent forward, head moving from side to side in a stalking mode. Ruth tried to clear her head. "Don't move!" She screamed.

Styles tried to climb out of the witness stand and Annieraptor straightened, her eyes riveted on him. With one quick movement she hopped across the floor and landed on the wooden rail of the witness stand, her claws shredding the wood. It groaned under her weight and Styles fell back into his chair. Behind her, the members of the jury screamed. She stood up and put her hands out.

"Everyone! Don't move. Don't scream!" She shouted.

The room fell into an eerie silence as Annieraptor leaned forward and studied Styles with a yellow eye. Ruth moved slowly across the floor. If she could just get to the reset button.

"It's the ID, isn't it?" Ruth said. "You programmed Annieraptor to stalk anyone wearing Dr. Darwyn's ID. That's why she came after me that night in the Institute and that is why she is stalking you now. You're wearing one of Darwyn's IDs."

"So are you." Styles whispered.

"No, this is a fake ID I brought in with me. No RFID. But, yours came straight from the evidence box. It's the ID Darwyn was wearing." She was four feet behind the dinosaur. "Why did you do it, Styles? Why?"

Styles stood up slowly and Annieraptor's snout pressed against his chest, nuzzling the ID on his lapel. "I didn't."

Ruth froze. "You lied about the programming. Why else would you have a memory chip slot in both the laptop and Annieraptor? The night Annieraptor killed Dr. Darwyn, you pulled the memory chip out of her and because the police were already there, you put it in your camera where it has been hiding ever since the police confiscated your camera. You programmed Annieraptor to kill Darwyn. You programmed it to stalk his ID." Ruth said. "Now, tell us why and I'll hit the reset button."

Styles' eyes widened and his face was red with rage. "It was her! The sister! Her and her backwoods, hard shell religion. She tracked him down for years. Finally found him. Played on his guilt. You know he watched his father die. Could have called an ambulance. He hated the man. Watched him die of a heart attack and then changed his name. But, she found him and reminded him of who he really was. A Wilberforce? Think that did it? No!"

Styles tried to pull away from Annieraptor's tooth filled maw. "No, she did something worse. She forgave him. Told him about the love of Jesus. Hallelujah! Smacked him in the forehead with the Holy Spirit for all I know. I'm not sure what she did, but he changed. The night of the unveiling, after the fight, I found them in his office. On their knees! Praying! On their knees!"

Styles' voice grew louder. "He gave his heart to Jesus." He said with disgust. "Found forgiveness and she left all weepy and crying and all. You know what he told me? Told me he was going to confess it all. The fraud, the fakery, everything. But what was worse, he was going to give all the money back. Close the Institute. We would have been ruined. Someone had to stop him before the world found out he had become a Christian. Well, I stopped him." Styles pounded his chest. "Me! The real creator of Annieraptor! I stopped his bleeding heart." He pounded his chest again. Annieraptor reared back, tilted her head to study his chest and then ripped his heart out.

32

Ruth tried to make her way through the raucous crowd toward Grace Pennington's library. She was stopped by her brother. She looked up into his frown.

"Looks like you proved me wrong, Sis. But, I always did have your best interest at heart." He lifted her in a huge embrace and her feet left the floor.

"Put her down, son."

Ruth gasped for breath and felt her father's hands on her shoulders. She smiled at her brother and turned to her mother and father. They hugged. Again. Her father smiled.

"We are so proud of the newest partner of Pennington, Foster, and Birmingham. You did well, precious." He said.

"Thanks, Dad. I just did what you said. I went for the truth. Now, if you'll excuse me."

"Honey," her mother said. "It's your party. You aren't leaving are you?"

"No, Mom. I think Ms. Grace wants to see me in the library." She made up the little white lie and pressed her way through more congratulatory people from the law firm. She reached the closed doors and quietly pulled them apart. Grace Pennington sat behind her desk talking to Frank Miller. Steel stood in the corner, his eyes directed out the window. Detective Citronella Jones waited just inside the door. Ruth's heart raced.

"Are you here to arrest me? If so, can we wait until after the party. Not in front of my family, please."

Jones put a hand on her hip. "Honey, it depends on what the D.A.'s office has to say. As far as I'm concerned, you just saved the justice system a whole lot of money."

Ruth tensed when she saw Bryan Nicholas appear at the door. He closed the doors behind him. "Well, Ruth, looks like you won. But, at what cost?" Nicholas walked slowly toward her. "You know, you might as well have picked up a loaded gun from that evidence table, put a round in the chamber, pointed it at Styles and pulled the trigger."

"Styles is responsible for what happened in that courtroom. Not me." Ruth whispered.

Bryan stepped around her and pulled a folded piece of paper from his jacket and handed it to Grace. "The D.A.'s office is not going to press charges. Their newest attorney managed to convince them to drop the charges as long as he joined their office."

"What?" Ruth blurted.

"Are you sure about this, Bryan?" Grace looked up from the paper.

"Yes. I hated to lose the partnership. But, to be honest, being on the prosecuting team was the thrill of a lifetime." He stepped closer to her and smiled. "Hey, Ruthie. I've got to admit, you rose to the occasion. The best woman won."

Ruth was shocked by his graciousness. "What's the catch?"

"The catch?" Nicholas shook his head.

"You've never been this nice to me."

"Hey, you beat me fair and square. You win. I'm not a bad loser, Ruth."

"So, there will be no arrest today?" Steel said.

Jones smiled. "Not here, honey. We already arrested Dr. Morrant. The two of them were planning on offing Darwyn long before the party. And, we found the accelerant from the fire in Styles' lab. I can't prove it, but I think they both worked on that little murder." She smiled at Ruth. "You did good, Ruth. What a comeback from Drake, eh? You took a heinous killer off the board this time." She turned to Steel and winked. "Come by and see me sometime, bright eyes. Now, if you don't mind, I am declaring myself off duty so I can enjoy this little party." She disappeared through the sliding doors.

Ruth could have sworn Steel blushed. Nicholas crossed his arms and studied her. "So, how did you figure it out?"

"It was his camera." Ruth said. "He had the thing at the party. Probably just to document the look on Darwyn's face when Annieraptor came to life. I imagine he had placed a program on the memory chip and installed it in Annieraptor. Obviously, he programmed it to stalk Dr. Darwyn at the party, probably as a joke. We all know how strange Style's sense of humor is. So, Annieraptor was programmed to track down Darwyn's RFID chip. Then, the argument took place and ruined everything. Miller had stolen the spotlight from Styles. So, he went up to his office to sulk and that is when he overheard Darwyn's conversation with his sister. He witnessed Darwyn's conversion and realized everything was in jeopardy. He must have put the plan together quickly. He already had the program for stalking Darwyn's chip. He popped the memory chip into his laptop and added the part of the program to kill. Then, he went downstairs and put the chip into Annieraptor's reset port."

"I wondered how he got to the display so quickly he could take a picture of me holding the claw." Miller said.

"Exactly! He waited for the kill and took the chip out of Annieraptor once she had returned to the podium. But, what he had not counted on was you showing up so quickly. And, he didn't count on the security guard calling 911 so soon and a patrol being just a block away from the Institute. When you showed up and he heard the police coming in the door, Styles put it where no one would suspect."

"In his camera." Steel said.

"Yes, and then he started taking pictures to draw attention away from his presence in the display area. What he never counted on was the police confiscating his camera before he could remove the chip." Ruth said.

"You knew about the memory port on Annieraptor?" Bryan said.

"Actually, no. That was a huge gamble."

Bryan's eyes grew wide. "Well, welcome to the new Ruth Martinez. I didn't know you had it in you."

"But, the stalking program means he planned to kill Darwyn long before the man became a Christian." Nicholas said.

"Jones is on the right track. I think Dr. Morrant and Styles had planned to kill him at the unveiling party." Ruth said. "With Darwyn dead and the Institute discredited, they could go off to the Caribbean and claim the offshore accounts they had been secreting away for months."

Ruth studied Nicholas. "Frankly, Bryan, if I had suspected anyone but Miller and I had been in your shoes, I would have reopened the investigation. You were blinded by the possibility of winning it all."

Grace Pennington handed Nicholas the paper she had signed. "Here is your release from your contract. Good luck with the D.A.'s office. You will do well."

Nicholas took the paper. "I guess you're right. I let my hubris blind me to the facts."

Ruth nodded. "That's where a conscience comes into play. It can be a valuable asset. You ought to try and rediscover yours."

Bryan nodded. "That's another reason I'm staying with the D.A.'s office. Prosecuting the bad guys might help me with my conscience." He paused as he walked past Ruth and turned to her. "There is one other thing, Ruth." He glanced around at the others and leaned in to whisper in her ear.

"What?" She said.

"I was wondering if we could have lunch sometime. I have some questions, you know, about God and the Bible and all that." He stammered.

Ruth looked at this face and found no guile there. "What?"

"Well, I'm afraid I am more like Dr. Styles than I'd like to admit."

Grace appeared by Ruth's side. "I hate to eavesdrop, but in view of what you just said, I think you should have this."

She handed him an evidence bag. "Detective Jones said she doesn't need it anymore. It was Naomi Wilberforce's Bible."

"I saw it in her motel room. It was the only thing to survive the fire." Steel said.

Nicholas took the Bible out of the evidence bag. It was covered with a fine layer of soot that instantly stained his hands. He opened it to the first page. "To my son from a concerned father." He read. "I know you don't approve of my devotion to God but do know that it is His love that compels me to love you so much. I am hoping this Bible will show you that we all deserve a second chance. Love, Father."

Silence fell in the room. Nicholas slowly closed the book and blinked. "Thanks, Grace. I'll cherish this. More than you can know."

Ruth sighed. Was this really happening? She had a hard time believing Bryan. This could be just another of his tricks. Then, she saw something shocking. Bryan hugged the Bible to his chest and the soot rubbed off on his shirt and jacket. He smiled at her. "So, lunch sometime?"

"We all deserve a second chance." Ruth said. Miracles never ceased! "I'd love to."

Nicholas swallowed and nodded. "Thank you. Thank you, both. I'll give you a call." He turned and left the library. Ruth blinked in complete surprise and turned back to Ms. Grace. "God never ceases to surprise me."

"Speaking of surprises." The other chair beside the fire turned. Cephas Lawrence stood up slowly and made his way toward Ruth. "You certainly pulled a rabbit out of the hat, my dear." He leaned forward and kissed her on the cheek.

33

J onathan Steel

I KEPT THE DIGITAL RECORDER. Gave the memory chip to Grace with all my notes. It's not a bad way to keep track of my findings in my search for my adversary. The trial was over and Cephas and I were about to examine the mask. I carefully carried the wooden cask from my car into the RV and placed it on the table. Cephas had moved the keyboard and monitor off the table so we would have a clear work area. I had charged up my high resolution camera to make photos of the mask.

"Before we open the cask, take a look at these carvings." Cephas bent over the wooden box. It sat about 18 inches tall and 12 inches square on top and bottom. The carvings reminded me of hieroglyphics although not as well formed.

"Recognize them?" I asked.

Cephas pushed his reading glasses up his nose and bent close to the wood. "Incan? Aztec? Maybe even Mayan? I'm not sure but they are reminiscent of Meso-American culture. Take some pictures for me, son."

I made over two dozen photos of each side of the cask, checking each image to make sure the images were well documented. I placed the camera on the table and reached for a bronze clasp that held the cask closed. My hands trembled.

"Are we ready?" I asked.

"Oh, yes." Cephas said. "After all you've been through the past few weeks, I'd say you are more than ready. Open the doors."

I undid the bronze clasp and pulled open the two doors exposing the interior. The mask sat on a wooden pedestal and the sight of it took my breath away. The nose was elongated into a beak and the crown of the mask was carved into feathers. Eye holes sat above the beak. Around the right eye, a dark spiral spun its way in an ever enlarging circle until it ended at the base of the beak. I could barely breath.

"Cephas, the spiral is here." I whispered.

Cephas was very still and he pressed his face close to the mask. "Do you know what this mask represents?"

"No."

"The Eagle Knights! If I am not mistaken, they were an offshoot of the Aztecs who rebelled against the Spanish conquest of those people. Could it be this creature came from South America or Central America?"

What happened next will forever be etched into my memory. The eyes blinked. Yes, they blinked closed for a second and reopened emitting a glaring green light that struck Cephas in the forehead. He fell back and I caught him before he hit the floor. We crouched there, halfway to the floor, our eyes riveted on the mask as the green light died out and the spiral faded from view.

"Cephas! Are you okay?" I asked.

"Yes. I see large purple spots before me." He pushed himself out of my arms and examined the mask. "I do believe we are on the right track, Jonathan. The spiral has gone and the light most likely came from some spirit guarding this mask."

"A spirit? As in, a demon?"

Cephas looked at me and rubbed his mustache. "Yes. Jonathan, you are on dangerous ground here. I beg of you to abandon this search. Come back to my loft and let us research this creature some more."

My face grew warm and I shut the cask on the mask. "If I had not have come here, Cephas, we would never have found out about the connection with the Eagle Knights. I will not quit. Not now! Not ever!" I reached up and touched the tiny cross hanging around my neck.

Cephas shook his head and we both jumped as a knock rattled the door to the RV. Cephas stumbled back and landed in the only chair in the RV, the one I used for the kitchen table. I opened the door and cold air poured in. Ruth Martinez stood in the door frame.

"Well, aren't you going to invite me in?" She said.

I rubbed my hands together and glanced at Cephas. "Where are your manners, son?"

I stepped back and she hopped up into the RV. She wore a pair of jeans and a fluffy white turtle neck shirt beneath a beige overcoat. Her cheeks were red from the cold. "Dr. Lawrence, I didn't know you were still here."

"Oh, just helping Jonathan check out his reward for being such a good investigator." He gestured to the cask.

Ruth's smile faded. "Oh. The mask." She looked at me and her eyes were full of questions. "And?"

"We, uh, determined that the mask definitely has a connection of sorts with my, uh, quarry." I mumbled. Gaaa! What was wrong with me?

Ruth reached a hand toward the cask. "May I?"

Cephas and I both bolted toward her at the same time. "No!" I said.

Ruth jerked back and glanced at me. "What is wrong?"

Cephas put a hand on her arm. "Ms. Martinez, some things are best left undisturbed." He stared at me with those piercing eyes of his. "I am sure that Jonathan does not want to drag you into his quest.

Let's just say that to do so might put your future in your law firm at jeopardy."

"At jeopardy?" Ruth looked back and forth between us. "You mean this thing is dangerous?"

I said "Yes" at the same time Cephas said "No".

"What we are trying to say," Cephas turned her gently to face him. "Is that Dr. Pennington has a strange taste in artifacts. There are things that are best not seen by his wife's newest law partner."

Ruth raised an eyebrow and put her hand to her mouth. She smiled. "Oh, like one of those fertility goddesses with exaggerated reproductive organs? No. I can do without seeing that in my sleep. Why, every time I would meet Dr. Pennington I would, well, see, well, never mind!" Her face grew red.

Cephas cleared his throat and his cell phone dinged. "Oh, my, my ride is pulling into the driveway. I must leave you two."

"Your ride?" I said. "I could have driven you to the airport."

"What? And, miss this time with Ruth?" He shrugged into his overcoat and picked up his small suitcase. He pulled a Dallas Cowboy wool cap over his unruly hair. "I knew she was coming, Jonathan. You have much to talk about."

A light passed across the front windows of the RV and Cephas stepped between me and Ruth. He smiled at her. "Ruth, I hope this is not the last time we talk. It has been a pleasure working with you."

She smiled and hugged him. "Thank you, Cephas. I mean everything I told you on the phone."

I glanced at Cephas. "What?"

Cephas frowned. "Not every conversation is about you, son." He faced me and placed a hand on my chest. "Guard your heart. Be careful. Consider my advice."

I felt my eyes moisten and stiffened as he embraced me around the chest. "Get out of here, old man." I said hoarsely. He winked at Ruth and disappeared through the door.

"Well." I said. I looked helplessly around the room. "Have a seat?" I gestured to the chair.

Ruth had this sly grin on her face as she settled into my desk chair. "You're not very good at this, are you?"

"Good at what?" I asked. My mouth was dry.

"I just wanted to stop by and thank you. I have a dinner engagement tomorrow night and then I'm off to Austin for a week of much needed vacation before the onslaught of being a partner hits me broadside."

"Who are you eating with?"

"Bryan."

"Really? I thought you agreed to lunch." I said.

"Well, he called me up today and said he'd like to take me to dinner. No hard feelings. And, he had some questions about something he read in that Bible."

"I told Grace he needed it."

"What? I thought it was her idea."

I looked away. "Shouldn't have said that. Look, everyone deserves a second chance."

Ruth stood up and stepped toward me, her eyes meeting mine. "You are truly a remarkable and confusing man, Jonathan Steel. Hard and flinty on the outside. Just as soon to slug someone as to shake their hand. Yet, sensitive enough to sense that someone as lost as Bryan Nicholas is not beyond redemption. I wish I could be more like you."

I nodded. "After the past few weeks you are. You were pretty skittish when we met."

"Yes, I was." She turned and sat in the chair. "I'm not done. The real reason I came here is because I listened to the recordings."

I blinked and then the realization hit me. She had listened to the recordings. "All of them?"

She nodded. "You didn't tell me everything that happened in that office with Drake. Those things he said. How did he know about this thirteenth demon you are searching for? How did he change his voice?"

I drew a deep breath as Cephas' words sunk in. I was placing Ruth's life in danger. She was being pulled into my world. "Drake is evil, Ruth. Very evil. He is in league with dark forces you cannot even imagine. You must avoid him at all cost. Be wary. Don't let him get near you. Put a restraining order on him or something. Talk to Detective Jones. She wants to hurt the man as much as I do."

Ruth's brow wrinkled. "I will not back down from that man, Jonathan. Not after what he did to me."

"Ruth." I took her hands in mine. "Are you a Christian?"

She blinked in confusion. "Yes." She looked down at my hands. "At least, I've always been once since I was ten. Sort of. Well, not totally committed, you know. I'm so busy and sometimes it's hard to think about God."

"This is you only protection, Ruth." I gently squeezed her hands. "Only God can protect you. What you see happening with Drake. With me. It's spiritual warfare. And, the forces that are lining up against you are not of this world. You can't put a restraining order on them but you can avoid their hosts."

Ruth pulled her hands from mine and rubbed them together. "Jonathan, the past few weeks have changed me. When you came into my life, I was scared and unsure of myself. What happened with Drake had cast a shadow of doubt on my professional life. I want to thank you for helping me get past that hurdle." She looked at me and then placed her hands on top of mine. "There was a time when I would have laughed you out of this room. But, I was chased by a raptor. And I looked cold, naked evil in the face. I saw Drake. I saw a dozen men and women just like him. I'm going back to Austin not just to rest. I'm going to do some spiritual inventory. I'm going to have that talk with God and try and get things straight in my life. So, don't worry about me. If God is going to protect me; give me a guardian angel as wonderful as Jonathan Steel, then I don't have to fear Reginald Drake." She leaned toward me and her eyes sparkled. "Instead, he better be afraid of me!"

My heart leaped. "That's my girl." I said before I realized it and she was standing and we embraced and she pressed her warmth against me and her face to my cheek and I felt the heat of her tears run down my neck until they touched the tiny cross. I couldn't do this. Not now. Not yet. I let her embrace slowly cool and I stiffened to show my discomfort. She slowly pulled away and turned her gaze toward the RV door. She wiped at her tears.

"Sorry. I know how uncomfortable that makes you." Her gaze drifted to the back bedroom and locked on the photograph in the hallway. She opened her mouth to speak and then closed it. "I had better be going."

"Yeah, I have to take this mask back to Grace tonight so I can head out for home in the morning." I said.

She looked up at me and placed her hand on my chest. "Jonathan Steel, you are the most unique man. If ever I need your spiritual expertise, I will be calling on you. I pray that time will heal your wounds and that one day you will find peace. Until then, guard this heart of yours."

I nodded and fought back the tears. She leaned up and kissed my cheek. "Take care my friend."

She walked out of my RV and out of my life. At least for now. I glanced at the cask and felt its evil seep into the room. I spoke a silent prayer of protection for Ruth Martinez and for my shattered heart.

EPILOGUE

"They say the most beautiful sunsets in Texas can be seen from this restaurant." Reginald Drake bit into his soft taco and gazed out over Lake Travis.

The man sitting across from him pulled out a meerschaum pipe and placed it between amber colored teeth. One side of the bowl bore the image of an angel. The other side the image of a devil. He wore a wide brimmed Panama hat and his turquoise eyes glowed against his deeply tanned wrinkles. "I hope the distance from Dallas didn't bother you."

"Oh, no. My buddy was strong enough to get me here. But, I'll have to hang around for a few days while we recover. I might look up the Martinez family. They have a house on Lake Travis."

The older man held a lit match to the bowl of his pipe and sucked the flame into the pungent tobacco. A waiter appeared behind him.

"I'm sorry, sir, but there is no smoking even out here on the veranda."

The old man chuckled. "You don't mind if I smoke."

The waiter blinked and shook his head. "I don't mind if you smoke."

"You'll keep the tables empty around us so we won't get interrupted."

"I'll keep the tables empty so you can continue without interruption."

The old man shook the fire from his match and puffed on the pipe. "You'll bring us a pitcher of margaritas as an apology."

"I'll fetch you a pitcher of margaritas. Sorry to interrupt you." The waiter stood there looking perplexed and then hurried into the interior of the restaurant.

Drake laughed and chewed on his taco. "You've been watching too many science fiction movies."

"No, Drake, like most simple men his mind is empty of any spiritual discipline. It is easy to manipulate. I believe it was G. K. Chesteron who once said, 'When a man stops believing in God he doesn't then believe in nothing, he believes anything.' An empty mind is truly the devil's playground."

Drake sat back and wiped salsa from his lips. "You quote our enemy."

"I know our enemy. A lesson you have yet to learn. Now, tell me about my son."

The waiter appeared with a pitcher of pale green liquid and placed it on the table. "I believe this is for you?"

"Yes. You did well. Now, go take some money from the till and party all night long." The old man said.

The waiter smiled. "I think I'll take some money from the petty cash and party all night." He walked stiffly into the restaurant.

"Now, that was cruel, sir."

"Cruelty is the worst sin." He stoked his pipe. "You can call me the Captain."

Drake nodded and picked up his second burrito. "Your son is looking for the thirteenth demon."

"Why was he helping this attorney?"

Drake shrugged. "Not sure. Maybe he needed the money."

The Captain sucked on his pipe and the fires from the bowl cast his face in crimson light. "Well, it will take time for him to track down number thirteen. I'll give him a few more months and then throw him a bone. Once he gets wind of the Council of Darkness, he'll be occupied for a few years. That will keep him away from the other thing."

Drake finished his taco and poured himself a generous glass from the margarita pitcher. "Speaking of the Council, you know I want a seat."

The Captain laughed and pointed the pipe stem in his direction. "Many men have wanted a place at the table. Your friend is a lower class demon bordering on insanity. Like you."

Drake guzzled the margarita and pounded the table top with a fist. "I have money. I have power. I have prestige."

"And, you have no self-control." The Captain hissed. "They will eventually discover what you did to your parents. And, if you continue with this hobby of yours with young women, you will eventually get caught and there will be no clever Ruth Martinez to get you off."

Drake's face reddened with anger. "I can control these urges. You just watch."

The Captain puffed on the pipe and studied him with half closed eyes. The sun set lower on the horizon and painted both their faces in fiery orange. "There are a couple of unstable hosts on the Council. Once my son goes after them, there will be vacancies. So, Reginald Drake, if you want a seat, then here is what you will do. Abandon these atrocious killing games. Accept the shortened sentence I will insure you will receive for assault and battery. Serve your time for a few months and I will get you released early. And, when you are released, you will be ready to do what I tell you. Agreed?"

Drake smiled and pieces of beef hung from his teeth. "Agreed."

The Captain stood up and slipped his pipe into his pants pocket. "And, leave Ruth Martinez alone. Go back to Dallas and wait for your trial. I'll see you get a lawyer who will get you a deal." The man looked into the setting sun across the rippling waters of Lake Travis and the rolling hills surrounding it. "My what a beautiful sunset." He disappeared from sight leaving behind a popping sound.

Drake shrugged and poured another margarita. "Whatever you say, pops." His eyes glowed with mischief. "But, I am not done with Ruth Martinez."

ALSO BY BRUCE HENNIGAN

Hope Again: A Lifetime Plan for Conquering Depression (with Mark Sutton)

The Homecoming Tree

Our Darkness, His Light

Shadow Merchant (Book 1 of Jack Merchant Medical Mysteries)

Merchant of Justice (Book 2)

Just a Bite of Something Sweet: At Christmas

The Chronicles of Jonathan Steel:

Death by Darwin (Jonathan Steel Prequel)

Book 1 - Demon 13: Dark Covenant

Book 2 - Demon 12: Wolf Dragon

Book 3 - Demon 11: Ark of the Chimera

Volume 1: Jonathan Steel Chronicles (ebook with books 1 - 3)

Book 4 - The 10th Demon: Children of the Bloodstone

Book 5 - The 9th Demon: Time of the Cross

Book 6 - The 8th Demon: A Wicked Numinosity

Books 7 & 8 - The Pandora Stone: Demons 7, 6 & 5

Book 9 - The 4th Demon: Trial of the 3rd Demon

Book 10 - The 2nd Demon: Tales of the Grimvox